PASS THE KRYPTONITE

RAZ STEEL

MATTERHORN PRESS

This book is dedicated to my children,

Kristyn, Xander, and Sarah, and Chris.

There're no scenes you need to skip in this one, kids!

There's a life message for you,

about the importance of friends and laughter.

I love you.

Dad

Acknowledgments

I really enjoyed writing this story because the characters could all be friends of mine.

Thanks to my original publisher and editor at Soul Mate Publishing, Debby Gilbert for believing in the magic of PTK. Thanks to Shannon Aviles, my marketing director at MoreThanPublicity and to her team. Thanks to editors Amanda Sumner and Eliza Dee; excellent job, ladies! And thanks to my great friends, Douglas Michael, MD., and Mimi Michael for their continuing support, research, and medical advice, and most importantly for their friendship. And to my friend, Miki DeBaise—here's one that's safe for you to read (no vampires)! And thanks to Cousin Janice for helping me maintain my balance even if she struggles to maintain hers and to my ex-wife who maintained her balance even when I struggled to maintain mine.

Chapter 1

How much remorse could any girl summon for a half-carat diamond? I wagged my fingers in the morning sun streaming through the apartment window, and the rock glittered. I loved Elliot Collins, I just wasn't *in* love with him anymore. Guys sensed the difference. They believed it. They dealt with it. And I imagined Elliot could begin this process if only we weren't still engaged.

Lela Thompson, my best friend/roommate, hunkered down on our tattered couch, studying for a test. Spring break was over—for one of us, at least. We were psych majors, juniors, hoping to attend grad school together; then we'd open a clinic here in Greenwich Village.

"Girl, why don't you muster the courage to tell him?" Lela didn't even look up from her notes, but she knew what I was thinking.

"I'm buildin' up to it."

"*Buildin'* up to what?"

She mocked my Tennessee drawl, Northernized, since I'd spent early childhood in Bucks County, Pennsylvania, before we moved south of the Mason-Dixon Line. "My life is in turmoil, and all you can do is make fun of my accent?"

"Just take off the ring and drop it in his hand. He'll get the message, Willow." Her New Hampshire accent sounded like a cross between Brooklyn and breathy. Maybe she'd lived too long in the Village, or she'd watched too many Marilyn Monroe movies.

"Elliot's a nice guy. I don't want to hurt him."

She extended her arm, palm up, still without looking. "Practice," she said.

I frowned because I'd never taken off the ring. I growled because the bugger wouldn't budge. I tugged harder and twisted, but my finger must've swollen in betrayal. The ring, like my social life, was going nowhere.

"Just text him." Lela glanced at me, and the devil danced in her eyes. She stroked our cat as he wandered by, an elegant line from his head to the tip of his curled tail—black fur, white chest and paws, all tuxedoed up.

I'd scribbled the list when I woke this morning, then memorized it: *The top five reasons not to marry Elliot Collins. Number five:* "You don't understand me."

Lela smiled without looking. "Did you say something, Willow?"

She'd heard me. "Practicing," I said.

We studied into the afternoon. Classes started again tomorrow. I'd transferred my work to the floor and milk and Oreo cookies to the coffee table. GREs were coming up soon, and I had a 3.9 GPA to protect. Lela wasn't far behind me. I accepted she had a better bod; I wasn't going to grant a better brain.

"I'm checking school e-mail," Lela said. "Want me to see if the psych department responded yet?"

We kept private e-mail addresses, but neither of us could afford smartphones, so for convenience we occasionally checked each other's official school mail. "Sure."

I had one required course remaining: Crimes in Psychology. I didn't even like the title. We were halfway

2

through March registration and the class was already closed. I'd discovered too late that the next academic year, Huntington University—for the first time ever—was offering Crimes fall semester only. I had one fall semester left. Administration would certainly understand and award me a place in the class. Just a formality for me to route through department channels.

Lela reappeared a few minutes later and leaned against the arm of the couch, hands on sculpted hips, and she was smirking. "You'd better read their response yourself," she said. "I closed your mailbox so you could enjoy the full Internet experience." I couldn't read Lela as easily as she read me. What could the e-mail say? *Of course you're in the class,* or *of course you're in the class and sorry we made you sweat this one.* The cat sauntered into the living room with his nonchalant "doorbell" look.

I scurried into my bedroom even as the bell rang. Lela answered, and Elliot's voice infiltrated its way into my psyche. "Be there in a minute," I shouted.

The e-mail was from Clarisse Naughton, administrative assistant for the psych department. I guess I didn't expect Professor Kirin—who taught the class and to whom I'd directed my request—to respond personally.

Subj: Re: special request for Professor Kirin
From: Willow Bolden, Junior

Professor Kirin says there's no need for him to meet with you, as that class is already full. In accordance with University procedures, I've put your name on the wait list. Your number is noted below, and you'll be contacted if the appropriate number of students drop the class.

3

Raz Steel

Clarisse Naughton
Administrative Assistant
Psychology Department
Huntington University
Wait list #208

Encouraged by the wonderful echoing of hardwood floors, I may have stomped once or twice on the way to greet Elliot.

Chapter 2

I wrapped my fingers around her neck and squeezed until the eyes of my ancient Malibu Barbie bulged. Barbie's boyfriend and my not-yet-ex-boyfriend gawked. How could I vent psych department frustrations on an innocent blonde in a sarong?

I straightened her clothes and combed her hair with my fingers. "Sorry," I muttered. Hearing me apologize to a doll probably explained Elliot's expression, if not Ken's.

Malibu Barbie had been my first, so I kept her for sentimental reasons. The same reason, I assumed, Barbie kept Ken.

My imagination replayed the e-mail like voicemail, and Ms. Naughton's nasal tone cackled like Barbie's wicked grandmother, which explained my expression.

"This message is for Willow Bolden. Professor Kirin says, 'That class is already full.' *Ah-ha-ha-ha-ha.*"

Elliot expected a kiss. I expected to be registered for a closed class. One of us, at least, would have to live with disappointment. But breaking up required a pittance more courage than I possessed in the moment, so I pecked him on the cheek. Lela collected her books and laptop and retreated to her bedroom, shaking her head.

"I have big news," Elliot said. He beamed, and his chest swelled.

"I have big news too, only mine's not so happy," I said. My stomach twisted into knots.

Focusing on the school issue for a day or two until it was resolved afforded me the perfect excuse not to deal with the emotional issue for a day or two. Breaking up with someone you didn't care about was easy. Breaking up with someone you loved required timing and sympathy and the right words. I didn't have the right words or the timing.

I angled toward my oversized iPod docking station. Stevie Nicks, with or without Fleetwood Mac, always commanded a smile.

"Don't you get it?" I shouted above the music.

Elliot slouched his shoulders—clueless. True, I hadn't explained the problem yet.

"There are more names on the waitlist than in the Bible. This setback could delay graduation by eight months and postpone grad school by a year. They never let grad students start in January." And it would blow the synchronization with my best friend/roommate/future partner-in-clinic.

Elliot smiled like he always did when I began a conversation in the middle. He flexed his fingers and scratched behind his ear. Flavor-of-the-month cologne swirled around him as he adjusted the music volume to a background level. "If the new job becomes official, I could help with…" Elliot's once-appealing Tennessee drawl grated like a telemarketer with a stutter.

"Just because the university named him temporary department head doesn't mean he can screw me." I twirled away, strangled the volume knob, then spoke below the music, fully aware Elliot couldn't hear. "Oh, and by the way, Elliot, here's your ring." I tugged—safe in the knowledge it was immovable.

Behind my back, Elliot adjusted the volume again, exhibiting more patience than I deserved. Elliot was several years older than me and several years—maybe more than several—more mature, and he projected Southern gentleman charm and a never-Northernized accent.

He lounged on the arm of our bedraggled couch, seated in his world, his beautiful cornflower-blue eyes failing to follow me as I stormed past, his mountain-man physique wasted beneath his clothes. I sighed. Three years ago, he'd encouraged my academic plans. Friendship before romance. Elliot was no longer on the top-three-friends list.

"I memorized the job requirements," Elliot said.

I trotted out my other list, concerning marriage and Elliot, but memory faltered.

"The final interview is a formality."

Roller'Rama in suburban Memphis—the site of our first date—had hosted our formal one-year first-date anniversary. By the time we'd skated one revolution, Elliot had been as eager as Rhett Butler to blow through the Union blockade. There's something irresistible about a guy in tails and roller skates on one knee, and I had accepted. But I was only a kid two years ago when he proposed, and it had taken a while to realize I needed a partner whose mind extended beyond business school logic, even if he graduated with honors and then followed me from Tennessee.

Top five, top five. I just needed one of them to pop up. Ah. "You don't know me," I whispered.

"Did you say something, Willow?"

I jabbered sideways with staccato movements and unintelligible gesticulations. I wanted a boyfriend as sensitive as Lela, who heard me when I spoke and when

7

I didn't speak. I desired a partner as passionate about my issues as I was about his. I craved a confidant who chose to dance to the music inside my head. Hell, I needed someone who *heard* the music inside my head.

My cheeks burned. "Professor Keeeer-inn"—my drawl exaggerated with stress—"won't meet with me."

"Starting salary is excellent," Elliot said.

"I can't afford an extra semester as an undergrad."

How does one break up with someone she likes? Texting didn't feel right. I needed to return the ring, and I felt obligated to explain why.

Face Elliot—I spun away—and confess reason number one, "You're a nice guy, but I'm not *in* love with you." Still whispering. That's how I *knew* the timing wasn't right.

"They want an assistant available to start soon."

"This will throw off my timetable," I said, voice normal.

"Dress is casual, two weeks off in the summer."

"Lela and I expect half our clients to be pro bono."

"Health care after ninety days."

Neck muscles knotted. I plopped on the sofa to encourage Elliot to rub my shoulders. He scooped the cat into his lap and rubbed its back. The cat purred. I growled. I needed health care now. I jumped up and snatched my iPod from the docking station.

Elliot stroked the cat into ecstasy and droned on: "Y'all are gonna be so proud and surprised..." He wanted strokes for a job he hadn't landed, and I just wanted the nod for rage at a professor I hadn't met. I needed to register now. The anxiety would cause sleep deprivation, and I couldn't afford lethargy with midterms coming up.

Lela snickered from her bedroom doorway. "Go," she mouthed.

I glanced around the apartment. Barbie—unbelievably my second-best friend—lay on her back, elastomer arm pointing toward the hall. "Go," she echoed.

I needed to escape Elliot in the moment, and may have closed the door louder than intended. I didn't even take my cell phone. An issue more immediate than breaking up without wounding the man dangled over my head.

"Willow, wait."

I peeked over my shoulder. Elliot's head poked past the doorframe. I really needed alone time, one of the facets Elliot *never* seemed to understand about me.

"Don't bother," I shouted up the stairs, "I'm going that way." I pointed right, darted through the lobby, and headed left. I knew Lela approved, and I'm sure Barbie would've signaled thumbs-up, had she been graced with opposable thumbs.

Clouds obscured the late-afternoon sun, the city already warmed far beyond pre-spring expectations.

The Corner Café served French vanilla lattes, naturally decaffeinated. A chalkboard described today's specials. The bakery aroma combined with the fresh-ground coffee beans and elevated my sour mood, if just for a moment. The café was a rendezvous for lovers and a haven for first dates, so a lot like the roller-skating rink back home—without the hippodrome ceiling or the rotating glitter globe.

An aproned high school girl offered a perky smile. "Can I help you, ma'am?"

Ma'am? Jeez. I don't know, *can* you help me? "I want a no-foam, nonfat, grande…" Romance with a guy who understands me without explanation or SparkNotes.

I added raw sugar and melted into a corner. A couple at a table nearby flirted. The girl's thunderous laughter pealed off the Formica, blowing empty sugar packets onto the floor. She caressed her companion's calves with her toes and whimpered when he massaged her foot.

"Mmm," I added in frustration.

They heard me. Damn. I confessed with a shrug and vanished in the spreading twilight like a good voyeur. I wanted understanding, I wanted validation, and I wanted to learn to face my problems instead of running away from them.

I headed into the bowels of the city. I'm a psych major. How could I not examine my behavior in terms of my education? Freudian analysis—"My father sent me into the basement too often when I was a child." Jung— "The subway served as a sexual surrogate." A more contemporary theory suggested since I'd failed once again to tell Elliot our relationship was over, I didn't know what I wanted. Sure I did.

I wanted Superman.

Beneath Washington Square, the A train rushed along the tracks, swept me off the platform, and dumped me at Columbus Circle. An unexpected rain washed the city, calming me and my third-best friend, the Cement Man. Like any reclining statue, the Cement Man lay on his side below other statues at the park entrance. No matter where I trudged, his gaze followed me. I cocked my head and gaped, frozen in time and space. He listened to the drops *tap-tap* on my arms and shoulders. Well, one of us heard the drops.

Rain soaked my hair and seeped through my clothes. A prepubescent boy in a Yankees cap stopped near the statue and ogled. I flushed, then snarled. The boy moved on. The Cement Man stayed. I slipped beneath the arches into Central Park.

The park was my refuge, a haven to sort out thoughts and express honest feelings, at least to myself. Central Park reminded me of home, like nothing else in the city.

Toxic pollutants that perfumed New York dwindled here, and I inhaled faux spring, the first flowers, freshly mown grass… sauerkraut and mustard as hot dog vendors wheeled away their carts for the day, thwarted by the weather.

Budding trees bowed in the breeze and whispered my name. "Willow… Willow…"

I rebelled against the predictable future, rebelled against my ordinary past. I raced beyond playing fields while my legs pumped, beyond the carousel as my breath labored, beyond the chess pavilion as my sides ached. I aimed for the park rock garden. Giant boulders, abandoned in the wake of a retreating glacier—or, the less romantic explanation said, imported when the park was constructed in the 1920s—dotted the landscape. I drained myself purposely, tears blending with raindrops.

The storm swept me onto my favorite boulder. I had dared to share this sanctuary with Elliot—before he floundered in not-quite-ex-fiancé abeyance—once, on a colder day. I lay at the top. My legs trembled. I flinched, startled to discover a dog huddled against the rock weathering my loneliness. A monstrous animal. Water matted masses of tangled hair. Brown saucer eyes inspected me. I thought he'd growl or at least bark, but he raised a ginormous paw and cocked his head. Resistance was futile.

I introduced myself and explained my curriculum problems, but the dog barked as if he knew scheduling obfuscated the real issue. "Okay, okay, I thought today was the day to break up with my fiancé, and I'm worried,"

I said. "I don't know what to say. And maybe today isn't the right day."

This time, the forlorn mutt listened without interruption. "I've stumbled for weeks, fumbling the typical signals. I stopped calling, I stopped holding his hand, and I stopped wearing clothes he likes. Nothing affects Elliot."

The dog stretched out, head on paws.

"I stopped talking to him about anything other than school and reality shows—at least when he can hear me. Doesn't matter. Elliot remains oblivious to my feeble efforts."

The dog sighed.

"I *may* have adopted a younger emotional age—though Lela, my best friend, claims it's the real me—and less socially acceptable forms of hinting at a breakup. I used *his* toothbrush, I quoted lines during movies just before the actors. I even flashed a mouthful of chewed food."

The dog whined, as if to say, "Eugh."

"Elliot won't go away." I bit my lip. "What happened to the emotional strength Mom promised I'd develop as I approach the big two-oh?"

The dog yammered like it was his turn to talk. The only problem was, I understood him.

"Yeah." I nodded. "Mom *could* be right." I chuckled. "Maybe I'll need a few extra days to mature."

I'm not sure if the dog caught my sarcastic lilt, but his stomach growled—I hoped it was his stomach—and his gaze never left mine. I patted my pockets. No food, so I flagged down the last of the retreating hot dog vendors and purchased two, no sauerkraut—the dog didn't need a gas problem on top of everything else—and I broke both into bite-sized wedges. I'm sure the dog could've wolfed a hot dog whole, but I didn't want him to choke, either. I delivered one portion at a time.

He scarfed as politely as possible, and we exchanged quandaries until a guy appeared from behind a tree. Clothing and backpack suggested he might be a student, grad school or high school, impossible to tell. His lips creased in a peculiar smirk, trapped between smile and frown. I expected the intruder to respect my privacy and move along. My gaze darted back and forth: boy—dog—boy—dog, but I retreated into my conversation.

"Did you ever have trouble breaking up with someone?"

The dog moaned.

"You look at me with those silly eyes, but you know what I'm talking about, don't you?"

The dog handed me his paw.

The interloping student flunked Privacy 101.

I wanted to ignore him; however, water dripping off his glasses captured my attention. His eyes were wide-set and darker than the dog's. He studied my face but seemed to avert his gaze from parts overexposed. In the Corner Café, I might've found him charming. But we weren't in the café, and I wasn't dressed for close inspection. His hands fumbled, as if he didn't know whether to hide them in his pockets or behind his back.

No rings adorned his fingers, nor a watch his wrist. He edged in our direction.

How scared should I be? My heart skipped, and my throat tightened. Spreading darkness and a thinning park crowd earned bonus fear points.

I patted the dog and scratched behind his ears to hide trembling hands. My nose wrinkled. The dog was in urgent need of a bath. The stranger infringed and leaned his hands against the base of my boulder, as if leaving a mark. Like the dog, Mark—I had to call him something—had dark hair matting his head. For his sake, I hoped he didn't smell as bad as the mutt. He seemed more like Mark Cutie than Park Creep, a guy with raw appeal. His distinctive jaw and the arc of his chin defined handsome. If we'd met at a party, I'd be drooling like the dog.

He tilted his head to see me between rain-streaks. I growled. Unlike the kid at the park entrance, Mark failed to back up. I refused eye contact.

"Isn't it obvious I want to be alone?" I whispered to the mutt.

"You're talking to a *dog*?" Mark said. Like discussing my personal life with an animal was so unusual. I'd swear Mark barked, or was it just the wind billowing his unbuttoned flannel shirt?

Heat rose in my cheeks, and I pushed off the rock. "Look at him!" I pointed.

Mark obeyed.

I glanced at the mutt too. "The poor creature is starving." The situation called for a white lie. "I bring him food." Butterflies swam the breaststroke across my chest, er, stomach.

I offered a sweeping gesture—"How'd you like to live here?"—and did what any female dog lover in the dark, in the park, wearing a clinging T-shirt would do. I mumbled something tactless and ran as fast as I could.

Chapter 3

The moment his gaze darted to her hand, the girl sprinted away.

He frowned. The dog angled its head as if to say, "Are you nuts, dude?" In retrospect, perhaps he imagined the fleeting connection. After all, she'd appeared from nowhere and swept him into the vortex of her passing storm, swirling rage and uncertainty in her expression. Rain soaked her clothing, pummeling her flesh as she sprinted in the spreading darkness.

She hadn't noticed him at first, but the fierce determination that overrode her other emotions surprised him and demanded his attention. He loved surprises. Curiosity propelled him along the park path. What drove her to folly?

Either this girl personified meteorologically attentive, fashion-conscious dressers—rain, white T-shirt—or a life-altering event blinded her to circumstance. He bet on the latter. The odd mixture of passions appealed more than the chic line of clinging clothes.

Her hair tangled, dangling to her shoulders and darkened by the damp. Did she realize running half-naked in Central Park shouldn't be on any girl's list of the ten best ideas she'd ever entertained? The striking combination of sharp emotional lines and soft carnal curves cast an intoxicating spell. Inattentive to where she was or what she was doing, focused instead on something so important it outweighed her safety. The girl might need protection, so he gave chase.

Rain blurred vision, but he sighed when he discovered her sitting on a boulder.

"You're talking to a dog?" Quirkiness added to her appeal before she raced away.

He glanced at the dog, then dashed after the girl. He was burdened by a backpack and out of breath, and pain laced his side. Angry horns resounded in the distance, and the steady patter of rain drowned out the usual city cacophony. A chill jogged along his spine arm-in-vertebra with fear. Not fear he was too shy to speak to her, or that the park wasn't the safest place after dark. His fear existed on a more practical level. *What if she runs faster than me?*

He couldn't let her escape. He stole between the trees like a convict in the night. The rain accelerated into a downpour, and in rivers that flooded sidewalks and streets, the blaring traffic splashed pedestrians without regard, and he lost her. Reluctant to admit she'd outdistanced him, he attributed her getaway to emotional denial.

What did it matter? She'd vanished.

Like every woman in my life.

The angst with Diana two years ago had sparked ideas and motivated him to write a romance novel about a liaison with a cougar. *Romance is supposed to end happily, right?* Since then, no time existed in his schedule for both writing and a relationship, so he avoided older women.

Hell, I've avoided all women.

Until tonight. Avoiding a relationship was the only way he'd have time to write a novel.

16

He balled his fists. "Ducking the possibility of a relationship doesn't matter."

What if it did?

He trudged home, unable to erase the park girl from his thoughts. His knee ached, perhaps from the weather, perhaps from a recurring tennis injury.

A deep bark from behind shot adrenaline through his system. Then the dog whimpered instead of growled.

Whew.

Snuggled next to a parking meter sat the bedraggled mutt that had caused this problem. Technically, the dog comment may've caused the problem, but he wouldn't have made the dog comment if not for the dog. His nose twitched.

"What'd you do, swim through the sewer to find me?"

The dog whined.

"What's your name?"

As if the mutt would tell him. No collar, either. The rain stopped, but few people traveled the street.

They surveyed each other. "I don't suppose you could tell me *her* name?"

The dog sighed and cocked his head.

"How about her address?" He arched an eyebrow and angled his head, mirroring the dog.

He sat on the stoop. Unbidden, the dog sidled next to him. "Okay, you tell me. How'd she get away? Why did my first words have to be offensive? 'You're talking to a dog?' Why didn't I say something nice like, 'I saw you lying on the rock and thought you might be hurt. Are you okay?'"

He stretched his legs and leaned back on his elbows. "I could've said something witty, like, 'Didn't you see the sign over there? It says no parachuting, no bungee jumping, and no rock lying in the park.'"

His knee throbbed, lying or sitting. Now elbows hurt too.

"Funny would've worked. 'Excuse me? I'm looking for my pet rock. He's short, hard, and kind of wet. Is he up there with you?'

"But no. I needed to open my big mouth and say, 'You're talking to a *dog*?' Lots of people talk to dogs, don't they?"

He sat up and hugged his knees. The mutt nuzzled his hand with its slimy nose.

"Are you cold? I'm cold. Come on. Let's go inside. By the way, what did you say your name was?"

The dog barked.

"Oh." He nodded. "Fish. I'm Ron." They shook paws and labored up the stairs.

~ ~ ~

"Lela, where are you?"

"I'm in the bathroom finishing my makeup. Come on in. You have some talking to do, girl." I liked it when she called me *girl*, like mortar solidifying our friendship.

I flipped on every light switch in the apartment, then marched into the bathroom filled with the scent of a patchouli candle balanced on the toilet seat. "He's gone?" I said.

"Elliot? Hell yes, he's gone. What would I do with him?" Lela glanced at my reflection. She brushed her hair, adjusted her sweater, then concentrated on eyeliner. "Date night." Two words and I understood all the primping.

I repositioned the candle on top of the tank and occupied the throne. A furry tail hooked my calf. "Hey, Dog."

I cuddled the cat and kissed his nose. I preferred dogs, but Lela loved cats, so we compromised and named our cat *Dog*.

"What're you going to do about Elliot?"

"Can we talk about it later? I'm starving." I hopped up. Dog flew off my lap.

"You're avoiding the issue again." A minute later, Lela followed me out of the bathroom.

She flipped off the extra lights, then imitated what she imagined to be my father's voice. "Who has more money, us or the electric company?"

I chuckled but scowled at the surrounding darkness.

"Your mom called again." Lela couldn't conceal her devilish grin.

"What'd you tell her?"

"You went to the park, and a strange guy accosted you." My wide-eyed reaction must've lent credence to her joke. She laughed harder than I did. "Don't worry, I've got your back, girl. I told your mom you went to dinner and a play with Elliot. You'd be home late. Of course, we talked about what a gentleman he is and about how you found such a nice boy."

"I need to misplace him."

Intimate conversations with Lela often pricked deep. I avoided these conversations, but she pulled them out of my thoughts so easily I found myself digging further to please her. She sat cross-legged on the floor, waiting.

"Lela, I did go to the park."

She frowned.

"It was dark."

"Did you get his name?"

"Look at how I'm dressed."

"Well, did you?"

An image of an innocuous intruder with rain dripping off his glasses sprang to mind.

"Yeah, Mark."

"Oh. Mark-in-the-Park."

"I guess I should explain myself to Elliot."

"You guess?"

Why couldn't I say what I meant? "I don't want to be his wife. I'm not ready for marriage."

"Why not?" She knew the answer. She liked to torture me.

I lay on my side, mimicking the Cement Man statue. "I'm so predictable. I need to capture the interest of one mysterious guy."

"You don't mean mysterious, you mean someone as strange as you are, girl. Tell me again how you got engaged." Lela reveled in teasing me, and I swallowed the Elliot-bait every time. Maybe a roller-skating rink was a more romantic locale in Tennessee than in New Hampshire.

~ ~ ~

Ron's simple plan couldn't fail. The girl said she fed the dog, so he'd take Fish back to the park, and they'd meet her. They waited at the same rock, at the same time, next day. Ron had treated Fish to a bed, a bone, and a bath, not in that order. Clean, hair combed—perhaps the dog wasn't recognizable? Perhaps he'd washed away Fish's ability to smell the girl? Maybe she'd lied about feeding the dog? Ron's insecurities existed on several levels. What if she didn't like him? He'd failed to ingratiate himself with the dog comment.

Emotionally surprising women appealed the most.

He was still inebriated by the splay of emotions in their brief encounter. Keyed to her signals, Ron was compelled to reconnect by the combination of earthy qualities and quirkiness. Running in the rain seemed so natural, though he had to admit a girl running in the rain in Central Park, wearing a white T-shirt, was a little less so. Still, she spoke to the dog, and she spoke to him, and he figured she liked the dog, so...

Not the girl, but the idea of the girl grew into an obsession. She distracted him at school and prevented him from completing assignments. Ron's already struggling writing came to a standstill.

On the sixth day of his simple plan, he thought a new plan might be necessary.

~ ~ ~

On the seventh day, Fish and Ron rested.

Chapter 4

The hike from Ron's West Village apartment to Huntington University on the east side of Central Park fulfilled Fish's requirement for daily exercise.

Dog and boy wandered beneath the statues near the park entrance. Ron contemplated falling in love. He balanced hands, juggling life. *Write fiction, or delve into a relationship?* His schedule precluded doing both. Besides, one heart stomping per lifetime was enough. He erected walls to surround himself, to prevent a woman from exposing his vulnerability. No matter how intimate, how connected he might feel to someone today, the loss of love always hurt too much tomorrow, so why risk the pain? The relationship with Diana had taught him that. He figured a woman's age shouldn't matter. Perhaps he didn't have enough experience to know.

Rows of street-hawking vendors intruded on his thoughts.

"Veee… nilla. Ice cream. Get it while it's cold! Veee… nilla."

"Fresh-roasted nuts. Don't be crazy. Get 'em while they're hot!"

"Watches. Get one before time runs out!"

Ron had started and stopped writing numerous times, filtering back five years into adolescence. Diana had shattered his heart two years ago, and renewed determination had flung him down a single-minded path to publication.

His stomach grumbled. Diana remained friendly, an occasional companion. He shook his head. Six times in two years was less than occasional. He'd grown accustomed to it, his callous soul. When would he venture beyond the walls again?

"Around perdition's moons and into purgatory, I stab at thee." That wasn't quite correct, but who can trot out an accurate quote upon command?

"Better to have loved and lost than… what? Never have a woman reach down your throat, rip out your heart, throw it on the ground, and stomp on it?" That couldn't be an accurate quote, could it?

Ron kicked a stone, and it careened across his single-minded path and down an incline. Fish barked and gave chase. His coat lustered after a few days of Frosted Flakes and milk—Fish had refused every brand of dog food, extra gravy or extra nutrition. He morphed in body and spirit, perhaps a happy animal for the first time in his life.

Not true. He'd experienced at least a moment's happiness beneath the caress of the park girl.

Ron stooped, and Fish licked his face. "We can't keep referring to her as 'the park girl.' She must have a name. I insist."

Fish gazed at him with—what had *the girl* called it—silly eyes? Fish seemed to wink, and what was worse, Ron understood him. In the background of shifting gears, tired brakes, and underground trains, one distinct voice squawked: a park vendor selling ice cream.

"Veee… nilla. Ice cream. Get it before it drips. Veee… nilla."

"That's what we'll call her, Fish—Vee."

23

~ ~ ~

Dog liked hanging in the bathroom with me more than with Lela. My singing attracted him. Sounded like cat wail.

My head ached this morning, perhaps because I hadn't slept well. I stepped from the tub and shook the curtain. The mirror revealed previously undiscovered flecks in my eyes. It reminded me of the number-four reason not to marry Elliot. "You *still* don't know me."

I toweled off, and my legs cried for warmth. I slipped on boxer shorts and curled in a ball beneath a crocheted blanket in the patch of Sunday sun streaming through the living room windows. My eyes shut, and I zonked.

Seemed like only moments passed before the creaking door woke me. The devil danced in Lela's eyes. She escorted Elliot. "Coffee, girl? You look beat." She winked and backed away.

I sat up, stretched, and squinted in the sunlight. Crochet-patterned sleep tattoos decorated my right arm. Elliot straddled my legs on his knees, and my nakedness dawned on me. I frowned and clutched the blanket to my chest, realizing what Lela had orchestrated, my wicked friend.

I meant to scoot back, to create a gap between us, but Elliot's knees stretched the crochet.

The lump in my throat hardened. I needed to tell Elliot I didn't want to be his wife. My stomach ached. A cloud blotted the sun. Now or never. Dreaming about Mark-in-the-Park in the park inspired me. "Umm, you know how in a forest you find all kinds of trees: maples, birches, dogwoods?"

Elliot tilted his head. "Why are we talking about trees?"

24

I forced a grin. "What I mean is, well, let's take you for instance. You're an oak tree in my forest. You're constant, you're strong, you're always there."

"But?"

Elliot was a brilliant businessman. I just never found him to be intuitive, and his insight surprised me; I hadn't said *but*.

Lela kicked open the door, carrying two mugs. "Here ya go. Need anything else?"

I nodded, acknowledging her stage-setting. "How about a shirt?"

She arched an eyebrow, more like I'd fallen into her next trap instead of forming a simple request. "Of course," she said.

Elliot waited until the door closed before he repeated his death sentence.

"But?"

I hesitated. Was there a nicer way to tell him? Mountain men identified with trees.

My frown stretched like the blanket, and perspiration slid under my arm. I didn't like this option any more than I imagined Elliot would.

"I, umm—"

The door swung open, and Lela tossed me a knit pullover, one of hers, two sizes too small for me. Her eyes laughed as she backed out again. I slipped on the shirt. Self-consciousness screamed and echoed off my bulging boobs.

"I want a redwood, Elliot." There. I blurted it out. I didn't want an oak.

"Oh."

This time, the engagement band almost fell off my finger. I centered the ring in his palm and closed his fingers over it.

Elliot raised his chin, and I watched the peculiar bob of his Adam's apple. His eyes misted, and I knew he wanted to say something, but he didn't want to cry. A wave of empathy washed over me, like sunlight breaking through the window again. I wanted to hug him, to tell him not to worry, he'd find his soul mate.

I often doubted that I'd find mine. I'd been alone for as long as I could remember. Even with Elliot, I was alone.

Silence surrounded us. It fit tighter than Lela's shirt.

~ ~ ~

Our class times didn't conflict on Tuesdays, so Lela and I didn't have to fight for the bathroom. Dog pranced on the vanity in front of the mirror. The coffee grinder whined as I stepped out of the shower. By the time Lela stepped out of the shower, I'd downed my first cup of coffee and dressed—T-shirt, skirt, sandals—ready to leave. I dabbed on jasmine.

"Rearranging your fall schedule today, girl?" Lela shouted from the bathroom.

I rolled my eyes. "What a mess."

Professor Kirin's reputation as a teacher preceded him. He'd transferred from the faculty at Rider University last fall, and all four of the courses he taught boasted a wait list.

I preened in the mirror attached to the bedroom door. "Any suggestions?" I yelled.

Lela flipped off the hair dryer. "You mean despite yesterday's e-mail from the mightier-than-thou professor saying that you can't ignore university policy?"

Lela peered around the bathroom door. "No one can dictate our future," she said.

I cleared my throat. "I e-mailed Professor Kirin again early this morning."

"Good. Don't give the man a chance to breathe."

"I used logic."

"By whose definition?"

"Plenty of students who made that class will be juniors next fall, and they'll have another chance to take the course." Perhaps I whined. "It's as if he anticipated my request."

"Don't tell me he answered already."

"Professor Kirin says, 'No way.' He won't move me or anyone else off the wait list and into the class."

Lela dressed in the bathroom. "March into his office, Willow. You deserve to be in that class. Tell him what you think."

Yeah, right. The sanctimonious tyrant. How much trouble could my thoughts cause?

Lela transferred her morning routine to the couch. Her hair covered half her face as she arched to polish her toenails peacock blue. "You've worked your tail off for three years. This is your last chance to take Crimes, and you don't care if he is one of the most respected psychologists in the country."

She glanced up. Devil eyes danced from across our apartment. They made me laugh.

"It doesn't matter that he's received the National Finest Achievement in Psychology Award. Twice," Lela said. "It doesn't matter that he holds two doctorates, or that he's published half a dozen psychology textbooks."

"Eight."

"Six, eight, what's the difference? It wouldn't matter if he'd published a hundred. Who's he to say you can't take his class?"

Her hair disappeared under a towel. She hopped up, and her perfect hourglass shape induced a pang of jealousy. She stood a head shorter than I did, but wow. When her head emerged from beneath the towel, her hair a study in disarray, she glanced at me. "Surprise him with your next request."

Dog hooked his tail around Lela's leg and purred. I waggled my finger at him. "Don't encourage the instigator." I shouldered my backpack, which was heavier than usual, and trotted down the steps.

Gray clouds frowned like a disapproving parent. What had I done now? Steel beams and concrete, overlapping buildings and sidewalks, iron bars fronting stores not yet open for business, steam rising from grates and trash, narrow doorways of restaurant kitchens, and people marching in crosscurrents so thick they blotted out the ground, all part of life in the city.

What about my predicament? Lopping off Professor Kirin's head would be one solution. Or two.

I entered the park past the Cement Man standing guard—well, reclining guard—near Columbus Circle. Street hawkers proclaimed their wares. "Vee… nilla."

Come on, who'd want ice cream at this hour?

Chapter 5

Acrobatic pigeons swam circles in the sky, bombing pedestrians. Fish and Ron sat on their rock—they'd claimed it since Vee hadn't been back—betting who'd be the birds' next target. Ron conceded major debt.

He lay down, hands laced behind his head, and yawned. Too many late nights struggling with the next chapter, the next paragraph, the next line. The manuscript required perfection. A writer's prerogative, and his father would demand nothing less. Ron shook an invisible Magic 8 Ball, spun it upside down, and pretended to read it.

Sources say, something is lacking in your life.

"Yeah... romance."

His heart twisted in anguish. Life without romance sucked, like eating a hamburger without catsup, mustard, pickles, French fries, or the roll. Who in his right mind wanted to survive that way?

Goals occasionally attached to a slippery slope, but Ron's mantra clung to him like dog business to park grass. *There's no time for writing* and *a relationship.* Ron chose writing.

Vee was nothing more than a blip, a vehicle ridden by fate to bring boy and dog together.

Ron yawned again and drifted into semiconsciousness, secure in the knowledge Fish protected him from would-be assassins.

~ ~ ~

A voice woke Ron. Something about the timbre lured his soul to awareness. A haunting voice, a voice that wound his stomach in rivulets of catsup and mustard and left his thoughts roiling with deprivation. Dreams unraveled, fantasies discovered new territory, and desires engaged hyperdrive. Ron pushed up onto his elbows, straining to hear more.

"Let's meet tomorrow. We can play in the sun."

Jasmine wafted across the park and wrinkled his nose. Sitting on the grass, scratching Fish's ear and laughing, was the girl of his tortured week.

Vee. A delicate goddess of perfection.

She nodded and inhaled a deep breath, then sighed, except her lips vibrated, and it sounded like a horse. Ron's grandmom called it faruffling.

Vee faruffled again.

Fantasies survived a dozen scenarios, but reality stumbled without words or any idea how to approach Vee without scaring her away.

Ron needed moxie and a mutt to ingratiate him. *Good boy, Fish.*

A toe thing—the word lost in a miasma of unraveling time—split her brown sandals in two, a string bracelet adorned her left ankle, and her skirt exposed endless pale legs. Her laughter peeled his flesh and placed a stranglehold on his heart.

Ron tumbled off the rock. She probably didn't notice, though her nose crinkled in a wide grin.

Ron balanced as best he could, having forfeited self-control, and he studied her without staring. Simple attributes lent her the aura of Aphrodite. The cast of her tawny hair in the morning sun, the sweep of her shoulders framed against the grass and rocks… the piercing frown, as if to say, *How dare you stare?* He'd already established he wasn't staring.

Ron's lips moved, but someone other than him must've spoken, because words emerged unrecognizable. "Would you like to dance?"

What! Where'd that come from?

"Excuse me?" Vee said.

Apparently she thought the same thing. Ron had no idea what words would flow from his mouth next. "Fish likes to watch dancers. He's always—"

"Fish?"

You're not much of a conversationalist, are you? He pointed at the mutt. "Fish."

"You named your dog Fish?" She did a double take. "He's your dog?"

Fish nodded. Ron's eyebrows shrugged. Fish nuzzled her hand, insisting she pet him.

Good boy. Remind me to give you extra sugar with your Frosted Flakes tonight.

Ron grinned, reinforcing his dorkiness. "Would you?"

"Would I what?" Her frown intensified.

"Care to dance?"

"You're joking."

Ron shook his head like Wile E. Coyote after running into a wall.

"There's no music," Vee said.

Stop being so practical. Of course there's music. It's all around us. Don't you hear it?

Ron spread his arms in dancing position. She gawped at him with dark, familiar eyes and pushed herself off the ground. Fish helped from behind.

31

Ron beamed, hands out, tempting her, unsure she'd engage—until she touched him. The electric jolt of a neophyte park dancer, sparks leaped across space as her fingers neared his, his transgressions absolved. He'd never come in contact with heaven, but this sure seemed close.

"If you don't want to take dancing lessons, maybe you'd consider analysis," Vee said.

Her heart thumped. No, that was his. They slow danced, her essence wrapped around his insides. Dizzy focusing on her, he leaned back.

"What?" Suspicion edged into her voice.

Not lengthy commentary, but at least they stayed on speaking terms.

"I want to look into your eyes."

"Why?"

"Eyes express thoughts from the heart." Ron allowed his thumb a single caress along her finger. Her glance unmasked his feelings. "We could have an entire conversation with our eyes. Few people understand that." His voice dropped to a whisper. "Who are you?"

Her face scrunched and she developed a funny little wrinkle in her forehead above her nose like he imagined a psychoanalyst might. "Can't you tell from the costume?"

Ron's expression made it clear he didn't understand.

"I'm a goddess of empathy with super powers. Insight. Understanding of people."

Only one goddess he knew with super powers of understanding, and she did start off as a mortal. A real name at last.

"Pleased to meet you, Psyche."

She mumbled something that sounded like "Mark-in-the-Park," then she drifted into him like night stealing into the city in early spring. Her breath caressed his cheek, their dance a lovers' embrace of promises yet to be made. She held him close or far, he couldn't be sure, sensory perception distorted by the faint scent of perfume rising from beneath her clothing. Rarely at a loss for words, but trapped within this perfect moment, Ron failed to conjure anything appropriate.

Fish intervened on his behalf. He pranced alongside them in time to the music in Ron's head.

Minutes or days passed.

Psyche smirked. "*Your* dog—Fish?—seems much happier now than the last time I saw him."

Ron winked at the dog. "I think he was having a bad day then, you know, with the rain and all. Right, Fish?"

Fish barked.

"Yes," Ron said, "I forgot. He hadn't been eating well at that time, either."

Psyche halted their dance. "You're talking to a *dog*?" She tossed Ron's words into his face.

Ron cleared his throat and accepted the gauntlet. "Fish has exceptional command of the English language and a unique insight into the human condition."

"Odd. He didn't act like he belonged to you that day in the park."

Fish took this opportunity to nuzzle Ron's hand.

"He doesn't belong to me."

"Oh?"

"Fish doesn't belong to anyone. Right now we're roommates. He showed up on my doorstep one day, desperate for a place to stay. Like Rocky and Adrian, we filled each other's gaps."

Ron remained ensnared on the analyst's couch, and Psyche edged forward. "What were you desperate for?" she asked.

"Not desperate so much as I wanted companionship, someone to share my thoughts, a hike in the park, or a discussion of a wonderful book. Fish fills gaps."

"What gaps do you fill for him?"

Ron shrugged. "The same ones." Fish barked in confirmation.

"He seems like a well-trained dog."

"I haven't trained him."

She smiled at Ron. Patronizing, but a smile none-theless. She stepped back, role-playing ended.

Psyche—he had yet to discover her alternate persona—glanced at her watch. "I'd better go. I'll be late for class." She gathered her backpack.

Ron glanced at his wrist. That's what people did when they checked the time. No need to wear a watch, however, with an internal clock.

Ron nodded. If he didn't hurry, he'd be late for his eight o'clock too.

"Where's your class?" he asked.

She hesitated before answering. "Huntington."

My school. Coincidence. Despite that clue, without her registered name, he could go an entire semester without finding her.

"I'm headed in that direction. If you don't mind, I'll walk with you."

She glanced at her watch again. "I'll have to take the subway."

Her insistence must be another coincidence. How many New Yorkers rode the train?

A lump welled into his throat.

What was he, anyway? A guy afraid of going underground, into closed spaces crammed with people? *Yes.* He hated the idea—dirt, rock, and concrete piled over his head. The subway would never figure into his travel equation.

"Good idea," he said. "Let's take the train."

What else could he do? Taxi drivers evoked images of crazed postal workers, and strange people jammed into cramped city buses. The vibration of skateboard wheels was like fingernails on a chalkboard, and his troubled knee prevented rollerblading or riding a bicycle to school.

Few traveling options remained. Perhaps moving to New York City wouldn't have been on the list of the ten best ideas Ron ever devised. He adjusted his glasses, and it struck him what she meant by Mark-in-the-Park. He was a superhero! Or, maybe a Dr. Seuss character.

His cape fluttered in the breeze, and resolve, unlike his passion, faltered.

The huge *M* stamped on his chest must stand for something.

She isn't going to shake me.

She hadn't offered her cell number or coughed up her address. He didn't want their next meeting dependent on another coincidence.

They navigated the crowds and the worn steps and arrived belowground. His breath came in gasps. The smell of sardine-packed humans twisted around his nostrils. Nausea aimed from his stomach toward his mouth. He should not have insinuated his way into her morning schedule.

People queued in front of a small plastic-enclosed cubicle, and a faceless but armed person compressed inside exchanged dollar bills for MetroCards. Psyche swiped a prepurchased card. Ron wiggled through the turnstile and tumbled onto the platform. Congealed noise disoriented him, and the cavernous dark that spiraled up a pair of tunnels spun him around and around until Fish leaned against his legs to steady him. He donned sunglasses as much to hide fear as to allow Fish to pretend to be a Seeing Eye dog so he could ride the subway. No one objected.

Ron didn't know if they waited two hours or two minutes for a train, but his life shrunk until he subsisted as a meaningless flea on the collar of the city transportation system. A 6 train whooshed into the station, and the doors flew open. A giant paw scratched the platform, flinging them, willing or not, into the bowels of the train.

His face paled, and his reflection waned in the glass windows. People crowded around them, yet Psyche seemed oblivious. She didn't have much to say during the trip. Fish's brilliant repartee also dried up.

Ron hesitated to ask for the info he wanted. He didn't want to appear forward or have his voice emerge as a high-pitched squeal.

Psyche tired of waiting for him to carry the conversation. She retrieved a textbook from her backpack and read—a bad sign.

Seeing Eye Fish squeezed onto the seat between them, licking Ron's hand with sympathy far beyond that of mortal dogs. No sooner had the train accelerated than it slowed with a screech.

"My stop," Psyche said.

"Mine too." Ron jumped up. Jerked forward by the braking train, he grabbed a pole for support. Fish remained seated.

Psyche opened the flap of her bag, but the book didn't want to go back in. She yanked out a folder and a wad of papers but had to put them down to maneuver the book. Ron picked up the papers to help her repack.

The staple drew his eye, *almost* the same way Juliet drew the eye of Romeo; not with a genuine grin, not with a flirtatious wink or a coy glance.

The staple stabbed him with brilliance. Psyche stabbed him with disdain, yet he was rewarded for the unrelenting efforts of a fortnight, and they consummated their meeting.

What was the staple doing there in the midst of her work, fastening a bunch of papers together?

Were he thinking clearly, his mind undiluted by irrational thoughts, he might've read the title, thereby gleaning one class Psyche took. More directly, he might've read the prof's name. More directly still, he might've spied the name of Psyche's alternate persona.

But Ron wasn't thinking clearly. Superfluous ideas deluged his mind.

Does she like me? I hope she doesn't ride this train every day. Why isn't she in one of my classes? Do my socks match? Is my fly open? Was that a question he wanted to ask in front of an empath? He glanced at his crotch to check nonetheless.

His eyes refocused. He glimpsed it then and, most importantly, recognized it for the salve for all his wounds: her on-campus e-mail address. LelaT@...

Psyche/Lela wrenched the papers from his hand, stuffed them sideways into her backpack, and disappeared into the throng of disembarking passengers.

Chapter 6

I charged off with clenched fists, unsure if my anger aimed at Professor Kirin and his provincial policies, or a stranger from the park pleased to dance with—what did he call me—Psyche? And that didn't count as an awkward goodbye because we didn't say "goodbye."

Not the man of my dreams. A true fantasy man would swoop in, serenade my mind and my senses. Einstein and Brad Pitt. Descartes and Chris Pine. Not Mark-in-the-Park and Fish. What a bizarre combination.

And he'd accepted role-playing so readily. He'd beamed, unfazed. I'd let him touch me. Wait, I'd touched him.

"Lela's gonna have a field day with this."

"Can I help you?"

Ms. Nausicaan Nasal. The Nausicaans, a particularly unappealing race on *Star Trek*, rivaled by Clarisse Naughton, administrative assistant and queen of the Huntington University Psychology Department. Impossible to speak with the teaching staff without confronting Nausicaan Nasal.

"Can I help you?" The voice of a frenemy.

I don't know. *Can* you help me? Do you have the ability? You mean, *May* I help you? Enroll me in the Crimes class. Please.

"I'd like to speak with Professor Kirin. Is he in his office?" I angled around her desk.

"No. Professor Kirin hasn't arrived yet." NN's words stopped me. "As soon as he does, he has a class. No time for office visits. You're not in any of his classes, are you?"

In a school this size, how could she possibly know all his students?

"No, I'm not, but—"

"You may make an appointment if you wish. I'm sure Professor Kirin can find a few minutes for you sometime next month."

"Next month? Registration ends this month. I have to speak with him now."

She tilted her head and squinted, shredding a few of my layers. "Are you the young lady trying to enroll in Crimes in Psychology without permission?"

How could she know that? I staggered, taken aback. An alien hand throttled my throat.

"Won't happen," she assured me.

I failed to regain composure, *joie de vivre*, nerve to tell this displaced person what I thought of psychology department policy. She glanced past me and waved to someone in the hall.

"Could you squeeze me in?" I asked.

"Next month."

"I need a favor. I have issues."

Alien eyes dissected me. "Professor Kirin has four classes and one hundred and ninety-three students, for fifteen of whom he is faculty advisor. His students take all his office time. Professor Kirin doesn't do favors, but if he did, it would be for a student he advised."

I tried to make one corner of my mouth touch the other. Nausicaans are tricky. "I need to see him."

"Midterms start next week, he has to prepare a guest lecture at NYU on the abnormal female mind, and another lecture at Columbia on relativity in day-to-day life. He has to meet with the chancellor because he was appointed acting chair of the department, not to mention sit on the interview committee for new faculty members, and he's writing for publication under a deadline. Seeing him requires a special dispensation from the pope." She peered at me over her glasses. "Won't happen."

Lela's words zoomed through my thoughts: *Tell them you've worked your tail off, you deserve a seat in the class.* I wanted to graduate on time. I'd figured out a life plan, and Professor Kirin blocked my path. I attempted to translate into Nausicaan. I had failed to arrange an appointment, I couldn't give up, and I didn't know what else to do. I fixated on the backward clock hung on the wall behind NN. The clock wasn't hung backward—the numbers were backward. Why would the psych department display a clock like that?

I gawked at the nameplate on her desk. I could e-mail Professor Kirin again, but *Clarisse* probably read—and answered—his e-mail.

"I-I…" Something NN had said nudged my mind, like a second-year French student in a fourth-year class. If anyone would do me a favor, it'd be my faculty advisor.

"I'd like to make an appointment with *my* advisor as soon as possible."

"Name?"

"Willow Bolden."

She typed, then glanced at the computer screen. "Dr. Coleman can see you Friday afternoon at three."

I grinned at my cleverness. Wait, how'd she know Dr. Coleman was my advisor? Nausicaans are even trickier than I thought.

~ ~ ~

The morning dragged.

I met Lela for lunch at our rooftop bench. We basked in sunlight that soaked through the thin cotton fabric of our pre-summer wardrobes, the temperature warmer than expected for mid-March in the city. The scent of vegetable soup and fresh-baked cookies rose from cafeteria vents. Lela laughed at my cowardice with NN, but agreed that asking my advisor for help seemed reasonable.

"Oh, I forgot to return your paper last night." I pulled it from my backpack. "Sorry if the edges are messy. I was escaping, and I crammed things back in."

Radar activated, Lela waved. "Don't worry, Dr. Preston won't care. She's the only professor I have who still insists on hard copies."

Lela's eyes caught every nuance, every crease of my clothing, every strand of hair misplaced. No sign I'd been bushwhacked. "Running away from someone? I know we're not talking about NN."

"No."

Lela arched her eyebrows, encouraging me to continue.

"He accosted me in the park again."

"The same stranger?"

My head bobbed.

"He waylaid you?"

"He forced me to dance."

"Dance? In the park? He forced you?"

"Uh-huh."

"You actually danced for him?"

"With him."

"Mark-in-the-Park?" Her evil smirk traced a line around her lips.

41

"Yeah. Same guy."

She spread her hands and arched her eyebrows higher, in anticipation of more info.

"I happened to be walking through the park, minding my business, and his dog distracted me."

"That's when he forced you to dance?"

"Music played an instrumental role."

"Music in the park?"

"Yes. No." I mooshed my face, trying to make my cheekbones touch my eyebrows. "Yes." Had he heard the music inside my head or his? Heat rose in my cheeks. "When he touched me, it felt like a thousand mosquito bites, and I didn't have calamine lotion."

"He *touched* you?"

"We slow danced."

"Mark-in-the-Park swept you into his arms and you didn't object?"

My lips pursed, and one side of my mouth curled up and the other side curled down.

"He's six feet two inches tall, two hundred and ten pounds of rock-solid rippling muscle?"

I shrugged.

"Okay, so he's a little shorter than that, but handsome, with steely eyes?"

I shrugged larger.

"Describe him."

"He's strange. Definitely strange."

"You could stay out of the park, girl."

"Yeah, right. You could stop ogling guys."

She stretched and plucked a moss-green pebble from the base of a potted tree and passed it to me.

"What's this?"

"Kryptonite. Just in case."

Chapter 7

In the crush of subway passengers and platform loiterers, he lost her again. But victory planted itself in his brain. LelaT@huntington.edu. The wheels clonked, air whooshed into the tunnel with the departing train, and the dirty concrete, worn smooth from a surge of trampling souls, greeted Ron's triumphant stance. He climbed the steps to the surface. Like taking cold medicine, escape from the city bowels into the sunlight restored free breathing.

All morning, he zoned out during classes, not sure if he answered questions correctly as his thoughts drifted in a sea of jasmine.

~ ~ ~

"Stay… Stay…" Ron said to Fish at the starting line, then backed away.

One stoop from their building, Ron called out, "Okay." Fish galloped. Ron hopped and raised his arms in triumph. "Oh, man, Fish, I win again."

Fish grinned like dogs do from time to time, as if he knew a secret Ron didn't.

They climbed the apartment steps, and Ron plopped on-to the best seat on the couch—the winner's prize, along with evening control of the remote. "What're we going to do?"

Fish stretched onto his lap and licked Ron's face. "Okay, besides this."

Fish barked, and Ron pushed him away.

"Eugh. We have to do something about your breath, and we need a plan." Ron massaged his chin. "A plan so simple it can't fail."

Fish eyeballed him sideways, igniting Ron's memory.

"Yeah, well, that was that plan. This is this plan."

Fish cantered to the computer, tail wagging.

"Right"—Ron nodded—"I have the e-mail address of a goddess of empathy. If anything goes wrong, I'll know it and she'll feel it."

A grin spread, and Ron's tail wagged as he typed.

Subj: Please read ASAP

Hi. You don't know me. Technically, that's not true. We've met, twice. We've danced, and we've shared music, a dog, and a subway.

My name is Ron, and I want to apologize about our first meeting in the park. I'm not a stalker.

I felt drawn to you. Let's call it quirky: running in the rain, talking to the dog, talking to me. Anyway, I don't believe in fate, but our paths crossed in a way that demands attention. I want to discover who you are.

Let's meet again.

I can bring Fish and the three of us can talk. If you'd rather, we can meet somewhere for coffee.

Fish can stay home.
(He doesn't drink coffee.)

I look forward to hearing from you.

His smile touched both ears as he typed the address LelaT@huntington.edu and clicked *Send*. He explored the net for less than two minutes, then checked for new mail.

No response.

Ron frowned. "Not fair to her, Fish. She needs to sign on, read my mail, decide where to meet, and write back." He signed off and noted the time: 1:15 p.m. "What if she's not home or doesn't read e-mail on her cell phone?"

He granted her two hours.

Never in world history had time crept as it did in the next 120 minutes. Even Ron's atomic clock defied the laws of physics.

Tiiiiihck… taaaaahck.

"Come on! It's supposed to be tick-tock, tick-tock." He swayed from side to side, hoping a different angle would improve clock efficiency. None of the twenty-three clocks on the wall or the eight clocks sitting on the armoire ticked faster.

He finished two loads of laundry, unloaded the dishwasher, wiped the stove and nuke machine, brushed Fish, lined up the shoes in his closet according to color, and drew smiley faces on all his tennis balls.

Tiiiiihck… taaaaahck.

He read the same page of *Blood Between Lovers* by Raz Steel four times. Perhaps because vampires scared the hell out of him, or because the sensuality of this book exceeded the sum of its parts.

45

He wanted to call the radio tower in Fort Collins, Colorado.

"There is no listing," the customer service operator droned.

"How can that be? Fort Collins emits the radio signal that controls atomic clocks everywhere."

"I'm sorry, sir, there is no listing," she insisted.

"They're in the middle of the United States." As if she required a geography lesson.

"I assure you, sir, I live on the East Coast. My watch says it's a few minutes before two in the afternoon, and the phone company won't charge you for wheedling the time out of me." Perhaps she pitied him—or she patronized him.

He closed his eyes and imagined Lela in the park. The next thing he knew, giant paws squashed his lap, and Fish's enormous tongue licked his face.

Wake up, sleepyhead. Time to sign on and check your e-mail.

True enough. Of his thirty-one clocks, twenty-two agreed: 3:15 p.m. or later. Majority rules.

He thought nothing functioned slower than his clocks this afternoon until the Wi-Fi carrier proved him wrong.

In his haste, he clicked the wrong button and found himself scrolling through 247 days of correspondence, unable to reverse the errant command. His stomach churned, and his toes stretched up to avoid leg cramps. Smile engaged, he might've been drooling. That might be Fish. Dampness suggested one of them drooled.

Where did Lela want to meet him?

Ron scrolled through the e-mail listing four times.

His disappointment existed on several levels and in no particular order. "How could there be no response?" Maybe she composed offline?

A new feature from the Huntington.edu server allowed him to check e-mail status.

Your mail has been deleted unread.

Ron stumbled around the apartment. "How will I arrange a meeting if she won't read past the subject line?"

Fish didn't respond.

A sinking weight bored its way through Ron's guts. The pressure of a thousand atmospheres pushed against his skull, and his temples pounded with migraine-driven pain. A simple solution eluded him. He dimmed the lights, popped three ibuprofen, and lay down until his headache subsided.

Fish stumbled around the apartment and finally stretched out on the floor next to Ron, head resting on paws. It appeared as if Fish rolled his eyes.

Duh. Draft a message to delay her deleting.

The back of Ron's neck tingled. He hopped up, copied the e-mail into another e-mail, and typed in a new subject line. *We talked in the park.*

He clicked *Send*, signed off, and went in search of two more hours.

Reversing the order of his books, tallest to shortest, took less time than expected. He cleaned the bathroom—not from necessity, but he liked the smell of minty pine. He did his best to avoid the clock wall. Ticking multiplied by thirty-one became inescapable. He grimaced. Fish barked.

"Right. Let's go."

They hurried out the door on their way to the park, with a backward glance at the atomic clock, an hour fifty-three to wait.

~ ~ ~

Fish managed the apartment steps in a single bound. Ron's troubled knee groaned and clicked, refusing to accept its full share of weight. He jumped and landed as any weak-kneed superhero would, glanced both ways for bad guys, then dashed toward the computer so fast no one saw him. Or no one saw him because he lived alone. Ron preferred the former explanation.

Wi-Fi carrier entanglements created the usual delays. He smoothed his cape and entered his mailbox, anticipation encased in each drop of sweat.

Where would they meet? The park? A coffee shop? A bookstore?

No new mail.

Ron leaned forward, adjusted his glasses, and checked e-mail status.

Deleted. Unread.

Again.

He laughed. He didn't want Fish to see him cry.

"Aghh." He twisted in the chair. Fish trotted over and sat next to him so Ron could scratch his head. "What am I going to do if Psyche keeps deleting my mail?" Ron pointed to the giant M embossed on his chest.

"I'm a superhero, aren't I?"

Fish moaned and rolled his eyes again.

"More like a superpatient?"

Duh. Send the letter from a patient.

"You're right. How can Psyche resist a message from someone brimming with emotion?"

Ron copied and pasted his e-mail with a new header when it struck him to take Fish's idea a step further. He wanted Psyche to see the real him, not a pretend persona. This message needed to be from the author he wanted to be, written by Ron.

He deleted and began again.

> Subj: Matterhorn Press Special Edition Edited for Psyche
>
> Walking through the city this morning—low clouds, so flying wasn't an option—I couldn't help but notice the chariot of a goddess parked in the park. What an incredible opportunity!
>
> I'm muddled in brain fog. I'm a writer who can't write, a storyteller moved by the greatest story ever, with no words to express my feelings.
>
> I've studied writing for a long time, and despite how this reads, I've developed a silver-tongued storytelling style. In person I may not always be this glib. On occasion it sounds as if there's a different "me" talking.
>
> People wear masks all the time. Superheroes and mortals. We disguise our faces and we disguise our feelings.
>
> I'd like you to see the real me.
>
> Ron

He clicked *Send*, hurried away, and thumped his chest, cape flapping in the wind.

Confidence overwhelmed him. He promised himself he wouldn't check back until morning.

~ ~ ~

Sleep proved elusive. He invented reasons to crawl out of bed and stroll past the computer, in case a crucial message couldn't wait until sunrise. Everyone knows kitchen water tastes better than bathroom water, and night monsters can't attack you if you're reading. He imagined closet lights also intimidated night monsters, and if his closets possessed lights, he would've flipped them on.

At three-thirty, his eighth or ninth time past the computer, impatience prevailed. He suffered fatigue running from monsters. Besides, in Iceland it was seven-thirty and the sun was rising. That Ron wasn't in Iceland seemed a minor technicality. He woke the computer, launched the browser, and signed on.

Entanglements minimized. He opened the mailbox and scrolled. Any inclination to remain calm disintegrated.

In a rare, perfect moment, life crystallized, thoughts narrowed in focus, breathing stopped, and telemarketers worldwide developed laryngitis.

A communication from Olympus, LelaT@ huntington.edu, yawned at him from the last line in his mailbox.

Chapter 8

Subj: Letter to the Editor c/o Matterhorn Press

Park air is clear, and city sounds harmonize with life that keeps to a steady pace. The soothing effect is like a salve upon my soul.

As comforting as a massage, the park embraces my heart and allows me to soar without a plane. It's a wonder I don't live here. What more might a girl want?

The other day, perhaps the day mentioned in the MP special edition, I thought I saw a man in a fluttering cape. He hurried away from me. Too bad, I've often thought it would be nice to meet a superego.

P

"Yee-haa!" Ron jumped out of his seat. "Lela—I mean, Psyche—wants to meet me." He hoped she wasn't schizophrenic.

He read the letter ten times. The middle of the night seemed an inappropriate time to respond. He didn't want to appear zealous.

He grabbed a water glass and another Oreo and scurried to bed ahead of the monsters. Fish didn't budge.

Ron yawned. No alarms in any of his thirty-one clocks. He relied on internal time-sense, which functioned even when he was asleep. Always.

~ ~ ~

Sun streaming through windows implied today wasn't part of *always*.

Enough time remained to brush his teeth, shower, and head for class. No time to compose an e-mail to Lela. Fish didn't appreciate rushing. He jumped, tugged Ron's pants, scratched the door, and wouldn't stop barking.

Ron eyed him, pointing an accusing finger. "If you wanted to go out earlier, you could've asked then."

Tail down, Fish stretched, rested his head on his paws, and sighed like an old man.

"Okay, okay, I give up. We'll walk through the park."

Fish wagged. Ron rubbed his chin, then Fish's chin. If they hustled they wouldn't be late, and he wouldn't surrender the possibility of another chance meeting with Lela.

The unwritten response distracted him during the hike to the university. The park displayed budding trees and ancient boulders and hundreds of people, none of whom drifted on the wings of a butterfly. A hectic Wednesday schedule meant no time to write until evening.

He sighed like Fish.

~ ~ ~

Fish and Ron raced the last half block home. Ron won, but conceded both couch and remote and parked himself at the computer. He'd enjoyed his day because he spent most of it in an eddy of e-mail induced euphoria.

Subj: Matterhorn Press—Late Editorial Edition

Where do we find empathy these days? Occasionally, analysis transcends the doctor. Couches as we know them will eventually become extinct, especially if social distancing continues. By the time we travel to the psychologist's office, wait in the waiting room—where else would we wait?— then finally become comfortable on the couch, time's up.

Years ago, people thought couches—well, analy-sis—was only for the ill. So, we redefined "ill". Now, analysis is for anyone with good health insurance. Couches have been replaced by easy chairs, and easy chairs have been redefined by ergonomics.

Soon, we will redefine the nature of the doctor/patient relationship. Social distancing allows the patient to sit behind the desk. If the psychologist then stretches out on their couch, who will I call Doctor? Or empath?

A quick response clicked into his mailbox.

Subj: Another editor

Whom.

53

Ron made a fist and punched the air. "My kind of anal girl."

~ ~ ~

Passion creates hunger, and hunger drives culinary sensibilities. Sautéed onions. How much worse could Fish's breath become?

The scent of olive oil and butter traced its way through the apartment. Fish diverted his attention from *Mister Ed*—his favorite TV show—more than once. Ron stirred more than once and foraged in the refrigerator. Blue-green and hairy described long-forgotten contents, and by the time he pulled his head out of the cold, smoke streamed from the stove.

"Layers of leftover cooking add additional flavor," Ron said.

Fish withheld judgment.

The level of smoke increased, requiring added ventilation. Ron flipped the switch on the range hood to start the fan. Nothing happened. He shut it off and tried again.

Haze distorted the ceiling. Experience told him what to expect next. Before he could reach *Romantic Times*—his favorite magazine—the smoke detector blared like an aircraft stall warning device. Fish shook his head. Ron fanned and considered purchasing one edition of *Backpacker* at the corner newsstand. At least it was a larger magazine.

Onions, mushrooms, black olives, asparagus, applesauce, and strawberries temporarily satisfied his passion. Sated, Fish returned to the couch, and Ron to the computer.

Subj: Matterhorn Press—Extremely Late Editorial Edition

Sometimes a publisher such as Matterhorn, or a writer such as yours truly, makes mistakes requiring retractions.

"How anal do I want to be?" Ron glanced at Fish, who kept his gaze narrowed on him.

"What do you think? Who or whom?"

Fish barked once.

"Gotcha."

This isn't one of those times.

I've checked with the highest authority available, who, after many years of dogged editing experience, assures me that the objective form of "who" used in the previous edition, is, in fact, acceptable.

Furthermore, former colleagues Carl and Carl preferred amiable contemporary prose to more formal syntax. We can trust my intuition. It's not like I'm crazy or anything.

Residual smoke set off the alarm again.

Tired of fanning, Ron collapsed onto the bed. Events of the past couple of days swirled into a collage of colors and sounds and smells, and he drifted into an altered-reality state in which pillowcases and Rorschach tests tangled hands and feet and mind.

Fish snored like Diana used to, and the night passed

like so many others: Ron needed a raincoat in the dream world.

~ ~ ~

Sunrise streamed through windows before the city could yawn, and Ron bathed in the briefest glimpse of an orange fireball. He nuked water and made Swiss mocha decaf. The browser allowed unusually easy access. He knew he'd find another response from Psyche.

> Subj: Letter to the Editor:
>
> Dogged editor needs glasses and a better dictionary.
>
> P
>
> p.s. Glad you aren't crazy.
>
> p.p.s. Anything else I should know about you?

However brief, the e-mail maintained further contact. She asked a question that demanded an answer.

> Subj: Straightforward and up front
>
> I listen to the same song twenty times in a row, I quote movie lines before the actors say them, all my clocks are set on different times, and I concede there exists the remotest chance I might be the slightest bit outside of the mainstream.
>
> Ron

He considered signing it Mark-in-the-Park. *Nope. I'm not in the park now.*

He called Handyman Dave to report the broken stove fan, connected with the answering machine, and left a message. Fish and Ron hurried to school—big day, the start of midterms.

The morning arrived directly from a painting— breeze, sun, deep-blue sky, and nearly breathable air, a rarity in New York City. Buildings appeared cleaner, streets less littered, people more considerate. Honking horns sounded politer. All equated to a good day to practice underground train riding without melting.

What if he orchestrated another meeting and Lela insisted on another train ride? *Dad always said, "Face your fears head-on."*

Ron had purchased a harness and donned sunglasses and used the Seeing Eye dog disguise so Fish could ride with him.

He swiped a MetroCard twice, fine manipulation being problematic for Fish, and they parked together on the narrow platform waiting for the express, pressed into the commuting crowd, surrounded by lilac and wild roses and Old Spice. Ron closed his eyes and opened his mouth, allowing senses to drift on the sea of perfumed New York multitudes.

He focused on voices, high and low, gruff and mellow, the whooshing of air vents, the metal-on-metal grating of an onrushing train, particles swirling in subterranean air. Everything added to the taste of the city.

His eyes popped open. It wasn't a good idea to stay in the dark for long in the Big Apple, even when escorted by a ferocious dog like Fish.

No milling in this crowd. People moved with

deliberate intensity. Rush hour. A train roared past. *Why didn't it stop?* The ceiling spun around. The walls closed in. People jostled him.

"Can't you see I'm blind?"

His head swam, and sweat streaked his skin. *What was Dad thinking?* More importantly, what was Ron thinking?

~ ~ ~

It seemed forever before he staggered into Goddard Hall and past the psychology department office. Dr. Coleman blocked his path.

"How's the paper coming, Ron? What if time slowed down? Wasn't that it?"

Ron winked at Fish, except he didn't rotate his head in time, and it's possible Dr. Coleman thought Ron winked at him. A wolfish smirk belied the professor's effectual posturing.

Dr. Coleman cocked his chin. "You look peaked. Are you all right? Would you like a drink of water?" He rummaged in his shoulder bag for a bottle.

Ron wasn't sure he answered the questions in chronological order, or that he answered all of them. His mouth opened and words tumbled out. "Yes. Exactly. It's coming along, slower than I'd like, but I haven't figured out if that's time relative to me, or time relative to the universe. Like right now, relative to the universe, I'm late for class."

Dr. Coleman leaned closer. "I have thoughts about relative time, if you have a few minutes."

Fish sneezed. Ron held a grin in check. "Sorry," Ron said, "not today. I have to tend a sick friend."

"Someone close?"

Fish sat, whined, and raised a paw.

Ron shot him a look. *What're you, nuts?*

"Very close," Ron said.

Dr. Coleman beamed unfazed, un-acknowledging Fish's response. "Your new class, Psychology of the Male Mind in Love? How's that going?"

Ron nodded, shrugged, and edged down the hallway. "Fine, fine."

"If you need help, let me know. I have experience in that department." Two rows of sparkling white teeth flashed at Ron. "Glad to work hand in hand with you."

Ron waved. "'Kay. I'll keep that in mind."

They hurried around a corner. Ron ruffled Fish's head and offered a horse-faced glance. "You almost blew that one. You know I was winking at you."

Fish seemed unfazed—his smile mimicked Dr. Coleman's.

~ ~ ~

Distraction pursued Ron, and Fish followed. Lela burned in his psyche. Had it been months, he would've thought about it in terms of months, but since it had only been days, he still tallied hours.

They strolled home through the park, and Ron calculated. He wanted to see Lela again, not like their previous park meetings, but a toe-to-toe, hand in hand, lost-in-the-fabric-of-her-being meeting that accompanies a first date.

He adjusted his pants. His desire for a date had no relation to the emanation spreading south of the border. He readjusted pants. Almost none. Arranging an encounter required finesse. It required subtlety. It required compromising his determination to have his novel published. *No way, right?*

He squinted at Fish. "Do me a favor. Next time we see Lela, tell her I only have time for writing *or* a relationship, and I'm committed to writing."

Fish didn't respond.

They continued in silence, hands behind Ron's back, tail between Fish's legs, heads bowed.

Ron scrunched his nose, pursed his lips, and jabbered out of the side of his mouth. "Come on, Fish. Wanna race?" He tapped the invisible *M* emblazoned on his chest. "Mark-in-the-Park can't wait to attack his keyboard."

They hurried past unflagging street hawkers.

"Veee… nilla. Ice cream. Eat dessert first. Veee… nilla."

"Fresh roasted nuts. Get 'em while you're sane."

"Watches. Get one before time ticks away."

Fish barked.

"Right. You keep an eye out for kryptonite vendors."

Chapter 8 ½

"You're typing a five-page treatise on the difference between redwoods and oaks?" Lela had a hard time keeping the laughter out of her voice.

"I'm e-mailing Professor Kirin," I said.

"You can't wait for your advisor to help?"

"I'm not meeting with him until Friday."

"That would be tomorrow."

"I'm making an impassioned plea."

"Impassioned or psycho?"

"Do you think Professor Kirin will know the difference?"

"One of the foremost authorities on adolescent behavior? I think you'll have difficulty disguising your true identity."

I smirked, and Lela grinned like a baboon. Dog pranced and Lela paraded, proud of an achievement I'd yet to discover. I needed to stay focused on my thoughts. Professor Kirin was no different than any other university bureaucrat who wanted to maintain control of his little world. Ego problems didn't plague me, so the issue boiled down to how to satisfy his need for power when he enrolled me in Crimes.

I was on page two when struck by epiphany. Professor Kirin must not have seen any communication from me.

Being an undoubtedly reasonable man, he would have already granted my request if he had. My appeals never made it past Ms. Naughton. It was *her* desire for power I needed to satisfy. What do power-mongers crave when they don't have an acknowledging title?

To be recognized as the person in charge. Our last conversation held the clues.

I punched *Delete* and started anew.

Subj: Special Dispensation

Dear Ms. Naughton,
I need your help. My postgrad plans are set in stone. I have to graduate with my class. I can't do that unless I'm granted admission to Crimes in Psychology for next fall. I'll sit in the corner, I won't interrupt, I'll hand in my assignments early. Professor Kirin won't recognize the difference between one hundred ninety-three and one hundred ninety-four students.

Please, enroll me in the class. I'll be eternally grateful.

Sincerely,
Willow Bolden, Junior

I clicked *Send* and directed my attention to Lela, but she was already engrossed in a textbook. I studied for an hour, until Dog rubbed my leg with the *doorbell* look. A bad omen—early evening, school night. If only I could teach Dog how to bark and scare away unwanted visitors.

I whooshed the door open and caught Elliot's micro-expression as he was about to knock. The corners of his mouth twisted down. Pained memory or pained anticipation? I invited him in against all wisdom. If Elliot needed to talk with me, I couldn't ignore him. I'd already broken his heart. What was left? Sweat rolled under my arms.

"Howdy," Elliot said. He appeared more uncomfortable than I felt, dancing from leg to leg like a kid who needed to pee. "It's been a long week. I'm burstin' with news. How 'bout a movie?" He sounded hopeful.

After our last conversation, the question seemed bizarre. I maintained a blank expression. Elliot realized his mistake and saved me the trouble of answering.

"I guess we're not just takin' a break, huh? I was kinda hopin'…"

Obviously not what I was hoping, but I hadn't thought of any better way to explain it to him. I hadn't thought I needed a better way. I maintained silence.

"You caught me nappin'," Elliot said, "like a bear sneakin' up on Davy Crockett." He forced a smile, perhaps proud of his analogy.

I sensed Lela *sneakin' up* on us.

"Can I buy anyone a drink? Hi, Elliot. This is a surprise, isn't it?" Lela said, glancing at us both.

"I'm a little unsettled, that's all," Elliot said.

Lela nodded. "That's understandable. Coffee? Tea? Moonshine?"

I kicked her, but Elliot ignored the jibe.

"I'm not thirsty. Guess I just couldn't drink past this lump in my throat."

I knew Elliot. It wasn't his intention, but now guilt wrapped around my spine.

Elliot blushed. "Ma always said I'd know when to

conquer a broken heart. Guess this isn't the time. My head's still poundin'. Kinda like wearin' a coon cap three sizes too small."

"Moms are full of wisdom," Lela said. "Especially Willow's mom. I call her whenever Willow's giving me a hard time."

I kicked her again. Harder, in case she indulged serious thoughts about calling Mom.

Elliot studied the hardwood floor. He glanced away, then at the floor again. "I wanted to invite you to a party on Saturday," he said. "Guess that's out of the question?"

This time, Lela saved me the trouble of responding. "Why, Elliot, that's so sweet of you," she said, "I'd love to go to a party."

Elliot's face scrunched in confusion. I was going to kick Lela a third time, but for a moment, it seemed like Elliot would do it for me, then he blanched.

"I-I-I didn't mean…"

"Wait, wait, I forgot, I have a paper due Monday," Lela said. "I'll be working all weekend. But maybe Willow wants to go to a party?" She sidestepped, anticipating my foot.

Elliot transformed from pale to blossoming scarlet. "I'm sorry," he said to me. "I didn't mean to embarrass you."

Elliot was apologizing when it should've been Lela and me requesting forgiveness.

"Guess I'm not over it as fast as you. It'll take time to work it out." Elliot failed to make eye contact with either of us. "I'd better go," he said. "Sorry to have barged in." He forced another smile and zipped down the stairs.

"I'm sorry too," Lela said to me. "I didn't want to miss the excitement."

"You didn't have to be part of the excitement."

64

Lela twirled, hands over her head. "I was swept up in the moment. Besides, I thought it would be easier on you if I did the talking."

Sometimes, Lela's peculiar idea of logic made sense.

~ ~ ~

Out of habit, I checked e-mail before going to bed. I'd sent my request after hours, so I wasn't expecting a response until tomorrow morning.

Subj: re: Special Dispensation

Dear Ms. Bolden,

I'm afraid you have me mistaken with someone else. It is not within my purview to grant dispensation to you or any other student, special or otherwise.

I remain yours truly,

Clarisse Naughton
Administrative Assistant
(Not yet queen)
Department of Psychology
Huntington University

Not yet queen. That only meant I ought to grant her perspicuity I'd formerly failed to recognize.

Chapter 9

Lela strolled around the apartment like a Cheshire cat for two days. I didn't ask and she didn't volunteer until I heard her moan at the computer, and not like she was in pain. She typed and tittered, her flirting giggle.

"What's up?"

"Oh, nothing."

Miss Innocent. "I know you better than that. What's so amusing?"

"I've met somebody."

"Online?"

Lela allowed a guilty nod. "We haven't met, met. He sent me an e-mail, and we've been writing back and forth. He's clever."

I rolled my eyes.

Lela hung her head. "I know, I know. He could be some wacko slasher. I haven't divulged our address, or my full name. This is just innocent fun. He hasn't suggested meeting or calling or anything else. He's been nothing but a gentleman, and like I said, a clever one at that."

"Be careful." Like telling your goldfish to stop swimming in circles.

Was swimming in circles anything like walking in the park? Since dancing with Mark, I marched through the park to and from school every day. I understood why,

I just didn't want to admit it out loud. I left Lela at the keyboard and headed to Huntington.

Today was no exception to my parade. Street vendors echoed in the background.

No Mark-in-the-Park in the park this morning. I laughed. Somehow, the name fit.

~ ~ ~

I rushed from class to class, my feet barely touching the ground. I planned an important meeting at three and arrived five minutes early, but had to wait since Dr. Coleman arrived ten minutes late.

I offered him my hand.

His chiseled jaw commanded attention, and killer peacock-blue eyes matched Lela's current nail polish. But perfectly coiffed hair and his damp, limp grip suggested all the girls swooning over him in class may have misplaced expectations.

"Hi. I'm Willow Bolden."

"You're in Psychology in Everyday Life? Good class, good class. You're…" He squinted, trying to recall information I thought he should know. "A sophomore?" He sat on the corner of his desk with one leg dangling.

"No, sir, I'm a junior, with a three-point-nine GPA. I need to take Professor Kirin's Crimes class, but it's full. I have one fall semester left, so I have to take the class in September. I'll bet a lot of those students are sophomores and could take Crimes the following fall. I hope—"

I didn't have to hope aloud. His hand shot out like a traffic cop to stop me mid-wish.

"Say no more. It's a required class for your degree, and if you don't take it this fall, you'll have to come back

67

after graduation. Professor Kirin and I are working together on a project. If I ask, he'll grant us a favor. I don't expect him to kick someone out of the class, but I'm sure he'll make room for one more serious student. Consider yourself in."

"Thank you, sir. Umm, there is one other tiny complication."

"Oh? What else can I do besides enroll you in the class with the longest wait list in university history?" He didn't sound annoyed. Yet.

"I, umm, haven't fulfilled all the requirements for the class. Actually, it's just one prereq I haven't met, and I can't see why I need—"

The traffic cop stopped me again, this time with a frown. "Which prerequisite?"

"Abnormal Psychology: The Disturbed Mind. I'm not interested in that class. Besides, it's also only offered in the fall semester, so there's no way I could take it before next fall when I take Crimes."

My advisor strolled behind his desk, plopped into a high-backed swivel chair, and spun 360 degrees like a kid. Or me. Smile reactivated, he rummaged in the center desk drawer.

"I'm sure I can convince Professor Kirin to squeeze one more student into Crimes. However, I know him well enough to assure you without the proper prerequisites, it ain't gonna happen. Like it or not, if you want to take Crimes, you'll have to take Ab Psych first."

He filed his nails. "I know Professor Kirin won't allow you to take the courses concurrently, so you'll have to arrange to take Ab Psych before the fall. That's his class too." He winked. "All you have to do is convince Professor Kirin to conduct a summer seminar."

Dr. Coleman's grin vanished. "Are you a professional lobbyist?" he asked. "You have a better chance of meeting with the President of the United States than of persuading Professor Kirin to present a private seminar this summer. Good luck with that." He spun 360 degrees in the opposite direction.

"Sir?"

"Sorry, Willow."

Fauxpology not accepted, I thought he might at least offer me cheese with my whine.

"You're on your own for arranging summer class. There's nothing I can do. Let me know when you've arranged it, though, and we'll add your name to the class list for Crimes."

My shoulders slumped. "Any suggestions how to convince him to teach a private seminar?"

"Talk with him."

"I can't. Ms. Naughton won't schedule an appointment for me."

"Go around her. Contact him directly. Try e-mail."

"I tried. She's the one who answers his e-mail."

"Not his *private* e-mail."

I glanced away. My toes tapped. "Yeah, so?"

Dr. Coleman slid open the center desk drawer again, pulled out a small directory, and thumbed through. He unpeeled a Post-it note, scribbled, and handed it to me.

"You didn't get this from me."

I faked a smile and accepted the crumb. I slogged away from my advisor's office, head down, scuffing the floor.

Lela wasn't home when I arrived, and I planted myself at the computer.

Subj: Crimes in Psychology

Dear Professor Kirin,

To take Crimes next fall, I need to complete Ab Psych over the summer. Can you teach me in a private seminar since there is no Ab Psych scheduled over the summer? I realize this is an inconvenience for you, but I promise to work hard and not cause problems.

Sincerely,

Willow Bolden, Junior

I didn't have long to wait for a response.

Subj: re: Crimes in Psychology

Dear Ms. Bolden, Junior,

You're already causing me problems. How'd you obtain my private e-mail address?

I've checked. You're not registered in my fall Crimes class. I spoke with Ms. Naughton, and she informed me you've already made this appeal. My answer remains firm. No, you can't enroll in Crimes. The class is full, there's a waitlist, and you aren't at the top of it.

And no, I definitely will not be giving a private seminar in Ab Psych this summer. It doesn't fit into my schedule. If Huntington doesn't offer a course you want, try another university.

Furthermore, I'll thank you to restrict your communications with me to my official university address.

Professor Kirin

Yikes. Not what I hoped for, but I clung to my advisor's promise. I googled other city universities. Only NYU offered Ab Psych during the summer. I lived within strolling distance of their campus. A class couldn't get any more convenient. Actually, it could. An 8:00 a.m., three-hour-long class five days a week for six weeks, by definition, couldn't be convenient.

Up before sunrise all summer. I could deal with that. But NYU cost three and a half times as much as Huntington for one course. Unaffordable.

I'd irritated Professor Kirin. At this point, I tossed discretion to the smog. I didn't want to grovel, but what choice did I have? I wrote to his private e-mail address.

Subj: one issue at a time

Professor Kirin, I wish to respect your privacy, and I understand what it's like to have a hectic schedule. Look, can't we make a deal?

I'll do research for you or proofread your next textbook if you'll teach the Ab Psych seminar this summer.

Please?

Willow

Dog strutted past but refused to let me pet him. Groveling didn't become me. In moments, a response appeared in my mailbox.

Subj: re: one issue at a time

NO!

A second e-mail appeared.

Subj: P.S.

Any further correspondence from you at this e-mail address will be deleted unread.

I screamed and pounded the desk. Dog jumped halfway across the room. I deleted every piece of mail to and from Professor Kirin. No trace of the bastard remained in my computer. I tore the Post-it into tiny pieces and brushed it into the kitchen garbage. If Elliot was an oak tree in a forest, Professor Kirin was a fire hydrant in a dog park.

Chapter 10

Fish woke Ron in the middle of the night. Ron was unsure who panted harder.

"Are you whining because you didn't understand your dream, or because I didn't understand mine?"

Ron grabbed the pad and pen he kept near the bed. A half hour later, he'd written more than three pages and couldn't stop. "Whose dream is this, anyway?"

Fish curled on the floor beside the bed. He glanced at Ron with a *What're you, nuts, dude? It's the middle of the night* look. Ron whispered the words he was writing.

~ ~ ~

Fish sang while Ron flossed, brushed his teeth, and shaved. Ron poured mouthwash into a bowl and placed it on the bathtub ledge. Fish eyed it surreptitiously and kept singing. Ron chose mouthwash by color instead of brand: red seemed like cherry-flavored medicine, which is good for you, tan looked like shampoo but he'd tried it anyhow, and now fish-tank blue because it reminded Ron of, well, fish. Same results. Any of them would've worked if Fish would lap it into his mouth and gargle.

What if Ron poured mouthwash on Fish's Frosted Flakes?

Ron showered, rubbed hand lotion onto his face, and dressed. Fish discovered an obscure cable channel that ran *Mister Ed* marathons Saturday mornings. He hopped onto the sofa, and Ron clicked the remote, volume up. Fish is a dog, of course of course, but hummed along with the theme song anyway.

The sun would rise soon, and Ron wandered the apartment. He sat next to Fish, TV volume down, and read aloud for two minutes—vampire romance—then popped up, peeked out the window, and paced. He read half a chapter, and finally, inspired by author Raz Steel, he seated himself at the computer, pounding keys, writing a romantic comedy. Previous attempts had produced partials of a murder mystery and a psycho thriller. Editors expressed no interest in his partials.

He typed for an hour, then wandered into the kitchen to nuke coffee water. He filled a mug from the spigot, and water sprayed from the top of the attached filter. Ron could never swallow the idea that New York tap water tasted great. When he'd moved to the city, Ron had sworn he'd never do certain things: dance with strangers in the park, adopt stray dogs, or drink unfiltered tap water. One out of three wasn't such a bad ratio. Mopping up reminded him he hadn't yet heard from Handyman Dave about the stove fan.

His thoughts jumped randomly from Psyche—who owed him an e-mail—to school to Fish.

This Saturday didn't totally belong to them. The chancellor of Huntington had scheduled a special luncheon at one o'clock—social, not an official school function—and Ron had promised to be there. He searched his memory but failed to retrieve any legitimate reason he'd made such a promise.

As his father used to say, "Keep that thing *in* your pants."

Ron squinted at Fish. "What does that have to do with making promises?"

Fish waved, barely missing a note. At least the quote was accurate.

Ron resettled at the computer. Words flowed, and thoughts coalesced long before dressing time for the luncheon.

He rummaged around dark closet recesses. Fish tagged alongside. Sunlight streamed through the apartment windows. Ron cursed the cheapskate builder who'd neglected to install closet lights. Nonetheless, he managed khakis, a black T-shirt, and a sport coat.

Fish grasped he wasn't on the invitation list, and Ron figured he'd be happy hanging around campus while Ron fulfilled his social obligation. The subway to Columbus Circle tempted them, but twice in one week seemed like overload. They left in plenty of time to walk through the park.

A magnificent spring day greeted them with a Manhattan zephyr and a steel-blue sky. Buildings swayed gently to the metropolitan music, a stark contrast to the weekday cacophony. To understand change in city sounds, one has to understand what remains constant throughout the change. In New York City, it's the street hawkers.

"Fresh roasted nuts. Get 'em before the squirrels do."

"Veee… nilla. Ice cream. Get it before it melts."

"Watches. Get one so you know when to eat nuts and ice cream."

Fish pranced along Fifty-Ninth Street as they passed the giant cement statue with little cherubs at the bottom.

Fish's tail beat in rapid motion, much like Ron's, and probably for the same reason.

They headed for their rock.

Budding trees compelled shadows to dance across the path. More pigeons meandered than flew. Daffodils and grassy knolls and joggers dotted the landscape. Couples strolled, children circled their parents, dog-walkers, cat-walkers, bird-watchers, fish-feeders—as distinguished from *Fish*-feeders—homeless, helpless, hapless. People read on benches, slept on benches, people-watched on benches; people threw Frisbees, caught baseballs, bounced basketballs; people loitered, littered, and lunched.

Every freaking person in New York City visited Central Park today—except Lela.

Ron's knee creaked, and a debilitating half limp accompanied him out of the park.

They arrived at the chancellor's home fashionably late. Ron chastised himself for being fashionable. The doorman frowned at them. Fish trotted onto campus, and Ron entered the den of the lioness.

Hilary Nixon administered a tight university and a loose home. Effusive, touchy-feely, domineering, married and divorced three times, a real charmer. Nothing happened on campus without clearing her office. Rumor suggested she hired everyone from interns to assistants as playmates; it was unclear if the hirelings were aware of the distinction. Today she displayed two: her newest assistant vice chancellor, and her newest best friend, Dr. Coleman.

Scuttlebutt said Hilary flirted with everyone and bedded the most delectable men. Either Dr. Coleman was a switch-hitter, or Hilary wanted the companionship of another psychologist. The reason for her continued interest in Ron remained unclear, and Ron preferred it to stay that way.

Ron drifted through the chancellor's magnificent Victorian home. *Seasick* was a good way to describe how he felt with so many people swimming around him. Who said he was obligated to face his fears head-on?

Waitstaff in formal black-and-white attire lent an air of stuffiness. Fine linen draped across tables laden with culinary delicacies whose names he couldn't pronounce and whose tastes he didn't wish to experience. Stupendous crystal chandeliers hung in both dining room and foyer. A string quartet and streaming sunlight reflecting and refracting through cut glass created a ballroom atmosphere of classical music and glittering rainbows.

French doors opened to a courtyard with a slate patio surrounded by early-spring blossoms in an ornamental garden. Immaculate. Pristine. Isolated except for the bar. Guests congregated until served, then most retreated inside the house, drinks in hand. Ron lingered on the patio opposite the bar, sipping bottled water, admiring a clematis, too early-bloomed for the rest of the city, when the serpentine arm of the hostess entwined itself with his and her song caressed his inner ear, searching for his spine.

"Ron, it's the little things in life that mean so much. Fancy homes, fine wines"—her hand skated across her dress—"delicate fabric."

His lower back made him moan and wince, a combination of a lousy computer chair, an altered gait on the hike through the park, and so many people so close. If Hilary noticed—and not much escaped her, except perhaps Ron's disinterest—she'd probably interpret the moan as sexual, the wince as orgasmic.

"Those things pale in comparison to the simple

company of a friend… or lover. I'm so pleased you're here." Like an expensive truffle, the words luxuriated on the serpent's tongue.

"It's my pleasure, ma'am." He allowed a slight tilt of his head.

"Ma'am? Really, Ron, you make me sound so old. I'm not, you know."

Conceded. Twice his age, she could pass for mid-thirties.

"You're standing alone in a corner. Is everything okay? I would've thought a student of psychology would find the mix of personalities here fascinating. How about taking a stroll through the guests with me?"

Through the guests. What an odd way to put it. He didn't seem to have a choice. She maneuvered him toward the bar. "Okay," he said. He wanted to believe he'd agreed.

They strolled through clusters of department heads; committee chairmen; the university president and his predecessor—though not the previous chancellor—deans of everything deanable; the financial proletariat; the university chaplain, a rabbi—Huntington is a New York-liberal university—half a dozen alumni whose names correlated with buildings, or at least building wings; a smattering of grad students whom Ron took to be either future buildings or Hilary's future conquests; and one perniciously beautiful woman wrapped in a black dress tighter than his escort's.

The woman glanced at him with a wicked shimmy from shoulders to hips. Seductive, charming, coy, subtle, suggestive, disarming.

He hated her.

And he loved her.

Chapter 11

Diana Burnett, the cougar who had once pried open Ron's mouth, shoved her arm down his throat, ripped out his heart, thrown it on the ground, and stomped on it, winked. Her gaze held him prisoner.

"Hilary. Gracious of you to invite me," Diana said.

No, it wasn't. *Gracious* was banned from Hilary's vocabulary. Hilary courted the company of women who challenged her supremacy, happy to go face-to-face or, as Ron glanced at their dresses, breast-to-breast, with the most pointed competition.

"Diana, don't you look ravishing," Hilary said.

"That dress makes you look ten years younger," Diana responded.

Claws in, ladies.

Hilary smirked. "I'm pleased you accepted my invitation. I hope you're enjoying yourself. There're so many eligible young men here, it's hard to know where to begin."

"You're monopolizing one of the most eligible. Perhaps I could borrow him for a while?"

Borrow him? Like a library book?

Hilary cocked her head and slithered from his arm, accepting the challenge and asserting her authority. "We need to discuss final details of the freshman open house. In my office, first thing Monday morning."

Diana, dean of Public Relations, nodded. Hilary glided away, casting a glance back at Ron as if to say, *we aren't done today*. Diana hooked his arm and guided him into a corner. Always direct, her hand slid down his sleeve until she touched skin.

"I've missed you, Ron."

He bit his lower lip. He hadn't pursued Diana to Huntington. It was a coincidence of circumstance that they were both here.

Diana leaned into him. "We've seen so little of each other," she said. "I hope we can remedy that. Get together for dinner? I'd enjoy an evening with you."

Clear enough. She meant: *It might've been a long time since we've reveled in carnal knowledge, but I miss you and want to enjoy your company and talk about old times.*

A beautifully sculpted leg peeked out from the thigh-high slit of her dress and disappeared into the curve of her hip. Sheer black nylons, strappy heels, hair up with a few dangling strands, and deliciously dark eyes that swallowed a man in a sea of feminine wiles—all posed the question.

He was, after all, only human.

"Okay."

"Splendid. You can take me home after the party. There's a new café in the Village I'm dying to try. Tomorrow we can sleep late, have breakfast and the *Times* in bed, and we'll see what the day brings."

Her pupils had long since dilated, her tongue traced a line around lascivious lips, and her hips swayed in a devious dance; he recognized the posture. He'd first seen it in a classroom when she'd guest lectured. He'd been sitting in the front row. Without touching him, she'd teased everything teasable that morning. Diana engaged his mind *and* his sex drive—there should be a word for that—before she ever took him for a spin.

She raised a brow as she caressed his hand and continued. "I wouldn't mind a day of being ravaged. Mondays are hectic, and I often have meetings into the evening, or I go to the gym late, but we can pick up again on Tuesday. Wednesdays are much like Mondays, but then I should be free Thursday evening. Of course, next weekend will be difficult with the freshman open house, but I'm sure we can work it out."

Okay, so he'd missed her meaning.

Diana wasn't missing him as in, *I'm lonely, and one evening reminiscing about old times will take care of that.* She'd planned his entire future. Old age flashed before his eyes: a doddering gray-haired man sedentary at the kitchen table; Diana in black heels, black pantyhose, and an apron, un-aged, her tongue outlining a lecherous smirk. *Finish your dinner, Ron, and come to bed for dessert.*

He refocused on Diana's swollen lips, well-defined cheekbones, the sensation of her fingers on his flesh. Discomfort confirmed his throbbing id. He wouldn't mind a whole day of ravaging. However, this was not the woman with whom he sought eternal bliss. One night, though? That would clarify his priorities for Diana. If she was just horny, she'd go for a one-nighter. She'd only object if she wanted more than sex. Diana? Not likely.

"How about if we—"

The image of Psyche dressed in a white T-shirt jogged around him. Psyche stretched, her hand almost touching his. Spring rain traced a delicate line across her shoulders, making her clothing cling. Her eyes sparkled, and the faint scent of jasmine wafted in the air. The earthy qualities that ignited a stranglehold on his heart in the park renewed their grip.

She whispered to the dog and she spoke to Ron; her laughter, her misdirected anger, her expression of single-minded determination cast an unbreakable spell.

Diana's touch stirred a single sensation, but an unseen Psyche evoked myriad feelings. He swallowed hard as resolve trickled toward his libido. Like a gardener cultivating the soil, Lela's laughter tilled his emotions, and the moment she faruffled, he understood what he wanted.

"I can't tonight, Diana, but if you just want to talk, we can have dinner tomorrow night. I have a hectic schedule the entire week."

"Just talk?" Disappointment dripped from her chin and drooled into the cavity between her breasts. Her hands anchored his biceps, reinforcing the sincerity of her words.

"Ron, I'm thrilled to have you tomorrow night, but I want more. I'm not suggesting a tryst. I crave the relationship we used to have. I miss that closeness, the intimacy. I want the one-on-one romance, with flowers and phone calls in the middle of the day and heavy breathing at night."

She paused and leaned close. "I know I hurt you before," she whispered in his ear, "but I promise I won't ever do that again."

Uh-oh.

Perhaps he'd lost something in translation, but that sounded like *Trust me.*

Psyche faruffled in his other ear.

"Diana, that's too much, too fast for me. If you want to hang out tomorrow night and talk, that's fine. I like you. I enjoy being with you. What you're suggesting is the romance that comes with love. I'm not in love with you." *Anymore.*

I can't believe I said that.

Suddenly he needed to clarify his feelings, for both of them. "I don't want to be in love with you. Friends, yes. That's fine with me. The physical stuff got in the way of intimacy before. Your friendship is far more important to me than having sex with you. Do you understand?"

She nodded, and sinking relief drifted below his waist.

"I understand. You're not in love, and you don't want to be in love. I don't want to be in love, either. I just want to savor a connection to someone—you. And yes, tomorrow night will be fine. We'll just talk. I promise. How about picking me up at four-thirty? We'll start early."

"'Kay."

Her grin spread in a victory Ron didn't understand. "You're sure you're not available tonight?"

~ ~ ~

Ron returned to the party like a seal floating on the Arctic Ocean, polar bears eyeing him from either side of the ice pack, one licking its fur to preen, another dipping its paw to test whether the water was the right temperature, both drooling through leers.

Every time Hilary sauntered past him, she touched his arm or brushed her hand across the nape of his neck. Diana knew him well enough to allow a measure of space but didn't refrain from shooting him coy glances. She peered over her shoulder and shimmied her derrière. She was a musician extraordinaire—he the instrument and, oh brother, she knew how to play him.

Cute as a penguin, a young redheaded woman in waitstaff black and white stomped toward Ron with a tray of hors d'oeuvres. Her sea-foam-green eyes narrowed, and her forehead furrowed. "Sir? Canapé?" Despite her obvious anger, her charming Scottish brogue dominated the first impression.

"The ones on your left are portobello stuffed with crabmeat in hollandaise sauce. To your right is classic pâté in béarnaise sauce."

She must be distracted by her feelings. No one puts pâté in béarnaise sauce.

"Thank you." He chose portobello. "Excuse me, is there anything I can do to help? You seem upset."

She studied him for a moment, and seemed to be gauging her response. "I'm here to work, not to be propositioned, and certainly not to be groped!"

"Someone has been acting less like a gentleman than one would hope at a function like this?"

"That's an understatement."

"He's a pig-ass?"

She nodded hard, but her expression softened, and the faintest of beams danced in her eyes.

Ron leaned closer and lowered his voice. "You're very professional doing your job. There's no excuse for rudeness."

She slid her tongue across her lips, and her pupils dilated.

Uh-oh. Not what I meant.

"Tell you what. Whoever the creep is, if he says anything else, come and find me. We'll march him out back and contract someone to beat the crap out of him. Deal?" He offered his hand. "Ron."

"Rhiannon. Raeburn."

"Ms. Raeburn, it's been my pleasure. Don't let an occasional pig-ass create distaste for all mankind. Remember my offer."

"You sound like my knight in shining armor."

"A knight? No, just a friend and a humble procurer of knights for damsels in distress." He plucked another portobello.

They disengaged. She radiated, head up, shoulders back, as she continued her job. He swallowed a long swig from his water bottle and studied the party guests. No time to admire all the beautiful people before trouble approached.

Chapter 12

Fantasies faded as my dream dissolved. I rubbed sleep from my eyes, listened for a moment, then realized Lela must not be home. I stomped off in search of a distraction from dream sex. Dog scooted out of the way. Too many high-calorie snacks to choose from in the refrigerator. I winced at the idea of gaining a few pounds but scrounged nonetheless.

The apartment door opened, and Lela's voice echoed in the kitchen. My radar activated immediately to the stressors in her tone.

"Are you dressed, girl? You have company."

I couldn't imagine what visitor would put Lela on edge. I backed out of the refrigerator.

Elliot beamed like Lela at a buy-one, get-one shoe sale.

"Elliot found me on campus and escorted me home." Lela's eyebrows shrugged. Tacit understanding—she would've tried to dissuade Elliot.

"Sorry to barge in on y'all. Can we talk?" Elliot flexed the mountain-man physique hidden beneath a dapper suit I'd never seen him wear.

"Sure, sure. No problem." I flashed Lela a "y'all're off the hook" smile. I could deal with the guy needing closure.

"Good." Elliot studied my nightshirt and bed hair, then glanced at his watch. "Umm, maybe we could go out for lunch?"

"Sure, sure."

Elliot's smile widened.

Another blip reactivated my radar. Lela had her radar, I had mine.

I dressed in loose jeans and a T-shirt, pulled back my hair, and left the cell phone on my desk.

Elliot didn't speak much on the way to the Corner Café. He asked a few polite questions about school and the classes I hoped to take next fall. I didn't go into detail about the Crimes predicament. He hadn't listened when we were a couple; I hardly expected him to be interested now. I let him ramble until food arrived.

"I spoke with your mother," Elliot said.

All chewing ceased. Good thing it wasn't a stand-up lunch, because I would've fallen down.

"My *mother*?"

"I took Lela's advice. I thought your mother could tell me what's going on in your head. One year to finish at Huntington, then grad school, a real job, and our wedding plans. You'd be changing roommates." He chuckled at that.

"Anyway, you're from a hick town, and this is the big city. Your mom explained it to me."

"She did?" I gawked.

"Oh, yeah. Your mom understands you."

"She does?"

Then he did an Elliot thing. He pulled his chin up, chomping his lips together like a chimpanzee, and nodded. Long ago, Lela tagged him "Monkey Boy," which she no longer needed to verbalize. She'd just curl one arm into a big O and scratch her ribs. We'd laughed so hard and done that so often, I couldn't help doing it now.

Elliot continued, unfazed. "When you backed away a couple of weeks ago, I wondered, how could I ever trust this person again?" He shook his head and shrugged his shoulders. "It'll take time, but bear with me.

"Your mom encouraged me to trust you. Brings me to why I'm here. Why we're here. Together.

"Your safety net has been jerked away. Well, I'll be your safety net, sweetheart. You don't have to worry. I'll catch you if you fall."

Elliot glowed. I barely breathed. He'd delivered this speech with all the inflections of true concern—and practice. He must've taken my shocked silence as acceptance and confirmation of Mom's theory. Good thing I stayed seated. I wasn't about to escape that easily.

"I love you, Willow. I love you so much. I know we were meant for each other. I know it's why you wanted me to come to New York with you, because you love me too. You just need to catch your breath, to grow into your big-city skin."

My jaw dangled. Catch my breath? I choked on the thought. I'd been there two and a half years.

Elliot cleared his throat. "A long time ago, you said one day you'd push me away. You said if I believed in you, I should wait, because you'd come back to me." His eyes grew misty, and his accent grew heavier. "Dang it all, I'll be here to catch you, no matter how hard you push. I have faith in your words." Elliot beamed so brightly, I thought he'd explode.

Elliot and Mom were wrong about most of this, and life would be a whole lot simpler if Elliot had misquoted me.

Damn.

My heart sank below my stomach, which twisted into knots and attempted to squeeze anything squeezable from any available opening.

I didn't need a second look at lunch in any format.

We finished the meal in awkward silence, despite Elliot chattering the entire time, conversation for an *us* that didn't exist.

Like a child, I slouched, pushed food around my plate, and didn't eat anything else. Words from an insightful—therefore fictional—Mom banged around in my head. *Sit up straight. Don't play with your food. And listen to your boyfriend, Willow. He understands you.*

I didn't want to hear it. My thoughts raced. I'd ripped out Elliot's heart once. Enough!

I ordered French vanilla decaf to go—something to carry in case Elliot thought his newfound understanding entitled him to hold my hand.

"Elliot, I think it's important that we come to a clear understanding. I don't want to hurt you. Please listen to me, and hear me. I need you to grasp this." I swallowed hard, holding the cup with both hands as we headed toward Washington Square.

"I'm not sure what to do now. All through the meal I wondered if I should apologize to you. For many things, yes, so here's my apology.

"I'm sorry it's impossible for you to ever trust me again. I'm sorry I didn't let you in on my thinking sooner. I'm sorry I made you change your plans, rearrange your life to come here and be with me, and then didn't follow through on my end. And I'm sorry what I hoped for with us isn't how it worked out. It isn't what I want, it isn't how I feel."

Elliot's lips pursed, his posture tensed, but no other reaction, so I forged ahead.

"I'm sure at least one of your friends must've asked, 'Are you finished letting her hurt you now?' I want to be finished hurting you too. That's why I needed to stop before things got horrible wrong, horribly worse.

"I don't want to mislead either of us. And I don't want to live regretting my decisions. I don't regret this one. This is what's best for me. If that makes me deceitful or a bitch or whatever else you're thinking, at least I know I'm listening to my heart." I peeked into his cornflower-blue eyes, but Elliot remained stoic.

I inhaled a chunk of New York City air. "I figured you'd ignore me, just let me wonder what you're thinking."

A dingy sky loomed over a pallid Saturday afternoon. Tons of NYU students milled and socialized. A few studied, but most didn't seem to be doing anything in particular. How many of these couples might benefit from hearing my soliloquy with Elliot? His obstinate silence chased us to the edge of the park. Elliot needed more, and I couldn't let this drag on.

"I remember you telling me once that loving is the easiest and the hardest thing someone ever has to do. It's easy because of the wonderful feelings and sheer joy generated by emotional intimacy.

"I agree. That is one of the best things about loving someone, and one of the easiest, but here's the thing—the joy wasn't mine, the wonder and the ecstasy weren't there. And I wanted them to be. I want them to be for myself. They will be. I just don't believe it can be with you.

"Again, I'm sorry, and it may not have been necessary for me to say that, but I need you to understand I didn't ever think the same way you did about us. I wanted to. I tried to see what you saw and experience what you felt, but I couldn't do it.

"It's no one's fault, it just is. I know you wouldn't choose to live your life that way, so I hope it helps you understand why I've chosen to do the same for my life, not settle, not just hope it'll happen."

I thought for sure this would make him cry. I thought it would make me cry.

Instead, my radar flashed, and a crash-dive alarm blared.

Elliot grinned.

So much for honesty and the straightforward approach. I squeezed my eyes shut before continuing.

"Elliot, I suspect you haven't heard me." I paused for dramatic effect, to solidify my resolve, and to open my eyes. "I will never be ready for you to catch me."

The all-too-knowing bob of his head confirmed his devotion to ME, the *M*om-and-*E*lliot theory: ignore everything she says, ignore her pushing you away; believe she still loves you.

I closed my eyes again and gritted my teeth, hard, mashing my face. "Please don't call me. Don't drop in. Don't look for me at school. One thing you can be sure of: if I want you, I'll find you."

I opened my eyes and tried to make a fist, but found my half-filled coffee cup in the way. I thrust my arm toward him. "Take this." The voice of authority—didn't sound like me.

Elliot seemed confused more by the cup than by my words.

I jerked away and called over my shoulder without a backward glance: "Goodbye, Elliot." I imagined his gaze boring into my skull.

Anxious to be out of sight, I dodged couples and scurried away. Tension raked my shoulders, souring my mood another notch. I kicked an empty water bottle. I knew what Elliot thought. *I get it, Willow. You're pushing me away again. Don't worry, I'll be here when you're ready.*

I slogged a half block before peeking to confirm Elliot didn't follow, then backtracked to retrieve the water bottle. Kicking it made it my recycling responsibility. A high-pitched whine droned in the background of my mind, and my ears rang as I trudged into our apartment ten minutes later. I flung the bottle into the green plastic bin. I opened and slammed the refrigerator door, then culminated my passive-aggressive outburst by flipping on every light. Barbie gawked with disbelief, Ken gazed with his usual disinterest, and I'm sure Lela pretended not to notice.

"How'd your talk go?" she asked, a strained attempt to remain casual.

My expression answered her question.

"You're not going out with him again, are you?"

My expression answered that question too.

"If he doesn't want to let go, he could grow annoying, you know?"

My eye roll answered that question.

"Too bad. He's a nice guy."

I managed a shrug.

"I don't imagine he'll be calling any time soon?"

My head traced a giant *Z*.

"Or that you'll be calling him?"

I traced a bigger *Z*.

"Your mom called."

Damn.

Lela arched an eyebrow. "I admire your sense of the dramatic, Willow." She glided around the apartment, switching off every light I'd switched on. Devilish eyes peered at me, and the serpent's tongue licked the apple before sliding it across the carpet with her foot. She'd gone to the trouble of highlighting the appropriate school newspaper headline: *Elliot Collins Named New Vice Chancellor of Huntington University.*

"Don't fret, Willow, it's not like the vice chancellor would have any pull to sidestep a prerequisite and enroll you in a Crimes class or anything."

Shit. Shit. Shit.

Chapter 13

Dr. Coleman waltzed up, champagne in hand and a familiar look in his eyes, like a polar bear on the prowl. Coiffed hair, polished nails, too-neatly trimmed mustache, and what appeared to be mascara lengthening his lashes.

Hilary couldn't be flirting with him.

"Ron, I'm so pleased to see you."

Dr. Coleman caressed Ron's sleeve like Diana had. Ron swigged from the water bottle more to disengage than to quench thirst.

"Dr. Coleman. It may not seem so, but I'm happy to be out of the halls and classrooms occasionally."

"*Dr.* Coleman? Please don't be so formal. Howard. Call me Howard."

"'Kay, Howard."

Ron pronounced his name, and Dr. Coleman's grin progressed from effusive to suggestive. *Howard* obviously thought Ron had winked at him and not at the dog the other day.

This discussion needed to be nonpersonal so as not to continue to give Howard the wrong impression. Ron waved to nebulous space. "This is a beautiful home, isn't it? I mean, look at the sculpted molding along the ceiling. And the folds of those drapes"—he pointed toward the front—"gracefully frame what would otherwise be harsh windows with the shimmering of diaphanous material."

What?

Ron may not have understood what he just said, but Howard seemed to grasp it. He flipped his hand at Ron.

"You're so right. Most men wouldn't appreciate such superb wainscoting. It's craftsmanship from another century. The wood is hand-sculpted, not milled by a lathe. There're so many things that can be done by hand and aren't. It's a forgotten art but one I'm adept at in several ways, I assure you."

Uh-oh. If that was a double entendre, that's not the signal I intended to send.

Howard's hand fluttered, like the drapes. "And I love the way the carpet picks up the color in those Louis Quinze chairs and the gold flecks in the mirrors. This is a magnificent home for entertaining. Hilary has performed wonders. I asked her if I could help with preparations. Set the table, perhaps cook, but she did it herself—at least the planning, and she hired these wonderful people to do everything else."

Someone called Ron's name, and he pivoted to wave. He wheeled back quicker than Howard must've expected, and caught Howard's gaze focused low, inspecting him the same way Ron had been ogling Diana. *At least I'm not wearing spandex.*

"Well, it's been a pleasure talking with you, Dr. Coleman—Howard. I'm going to wander around. There're a few people I need to speak with."

Howard wasn't ready to disengage. "I'm interested in the paper you're writing, 'Relative Time and the Human Mind'? Isn't that it? Perhaps I could read a rough draft? We could sit down over a glass of wine one afternoon this week and discuss the subject. I'd like to offer my thoughts and find out more about what you think."

I think whoever becomes involved with you will be a lucky guy, but I'm just not interested.

"I'll e-mail you a copy of the rough draft as soon as I finish it, Howard. With my schedule this week, we may have to put off the discussion."

Howard's smile expanded. Ron had conceded a paper, and in that, Howard found victory.

"Excellent. I look forward to reading it. And please, do let me know when it would be convenient to meet. An evening works for me as well as an afternoon. And of course, it doesn't have to be on campus."

Dr. Coleman winked, kind of like Fish. Could've been a blink; there's no instant replay at chancellor parties. Where were Diana and Hilary when he needed rescuing? They hadn't been out of sight for more than thirty seconds in the past half hour, but both had now disappeared. Ron massaged his temple; the crowd closed in around him.

The front door opened. Ron recognized Elliot Collins from his picture in the school newspaper. A fortuitous arrival, Elliot headed directly toward the bar.

"Oops, that's Elliot, the new vice chancellor," Ron said. "Excuse me, Howard, I have to talk with Elliot."

"Of course, of course. I'll catch up with you later." Howard radiated pleasure incommensurate with events.

Ron intersected Elliot at the French doors.

"Elliot, hi." He offered his hand. "I'm Ron. Ron—"

"Yes, I know. Pleased to meet you. Elliot Collins. The chancellor pointed you out to me the other day and said if you ever needed anything, I should bend over backward. What can I do for you, sir?"

Not what Ron expected. "You're doing it right now."

Lines crinkled around Elliot's eyes.

"You're rescuing me. And like any marine carnivore not at the top of the food chain, I'm greatly appreciative."

"Marine carnivore?"

"It's a long story. At the chancellor's parties, you have to watch out for polar bears."

Elliot didn't understand this conversation, so Ron moved on. "Congratulations. On your appointment as assistant to the chancellor."

"Thank you. Thank you very much."

Ron shook his head. Elliot sounded like *the* King, twang and all. *Thank you. Thank you very much.*

"If you don't mind my mentioning it, you seem young for such a post."

Elliot flashed a smile. "I don't mind. I hear it all the time. I'm not as young as I look."

"Where're you from, Elliot? Around here?"

"Nope. I mean, no, sir. I'm from Tennessee."

"Where'd you attend school?"

"Went to school back home, but my fiancée came to school here, so I followed her."

"That's romantic. You must've swept her off her feet. How could any woman resist? When're you getting married?"

A frown clouded his face. "As of now, the wedding's off."

"I'm sorry." Over Elliot's shoulder, Howard sipped a drink with a floating umbrella and winked at him again. Ron nodded at Elliot and aimed him in the other direction. Elliot didn't seem to be having any difficulty with this conversation, so Ron pressed on. "Tell me, what happened? Did she call it off, or did you?"

Elliot bit his lip before answering. "She did, but I'm convinced she's scared by the idea of marriage. Moved to the big city, adjusted to life here—you know, it's different than back home in Tennessee."

"I don't know, since I've never been to Tennessee. However, I imagine there are differences between life in New York City and 'America at its best.'" Ron remained straight-faced.

"She pushed me away, but I know she's still in love. She needs time. I'll be right here when she's ready."

"She must be an extraordinary woman to inspire such devotion."

"She is."

"You sound like you have this well thought-out. I'm sure she'll appreciate that too."

Elliot shrugged. "Not yet, anyhow."

Howard peeked around a corner. Ron pretended not to notice. "How'd you meet this woman?"

"Her boyfriend lived in the apartment above mine in Memphis. One day I was having a party, and I invited them to join us. We were all in shorts and T-shirts, but they were on their way to a wedding, and she wore a tight dress and high heels and she kept staring at me." He scratched his head and pointed with his chin. "Kind of like the woman over there who keeps smiling at you."

One-third of the polar bear club. Of course she's back, now that I don't need her.

"Yes, Ms. Burnett. Dean of Publicity. I'll introduce you if you like. Anyway, you were saying?"

"She looked fantastic, like a pheasant on its way to Sunday dinner. And the two of them, well, they weren't exactly paying too much attention to each other, you know what I mean? Unhappy together. Anyhow, I had so much food, I invited everyone back for another party the next day.

"She came without him. Apparently, he had cheated on her. She and I talked a lot after that, finding excuses to meet each other when he wasn't home. She'd sit on his balcony right above my balcony—I swear, not wearing too much—and we'd chat. It seemed kinda like *Romeo and Juliet.*

"I finally got the nerve to ask her out, and she accepted. The two of us remained inseparable after that."

Ron arched an eyebrow. "You mean, with her ex-boyfriend still in the apartment above you?"

"Yep."

"Wow."

"Well, we didn't tell him."

"You didn't?"

"'Course not."

Silly me. 'Course not.

Ron offered his hand. "Elliot, you have an impeccable sense of irony." They laughed.

"A year later, she decided to come to school here." Elliot massaged his chin. "Found an apartment with a roommate, and she seemed happy I followed.

"That was almost two years back. A few weeks ago, she told me I was an oak tree in her forest, but she wanted a redwood." He chuckled. "Mixed-landscape metaphor. You'd think a country girl would know better. Oaks and redwoods don't grow in the same forest."

"Did you understand what she meant?"

Elliot pulled his chin up and pressed his lips together. "I think subconsciously she used the wrong trees because, deep inside, she's confused. She's in love with me but doesn't want to admit it. The city has her mixed up, that's all. Like a visitor who doesn't know whether to take the subway uptown or downtown. She's not sure what she wants, but when it strikes her that it's me, I'm gonna still be here."

Hmm. Do I want to go there? Elliot seems like a nice guy, and somebody should tell him.

Ron decided to proceed, but to tread softly. "That's one possible analysis. Look, I don't know this woman, but from what you've told me, she sounds like someone capable of making decisions and following through.

"What I mean is, it sounds like she understands herself. When she says you're an oak in her forest, metaphorically, she means you're as solid as that tree. She knows she can rely on you."

Elliot beamed, and his eyes misted. *I did say I'd tread softly.* Ron forged on nonetheless.

"When she said she wanted a redwood, metaphorically again, it's possible she meant something different than your interpretation. When you think of redwoods, what springs to mind?"

"Big?" Elliot glanced at his crotch. "I'm pretty well—"

"No, not big." Ron glanced too, and fought a smile. "I mean, yes, we think big when we think of redwoods, but she's probably referring to something else. Redwoods are magnificent. There's beauty and grace and majesty in the giant trees, the stuff songs are made of. Have you ever been to the Redwood National Park?"

Elliot shook his head.

"It's America, and it's the Earth, and it's humanity wrapped in one. It's the mountains and the lakes, and it's the thickest air you've ever breathed. The forest towers over you, and envelops you, and cuddles you. It's awe-inspiring and safe, and it's the womb of life. It takes your breath away." Ron paused to let the words sink in. "Do you understand what I'm saying? Do you understand your fiancée's more likely meaning?"

"Yep." Elliot chomped his lips and pulled his chin higher. "Thanks for clearin' that up. She wants me to inspire her and keep her safe because she's out of her forest. I mean, our forest. She's here in New York. Back home we boasted mountains and lakes and butterflies. But here, she can barely see the sun. There's plenty of rain, but where're the rainbows? And she sure as heck can't breathe this air. Yeah, I get it. Thanks, Ron. You sure understand women."

Ron needed to find one of those super-thick dictionaries with foreign languages in the back and locate the translation section for English to Tennessean. For himself or Elliot, he wasn't sure.

"Umm, that wasn't *exactly* what I meant."

Southern-boy charm dripped off Elliot's chin. "Close enough."

Before Ron formulated an answer, a serpent entwined his arm again.

Chapter 14

Hilary pressed her breast tight against his elbow.

"You two look as if you're having a serious conversation. I hope I'm not interrupting."

Elliot answered for them. "No, ma'am, Ms. Nixon, you're not interruptin'. Ron helped me understand a few psychological issues." Elliot's wink didn't have the same meaning as Diana's or Howard's. "I better circulate and meet the other people I'll be workin' with." He hitched up his trousers. "By the way, Ron, my fiancée has a beautiful roommate. I could introduce you."

Ron held up his hand to stop any such notion. "Thanks, but no thanks, Elliot. Enough women already complicate my life."

Like a viper, Hilary tightened her grip. "You should accept Elliot's offer." She softened her tone and deepened her voice, pitched for Ron. "You have no idea what complicated is… yet."

Did she lick my ear?

Ron sucked in his cheeks. Howard peeked and licked his lips. Ron pivoted, and Diana treated him to a shimmy too sadistic for public consumption. Hilary may have left marks on his skin. Where were the referees? Where was the instant-replay camera? Ron managed a smirk. Enough partying for one afternoon; he needed to escape, sign online, and send an e-mail to Psyche-Lela.

"Thanks again, Elliot, but I'll pass on the roommate."

Elliot offered his hand. "Nice meeting you, Ron. Let's talk again sometime." His gaze swept over Hilary and back to Ron. "Y'all enjoy the rest of your afternoon." Elliot melted into the crowd.

Hilary glided into a private alcove. Attached as they were at the hip, Ron stumbled beside her, though distancing the crowd spurred a sigh of relief.

The chandeliers glistened in the midafternoon sun. An overlapping mix of hair spray, deodorant, and perfume floated on the air, intoxicating many of the guests, but hobbling Ron, like various flavors of garlic at a vampire ball. Tuxedoed employees maintained decorum and a steady supply of hors d'oeuvres. The party attained a level drone, loud enough to be heard above the string quartet. If Hilary imprisoned Ron, perhaps he could accomplish research.

Ron proposed a theory: In Western culture, in a social setting, groups with an odd number of people are more likely to discuss controversial topics than groups with an even number of people. A twosome didn't count as a group in this setting. Twosomes were more likely to be flirting. Ron wanted to drift and eavesdrop, at least gather anecdotal evidence for his theory. Hilary kept him entwined in a group of two.

Uh-oh.

He needed a simple plan to extricate himself.

"Who is the most interesting person at this party?" Hilary said *person*, but Ron heard *woman*.

"You mean besides yourself?"

Hilary pretended that wasn't the answer she wanted. Her tongue flickered, and she wound herself tighter around his arm.

"You've met most of the *people*"—Ron heard *women*—"here at one time or another."

103

Unprepared to feed Hilary the answer she wanted a second time, he formulated a plan. A sly smile curled his lips. "Rhiannon."

Wheels churned, gears ground, synaptic relays overloaded. Hilary must've searched in vain for a Rhiannon. Any Rhiannon.

"There's no one here with that name," she said.

Ron arched an eyebrow and, with a flick of his chin, indicated the striking redhead marching group-to-group gripping a canapés tray, her sea-foam eyes daring anyone to misbehave. Ron neglected to mention that one of Hilary's guests had groped Rhiannon's backside.

"She's the most interesting person here?" Hilary resonated disdain.

Ron pushed his head forward and nodded, as one speaking to someone who stands aghast. "She likes to brag." All that time he spent with Diana, Ron couldn't see Hilary, and presumably Hilary couldn't see who else he spoke with or for how long.

"Ms. Raeburn, Rhiannon, isn't an American citizen. She's been expatriated from England. Suspected SDN agent."

"SDN?"

"Scottish Democratic Navy."

Hilary squinted. "Never heard of it."

"They're in our country to raise money. American universities have been a haven for the SDN, New York and Boston universities in particular, and Huntington is endowed with wealthy liberals. Perfect targets. According to Rhiannon, the SDN has maintained an on-campus presence for years. I wasn't aware of it. Were you?"

Ron didn't wait for an answer. "The SDN makes a practice of attending high-profile events that attract the wealthy and powerful, and they solicit donations. That's what Rhiannon is doing here, now. It's why she's angry. She's not having much success."

"Right now? She's soliciting donations here? Among my guests? She can't do that. I've never heard of the SDN. I'll have her arrested."

"Based on what, Hilary? You haven't been personally solicited, have you? You haven't heard anyone being solicited. You can't have her arrested on my secondhand testimony."

"I'll speak to the people she's spoken to. They can testify."

"I don't think so. It's made clear to those people what would happen to them, to their families, if they mention an encounter with Rhiannon. They're not going to talk."

"I can't believe this. At my party. At my university?" Hilary arched her back, hands on hips. "She's threatening people?"

Ron managed a one-sided shoulder shrug. "SDN operatives take positions with caterers, janitorial staffs, entertainment groups. They do their research. Do you think it's a coincidence Rhiannon hasn't solicited you? And you can bet she obtained a copy of the guest list and devised a plan of whom to approach."

"She contacted you?"

His head bobbed. "Rhiannon solicited my help. Rather eloquent. Compared me to a knight. She made it clear I wasn't to discuss the incident. If I decide to contribute, I won't want it known, and if I decide not to contribute, the contact needs to remain discreet. We talked about going out back and beating the hell out of someone. Unclear whom. Apparently, it happens all the time, and no one knows about it."

"What can I do?"

He offered a full-body shrug. "I don't think there's anything you can reasonably do, Hilary. Face it, you're being manipulated."

Hilary winced. He'd found a button.

"You can't run the university without caterers and janitors. Suppose you insist the caterers don't bring Rhiannon to your next function. The SDN will send someone else, only you won't know who. I think you're better off insisting they do use Rhiannon—you can keep an eye on her. You'll know what she's up to, whom she speaks with."

Ron massaged his chin as though an intriguing idea occurred. *What's the point of having a button if you don't press it?* "Instead of being *manipulated*, you could reverse roles."

"Manipulate them? How so?" Hilary was caught up in it now.

He rubbed his hands together. "You control the guest list so you restrict access to potential contributors. Actually..." He narrowed his gaze, leaned closer, and lowered his conspiratorial voice. Ron cast a surreptitious glance at Rhiannon. Jason Storm—AKA Raz Steel—was an author full of helpful ideas for various situations. "You could bring plants to your functions."

"Plants?"

"Invent people—*plants*. Give them backgrounds that attract the SDN, and then let the SDN spin their wheels trying to solicit donations from people who don't exist. My guess is, they probably obtain most of their information from our database.

"Invent trustees, administrators, alumni. Insert them in the computer and on the guest lists. Rhiannon will never know why you're laughing."

106

Hilary nodded, as if this sounded like a great idea.

Ron sunk the hook deeper. "They usually work in pairs."

"There's a second person soliciting donations at my party?"

"Uh-huh. You can bet she's got a partner here. This is a real opportunity for you, Hilary. If you watch, you can figure out who her partner is. Keep a log: partners, the people Rhiannon solicits, their reactions. Go to the CIA with your information, as long as it's documented."

"CIA? I thought it would be the FBI? Internal and all?"

"This concerns foreign relations, and even though it's here in America, it's still the purview of the State Department."

Ron's smirk reflected off a gold-embossed beveled mirror. The SDN would distract Hilary's unwanted affections from him and provide Rhiannon with a shield. If Hilary kept Rhiannon under scrutiny, she'd notice misbehaving guests. SDN or not, Hilary wouldn't tolerate pig behavior. Polar bears hunting on university grounds? A different matter.

Hilary peered at him. "Are you serious?"

He rocked several times, from heel to toe. "Are you going to let them infiltrate our university, or are you going to stand up to their social-terrorist tactics and fight back?"

She giggled, trying to hide her true feelings. "You're pulling my leg, and I totally believed you."

Ron glanced away, then gazed into Hilary's eyes. "How long will you allow yourself to be manipulated?"

Button, button, who's got the button?

Chapter 15

Dog jumped on my pillow and danced around my head. Not ideal, but better than a buzzing alarm clock. I rubbed my eyes and fought against dreary fingers ticking off the morning routine. Earlier classes Monday meant earlier bathroom privileges. I stepped into the shower. Lela banged cabinets and puttered in the kitchen, brewing coffee.

Last night's thoughts recycled: Professor Kirin's hard-nosed position, the new vice-chancellor ex-fiancé who could probably override Professor Kirin's hard-nosed position, my partial lack of preparation for today's oral presentation in Dr. Coleman's class, my total lack of preparation for midterms, and Mark-in-the-Park, for whom no preparation seemed possible.

A warm towel offered comfort. Small chunks of French vanilla decaf floated in my coffee, a telltale sign that Lela sprinkled the powder into hot water instead of pouring hot water over the powder. My back ached, either the result of a restless night or the beginning of my period. Life conspired to push me off-kilter.

One of those Monday mornings when time refused the *hold* button, so I had to deal. I dressed and packed for school while Lela showered. My clothes pinched, and my backpack drooped, heavier than normal. I draped my towel across the chair to dry and left Lela chunkless coffee. This restated what we already knew—my middle initials: OCD.

Warmth spread from my stomach, but knotted before going far. My mind wanted to shut down and abandon me to sleep. I forced myself to stay awake on the train. I'd decided not to walk through the park today. Exercise might stimulate my sluggish mind and focus my thoughts on the day's first obstacle, the oral presentation, but off-kilter spread outward, its tentacles latching onto all bodily functions. I didn't dare distance myself from a bathroom.

Another reason for staying out of the park—I didn't want to meet *him*. The stranger. Mark. Not today. Too much of a challenge.

I arrived on campus and found bona fide coffee, probably my second mistake of the morning.

~ ~ ~

I left the bathroom and glanced at my watch. Enough time to reach the psychology department office and return before class. I hurried along the corridor. Professor Kirin hadn't responded to my most recent e-mail. I wanted to leave a real-world note and entered the office without knocking.

Before I spoke, Nausicaan Nasal jumped down my throat.

"Ah, the young lady who thinks university protocol includes an addendum: 'No rules apply to Willow Bolden.' Well, what can I do for you, Ms. Bolden? Present your doctorate without the necessity of classes? That would save time, wouldn't it?"

The biggest problem with being off-kilter was my

inability to produce snappy responses. "I'd like to leave a note for Professor Kirin."

"Too late."

"Too late?" How could it be too late to leave him a note?

"He left you one."

"What? A note?"

True to her word, NN pointed to a sealed envelope cornering her desk, my name scrawled across the front.

"Professor Kirin left me a note? Here?"

"Your powers of observation defy the usual psychology department acumen, Ms. Bolden."

I snarled and tore open the envelope. How could Professor Kirin have the nerve to leave me a note in the psychology department office? Counting today, I'd been here three times this semester. How'd he know I'd be here now? I didn't know I'd be here now.

"When did Professor Kirin leave this envelope?" Probably last week.

"He dropped it off first thing this morning. I asked if he wanted me to contact you. He said that wouldn't be necessary."

How could anyone know what I'd do before I knew? How could a psychology professor know what I'd do? How could a nationally renowned, textbook-writing geek *know* what I was going to do?

I glanced at the backward clock. Predictably, numbers stared at me—backward. I squinted into focus: three minutes after four. How about three minutes before eight? I muttered a few choice words and angled out of the office toward Dr. Coleman's class and my oral presentation, reading Professor Kirin's note as I jogged.

Dear Ms. Bolden,

NO!

A brief and totally unacceptable answer. I screamed inside my head, and in a feeble attempt to hide, I flopped into my usual seat behind Derek Dunker, seven feet whatever inches of basketball jock whose real last name I couldn't remember, just as Dr. Coleman strolled in, his usual cheery Monday morning self. Derek twisted in his seat and scanned my row, roving over me twice, though not like a horndog.

"Here." He thrust a sheaf of papers into my hands. "My report. Hand it in for me. Thanks." He shouldered his backpack, towered over me, and headed out. "Forgot. Team meeting," he announced without looking back.

I opened my mouth, but lengthy strides speeded him from the room. I don't normally do favors for jocks. On the other hand, what's the big deal? I'm passing in a paper for him.

"Everyone, settle down," Dr. Coleman said. "We have two oral presentations today. Let's see…" He fumbled through notes. "Ms. Bolden. The podium is yours." His grand flourish waved me front and center.

I began where my notes said to begin. My voice cracked due to insecurities. Normally, I don't have issues standing in front of a group. I stumbled, did my best to cover it by asking questions and fielding answers, allowing me a few moments to collect my thoughts. Dr. Coleman must've recognized my strategy, because he asked me questions at the end. I scrounged answers and fell into my seat, relieved that I'd coped with the worst of today.

111

"Mr. Forrester, you're next," Dr. Coleman said.

Forrester. That jogged my memory. The absent Derek Dunker Forrester. Like sunrise over Verona, dawning awareness confirmed the unlikelihood of an 8:00 a.m. jock team meeting.

"Mr. Forrester? Anyone know what happened to Mr. Forrester? He was here when I arrived."

Awkward. If I said he attended a team meeting, it would sound like truth. The class knew I didn't associate with DD. On the other hand, since I knew there wasn't a team meeting…

"Umm, he couldn't stay." Lame, but the best I could offer. "He left his report." I waggled the loose papers over my head and leaned to pass them forward.

Dr. Coleman nodded. "Ms. Bolden. Seems you're up again. Front and center."

"What?"

"You're up, you're up. You've got Mr. Forrester's report. Let's have it. The podium is yours."

"I don't want to give his report."

"Doesn't seem to be an option at this point."

"But—"

"You agreed to hand in Mr. Forrester's paper?"

"Yes, but—"

"The stage is yours again. Front and center."

"But—"

"Ms. Bolden, you're holding up the class." He gestured with another grand flourish.

The class didn't help. Every face gaped at me and multiple voices called out.

"Come *on*, Ms. Bolden."

"You're holding us up."

"On stage, Ms. Bolden."

That's what you merit in an advanced psych class: encouragement.

Little wonder DD didn't hang around to deliver his report. The jumble of thoughts that held my report together seemed smooth and well written by comparison.

Dr. Coleman frowned. "Interesting would be one adjective to describe that, Ms. Bolden. Next time, review the paper before you present the report."

I wanted to argue with Dr. Coleman and remind him I had nothing to do with this paper. I didn't even like DD. Instead, I plunked back into my seat.

I drudged through the morning like one of those ugly rodents trying to cross a busy highway. I decided to forego my packed lunch in favor of soup and entered the cafeteria ahead of the midday rush. I still waited in line to pay, tapping my foot, fidgeting, uncomfortable in my skin, impatient to meet Lela at our bench.

"Hey, psych-girl." I wasn't sure why the label attached to me.

Eye level penetrated dead square at a belt buckle. My neck stretched backward until I saw DD's elongated face. Maybe it wasn't elongated, but so far away, I couldn't tell.

"I heard what you did this morning. Thanks for presenting my report. I hate standing in front of a class."

But you can walk onto a basketball court in front of ten thousand screaming fans?

DD glanced at his feet. I followed his gaze, then quickly readjusted to eye level/belt buckle. Could his entire body possibly be in proportion? I couldn't swallow.

DD cleared his throat. "Could I ask a favor?"

On a normal day, that request from a stranger would incite my radar, sirens would scream, horns would honk, and a lightning bolt would split the ground between my toes. Today I barely shrugged my eyebrows.

DD continued, smooth, suave, practiced. "May I copy your notes from today? It's tough, the demands on athletes: practice, team meetings, programs, press conferences, luncheons with alumni, dinners with major contributors, secret meetings with sponsors who aren't allowed to sponsor us. And expectations: engage a full academic load and maintain a three-point-oh. There isn't time for everything. I'm lucky if I have a half hour to myself some days."

"What do you do with your half hour?"

"Read. If I'm in the mood, play the sax."

"You're a musician?"

"Since third grade. School band, orchestra. I organized a jazz ensemble here. I write music, and we play at coffee shops around the city."

My lips pursed together, kind of like a fish. "What're you reading?"

"*Love and Other Sides of Sex*. Professor Kirin assigned it for class. The author, Raz Steel, offers a unique understanding of the male psyche, about creating walls, keeping people at arm's length, and searching for a soul mate. It's also hilarious."

DD's hip at my shoulder served as a nagging reminder that I spoke with DD. He didn't sound jockish; he sounded intelligent, all evidence from his report to the contrary. DD's world unfolded as the lunch line inched toward the cashier. He didn't carry a food tray. What did he ask me?

"May I? Borrow today's notes?"

I rolled my eyes as if I hadn't forgotten the question.

"I'll bring them right back. I'll photocopy them and make my notes later."

"Okay. I suppose. Here." I passed him my tray,

unslung my backpack, and rooted for my psych notebook. I re-hoisted the backpack and traded notebook for the tray. "I'll be on the roof for the next half hour, on a bench in the sun, kind of on the library side."

"Thanks. I'll find you." He raised my notebook like a salute, and three, possibly four strides transported him out of the cafeteria and halfway down the hall. Memory tugged at my scalp, a certain promise made to myself about never sharing notes or doing someone else's work.

My feet clunked on the metal steps to the roof. Sunshine burned away the memory, leaving me warm but scarred. DD had entrapped me in the class this morning. He'd sneaked up on me in the lunch line. I'd been amazed to discover an enlightened reader and a self-fulfilled musician, and I'd been caught unawares when he asked for my notes. And Professor Kirin's note was unexpected. Otherwise, it hadn't been a surprising day.

Lela wasn't at our bench. Surprise. I expected her to be waiting for me with sympathetic understanding of DD's intrusion into my world. Instead, I sat alone, sipping soup. I foraged in my backpack to find Professor Kirin's note, then remembered I'd memorized it.

No.

It irked me that Professor Kirin had anticipated my visit to the psych office. What could he have been thinking? *No.*

What could I have been thinking? Do I take that for an answer? Okay, it is an answer, but is it definitive? "No. No!"

I'd just finished my soup when Lela strolled along, flashing a silly smile. A guy. Had to be.

She sat close. Her radar zeroed in. "What's wrong?" she asked.

My head wove from side to side, doing a dance

without the rest of my body. My mouth curled up at one corner and down at the other, my lips mooshed sideways, and I squinted one-eyed at her.

"Oh. You're off-kilter."

An understanding friend—a necessity of life. I purred.

"Your oral report?"

"Grrr."

"At least it's over, Willow." She leaned back to inspect me. "Looks like you survived. Did it sound okay?"

"It sounded better than DD's."

"Your competition? Can he speak and dribble at the same time?"

"We still don't know, but I can."

"I'm sorry Dog and I missed that."

I explained how DD had hoodwinked me into giving his report.

"Girl, I know it's a bad day if you fall victim to a jock. And I can't believe *you* didn't argue with Dr. Coleman." Her broad grin let me know she teased. My frown let her know I hadn't told all.

"What else?" Lela asked.

"The 'what else' is approaching as we speak."

Derek reached us from halfway across the roof in five strides. The building shook, the noon sun blotted out by a DD eclipse. Lela and I had to look straight up to see his face. He tossed my notebook onto the bench.

"Thank you for letting me borrow your notes." He extended the largest paw I've ever clasped. "I don't think we've been properly introduced. I'm Derek Forrester."

Yes, Mr. Forrester, DD, I know who you are, and I'm sure you know who I am. "Willow Bolden. This is my best friend, Lela Thompson." Ahh.

116

He re-aimed the paw, simultaneously offering an elegant bow that elicited a giggle from Lela. He spoke, stooped in Lela's direction.

"Best friends are the essence of life. They hold us, comfort us, understand us in a way no one else possibly could. Best friends engage our minds in an intimate embrace of emotion and intellect. They're sympathetic and willing to share themselves as we share with them. They know when to talk, they know when to be silent." DD spoke with an eloquence uncommon among college students. Hell, uncommon among human beings.

His glance included me, then focused on Lela. "They know when to push and when to lay off."

I don't think Lela noticed DD hadn't disengaged her hand.

"It's a pleasure to meet you, best friend." He finally released and straightened to full DD height. "I'll see you in class Wednesday, Willow. Thanks again." He strode away, swallowing the roof in a few easy strides. I climaxed in an eargasm of epic proportion.

Lela remained open-mouthed with her first DD surprise of the day. I was a veteran, my mouth almost closed.

Few people have an introduction-to-best-friends speech like that.

Lela finally cleared her throat. "You lent your notes to a jock?"

"Come on, Lela, you have to admit he has an unjockish quality."

"I think you're missing the point. You lent out your notes. A jock recipient merely adds insult to injury."

"H-he surprised me. You heard him."

"He asked for your notes that way?"

"Uh-huh."

Lela considered for a moment. "Too bad. I've seen you help people. I've seen you tutor from your notes, but you never hand them over to someone. Ever."

"Okay, okay, I understand who I was. The question is, who am I in this moment?"

"I guess the answer will have to wait till class on Wednesday. You didn't do anything silly, like confess your phone number or our address?"

I made a *You've got to be joking* face and squinted until the sun ducked behind a lone cloud. "Speaking of guys, what has you in such a fine mood today?"

The combination of Cheshire cat grin and devilish eyes endeared Lela to me. "Another e-mail this morning from my clever friend."

"You two haven't agreed to meet or anything, right?"

"Just online, but it's a lot of fun."

She extracted a folded paper from her backpack and handed it to me. E-mail, printed this morning. The address seemed familiar, but memory remained blocked.

Subj: Unremembered Memories

Tell me a story from your childhood and I'll tell you one from mine. Not any story, though. Not one of the "big" events you recall vividly, but something you haven't thought about for years.

I noticed someone's car dripped oil on the wet pavement this morning, creating a rainbow.

An early childhood memory flooded my mind.

Dad organized everything in our storage shed and tried to track how much oil he used for the cars, the lawnmower, and his projects.

After rainstorms, I'd "borrow" his small oilcan, sneak up the street out of his sight, and drip oil onto the pavement to create rainbows of assorted sizes and shapes. I traced trails across the road, unusual patterns, isolated rainbows, overlapping rainbows, one-drop rainbows, and gigantic rainbows.

I learned quickly that while Dad knew when the small oilcan should be full, he didn't have a clue about the big oilcan he used to fill the little one, so I refilled the little one after each adventure.

I confess to doing my part as a five-year-old to keep oil companies in business, and to whatever extent that incriminates me in the Deepwater Horizon oil spill, I apologize.

It's probably why I blotted out this memory: the harsh reality of creating oil spills across the road implicates me in the worst accidental oil spill in history.

The memory has resurfaced because of you. The anguish. The agony. The psychological damage to my psyche may be irreparable.

Ron

I giggled. Lela dove into her backpack and withdrew a second paper, this morning's e-mail, also from Ron.

Subj: P.S.

I hope you're not laughing at my expense.

Lela laughed at my reaction. My stomach settled suddenly, and the weight of the world had eased off my shoulders. Maybe the soup kicked in. I headed toward afternoon classes in a more normal universe, fighting through PMS. Professor Kirin's pre-response notwithstanding, my best option remained the original idea to leave a handwritten note, and Lela's e-mail inspired an idea.

Subj: Inspiration

Professor Kirin, I've researched this. Of all the city schools, county schools, state schools, public and private institutions, colleges, and universities in the city, only NYU offers Ab Psych this summer.

I can't afford NYU.

I don't need to remind you that Crimes is a required course. If you don't teach me Ab Psych this summer, I won't graduate on time, and I'll have to return for another semester just to complete your class.

Give me a break. Please.

We're talking about my career. My psychological future rests in your hands.

If you don't say yes, I could become emotionally scarred for life. I could become a subject in the next Ab Psych syllabus, instead of a student in the class.

Save me that fate.

Hopefully about to become your newest favorite student,

Willow Bolden

I headed for the psych department office.

NN shuffled papers on her desk. She spied me, then glanced over her shoulder at a closed door. "Ah, Ms. Bolden. Professor Kirin has been expecting you."

"He's here?"

Chapter 16

The queen of the psych office smirked, as if I were nuts. "Of course he's not here." She packed her desk as if I weren't here, either.

I waited a moment. Hands out, head forward, eyebrows up. NN paused and flicked her chin. I followed the flick.

An envelope with my name flourished across the front sat cornered on her desk. Not possible. "Professor Kirin left another note for me?"

"No trained psychologist could be any more observant. You're sure I can't award your doctorate now?"

I didn't have to take this. My mother taught Guilt 101. "I'm learning impaired. I can't believe you're making fun of me." As a child, I'd tested negative for dyslexia, but being tested satisfied my need for truth-telling now.

The Nausicaan was unsympathetic.

I pretended to struggle with Professor Kirin's envelope. No salutation.

Consider this professional curiosity, Ms. Bolden.

It's not my intention to leave you emotionally scarred, but which part of my previous note didn't you understand?

Anticipated again! I sucked in my cheeks but failed to make the insides touch. Could I be this predictable?

I clomped out of the office and headed toward Central Park. Rock time.

I needed a plan so simple, it couldn't be anticipated. Did I mean simple or bizarre?

The late-afternoon sun caressed my shoulders. I tuned out grinding bus gears, honking horns, and construction machinery and drifted into my world of spring flowers, pigeons strolling instead of flying, and people flying instead of strolling. Bicyclers whizzed past, chased by skateboarders and rollerbladers, and after 3:00 p.m., East Drive reopened to cars.

I rejoiced in them all, climbed my rock, and surveyed my realm.

Professor Kirin had anticipated my notes twice. A third attempt loomed on tomorrow's horizon. Would it be obvious to him? I considered delaying a day or two, so he'd be wrong. But delaying would hurt me more than him. I conceded he'd expect me to drop off another note tomorrow morning; I refused to concede the contents of the note.

I scribbled ideas, searching for the unexpected till a dorky glow creased my face.

> Professor Kirin, here's an idea that may satisfy both our needs. I'll teach Ab Psych this summer. I'll do the research and present a lecture to you twice a week.
>
> Listen to my presentations, recognize all the required material is covered, and offer congratulations for a job well done.

I'll prepare tests, write essays, and grade them. This will take virtually no time from your hectic schedule.

A future arbitrator,
Willow Bolden

The breeze graduated to wind. I blew from rock to rock, exiting the park near the Cement Man standing guard over the street vendors.

"Vee... nilla. Get your vee... nilla ice cream before someone else does."

~ ~ ~

Patchouli filled the apartment. I flicked on all the lights as I entered. Dog pranced, tail up, and caressed my leg.

"Lela. Where are you?" As if I didn't know.

"I'm taking a bath. Come on in. You have some talking to do."

I transferred her candle to the top of the tank so I could occupy the throne. Dog accompanied me, purring, demanding attention. Lela stretched out, submerged to her chin in bubbles. Humidity hugged me tighter than I hugged Dog, caressing my flesh in a warm embrace. Childhood memories flooded my mind.

Eyes closed, Lela displayed the longest eyelashes and an expression between demure and sly. "Do you have a lot of homework tonight?" she asked.

I knew Lela. Her question had nothing to do with demure or sly. "Yeah," I said, "all my profs loaded up today."

"Did you work out the Crimes thing?"

"Almost. One or two details to settle."

"You have to keep up with me, girl. We're facing grad school together. I heard Professor Kirin is an amazing teacher, and considerate of his students."

"All evidence to the contrary."

"You're not one of his students yet."

I shrugged my shoulders. "The bastard could still be understanding." I scratched Dog's ear. "I'm challenging his psychological abilities."

"I bet you are. What're you going to do about DD?"

Demure and sly blurred mid-conversation. "What do you mean? There's nothing to do. He returned my notes."

"I saw the way he glanced at you and the way you gawked at him."

"I was not gawking at him."

"Were too."

"Not."

"Were!"

"What if I was? Look at how…" I fumbled for the word on the tip of my tongue. "*Big* he is."

Lela flashed a mischievous glow, and I laughed.

"Hey, he's over seven feet tall," I said. "You've got to admit you're as curious as I am. Is *everything* in proportion?"

"And if so, what exactly does 'in proportion' mean?"

We both laughed. I held up my hands, palms out. "I have no plans for finding out." Time to redirect the conversation. "Did you write to your e-mail friend?"

Lela sulked, her mouth barely above the water. "I couldn't think of anything. If it's a forgotten memory, how am I supposed to remember it? I hate to send him a message without a story."

"Why don't you invent something? He'll never know."

125

She tapped her teeth with her fingernail. "I thought of that, but I can't think of a clever made-up story."

"Want me to write it for you?"

Her eyes widened. "Would you?"

I hopped off the throne. "I'll take care of it. Do you have a lot of homework tonight?"

Her head bobbed.

"I'll write the note now so your computer will be free when you're done with your bath."

"Girl, you're a sweetheart."

Dog circled Lela's desk, and I signed on to Lela's account. We shared passwords to save time. We often checked each other's e-mail from professors and classmates and my mom, but agreed boyfriend e-mail was off-limits unless expressly authorized.

I found the message titled "Unremembered Memories" in her mailbox and double-clicked to reread it. Just as funny. I hit *Reply*.

"What do you call him?" I shouted through the closed bathroom door. We rarely referred to anyone by his real name.

"Who? My online friend? His name is Ron." Duh.

Dog lay at my feet in scratching position, belly-up. "Ron it is."

I peered past the legs of the desk, across the hall, into my room. My anally organized closet—arranged first by color then by hanging length—stared back.

Subj: Closet Monsters

Switching on the closet light before I begin…

Closet monsters have existed since the dawn of closet building.

126

Please check if universal closet-monster rules apply to you:

Rule #1
Closet monsters can't confront you if you're under the covers.

Rule #2
They can assail you the second your feet reach the floor.

If you're on the bed but not under the covers, they're allowed to drag you off the bed, and as soon as your feet touch the floor they can strike.

Have you ever dragged anyone off a bed?

Lights help, but they have to be specific. Night-lights make it easier to see monsters but do nothing to deter them.

If monsters are going to attack me, I'd as soon not see them.

Ceiling lights keep monsters from appearing altogether.

Unfortunately, it's difficult to sleep with the ceiling light lit.

Fortunately, there's a reasonable solution to closet monsters.

Closet lights.

My father did one of the nicest things ever when he installed a closet light in my room. He did one of the meanest things ever when he refused to allow me to use it.

"Daddy! What's it for?"

"So you can see your clothes when you're deciding what you're going to wear in the morning."

"I don't need the light in the morning."

"Then don't use it."

In defiance, I put the closet light on every night before I climbed into bed, thrilled to confirm closet monsters were being thwarted.

Around eleven o'clock every night, my father stopped on his way to his bedroom and switched off the light. If I complained, he scolded me for being awake.

"I can't sleep without the light."

"You won't know if the light is on or off. You'll be asleep." Dad's idea of logic, not mine. More of Dad's logic followed. "Who has more money, us or the electric company?"

Most nights I pulled the covers over my head and hoped to make it till morning. A handful of nights fear of being alone in the dark won. I needed the closet light on at any cost.

The switch, six feet away, might've been six hundred. I tossed my pillow on the floor to use as a buffer to keep my feet from touching.

I paused at the end of the bed, gauged the distance, and leapt into the dark. The pillow cushioned the landing, and I slid across the slippery wood, leaned into the doorjamb, and flipped on the closet light switch.

I jumped into bed and snuggled, basking in the warmth of closet light bathing my feet.

Excess revenue generated from unnecessary use of closet lights enabled the electric company to construct additional power plants that pumped out pollutants.

If I weren't so scared, had I been willing to face closet monsters in the dark, the electric company wouldn't have reaped enough profit to build so many pollutant-pumping power plants.

Thinking about my role in power-plant pollutant pumping projects makes me shudder. I've been repressing this memory for the sake of my psyche. It's a good thing I'm sitting as I type this— otherwise I'd collapse from guilt. You should feel ashamed having unscrupulously forced me to remember closet monsters.

How can you be so heartless? You monster.

p.s. Inasmuch as power-plant pollutants are significantly more widespread than oil spills, I claim greater emotional scarring.

Cheeky, but Ron believed he corresponded with Lela, not me.

I reread several times for errors, ran the spell-checker, and clicked *Send* before I changed my mind.

Lela emerged from the bathroom robed, hair up.

"The computer is yours whenever you're ready. Want to read this before I send it?"

"Nope."

"Good thing." I hadn't signed off yet, and set up another e-mail to Ron.

Subj: p.p.s.

Thought you'd like to know, my Internet provider has presented me with an award for the most damaged online Psyche.

I thought it was clever to capitalize Psyche. This stranger didn't know me by that name, so it would be a double entendre, at least to me. I waggled my head and clicked *Send*. "I'm adding a postscript. Want to read this before I send it?"

"Nope."

Whew.

Chapter 17

Fish expected him home Sunday night by eleven. Sometime between three and three-thirty Monday morning, Ron stumbled into their apartment, and bed gravity sucked him into a black hole. Fish managed a disgruntled sigh to let him know he wasn't being respectfully quiet.

Sunday with Diana hadn't gone the way Ron expected. Nor had it gone the way Diana expected. He'd arrived at four-thirty to pick her up for dinner. They never left her house. She tried to keep him in the bedroom. She tried to kiss him. He fended off the kiss and any further advances.

Diana expected him to stay overnight and become Mr. Diana, but he had plans for early Monday morning and preferred to remain unattached.

The list of Monday's best ideas didn't include rising with the sun. Nor did it include waiting so long to walk Fish. Ron's shoulders drooped, and he growled at anything that moved.

He struggled with his writing, then added one more bad choice to today's list, opting for the subway instead of walking to school. The platform spun around him, ceiling dangerously close, noise profanely loud, multitudes multiplying as he waited for the express.

Face your fears head-on, son. He cursed Dad's unswerving approach to life.

Ron finished midterms in two classes and began the second half of the semester in the other two. Howard flagged him down in the hall to remind him of his promise to deliver a rough draft into his smooth hands. Fish had refused to come to school with him, opting for couch potatoism. Ron recalled hearing something about a *Mister Ed* marathon.

He arrived home Monday night, stomped up the stairs, and banged around the apartment, too tired to fall asleep. He signed online more from habit than desire and found an e-mail from Psyche. His smile disintegrated as he read, the last two lines lodged in memory.

How could you be so heartless? You monster.

What's missing in e-mails, even from people you know, but especially from people you don't, is inflection. No nuance to catch sarcasm or a lilt. Psyche must be joking about him being a monster. He glanced at the wall of clocks; nineteen of thirty-one said he still possessed time to add to the list of Monday's *not the best idea*s.

Majority rules. He clicked *Reply*. Afterward, he remembered one line. *A noted psychologist who wishes to remain anonymous stated that Psyche is emotionally scarred.*

The message was too acerbic, and he retained the good sense not to send the e-mail. He needed to read it when his mind cleared and most likely edit or rewrite the whole thing. He did something he never did with e-mail: he clicked *Send Later*, and trudged away from the computer in search of dinner.

~ ~ ~

Tuesday morning found Ron slightly less tired and slightly less cranky. He slept later than normal. Monday

132

memories blurred, probably a good thing. His usual lightning-quick reflexes slowed down, and the water filter drenched him. By the time he changed shirts, packed his backpack, gulped coffee, and brushed his teeth again, nineteen clocks declared him behind schedule. Fish agreed to accompany him to school. He tried to sign online first. Fish barked.

"I know, I know, we're gonna be late." The sign-on screen flashed: *You have mail waiting to be sent. Send now?—or—Review?*

Fish barked again.

"Okay, okay. Why do I have mail waiting to be sent?" Nothing he could think of. No time to read, and he couldn't reach his school mailbox if he didn't choose one or the other. If he'd written an e-mail, he must want to send it. He clicked *Send Now.*

~ ~ ~

I kissed Dog goodbye, waved to Lela, and headed for the psych office early enough Tuesday morning to arrive pre-NN. No such luck. I warped in, and NN beamed like an alien with the drop on Captain Kirk. The official psychology office clock ticked off defiant backward seconds.

I nodded. "I know, I know, there's a note for me. Well"—I extended my note—"I have one for him too."

"Professor Kirin said you'd be in this morning to drop off a note."

I had conceded that yesterday.

I squinted and twisted my head. "I thought the psych office didn't open until seven forty-five?"

"That's correct. Professor Kirin asked me yesterday if I'd come in early today. He said you'd be here first thing."

Even renowned psychology professors made lucky guesses. I extended my note farther.

"You better read his note before you leave yours."

"Why?"

"Professor Kirin said that's what you'd want to do, even if you pretended to protest. You need to read his note before leaving yours. After you read his, you'll change your mind about leaving yours. He said he knows what you're going to say, so you might as well read his answer first."

I *knew* that was what he'd think. No way *he knew* what I wrote this time. I scrutinized my name flourished across the envelope cornered on NN's desk. No point in protesting— that was what he claimed to expect. I stuffed my note into a pocket, grabbed his, and tore it open. NN's smirk broadened as she pretended to concentrate on her work.

> We both know you're going to be here this morning, Willow. You considered waiting a few days so I'd be wrong, but you couldn't stand to wait twenty-four hours for the answer you want.
>
> I know you. Without ever seeing you or reading your file, your behavior makes you predictable and understandable. Want to hear what I can surmise?
>
> You're undoubtedly a great student and never wait until the night before a due date to start an assignment.
>
> You have huge issues with one of your parents— probably your mother—and I'll bet you feel emotionally scarred from childhood.

If you have a pet, it's a cat.

"Yeah, but I call him Dog."

You probably have short hair.

I fingered hair that swished against my shoulder blades. "Ha. Got one wrong."

True, Ms. Naughton might've told me that, but I assure you, she has told me nothing about you. I know you, Willow. The next thing you're going to suggest is that you lecture me on Ab Psych.

No, no, no.

I'd have to devote way more time than you realize or I can afford. Just as you want teachers who challenge you, I want challenging students, and we represent both parties.

So, in the interest of fairness, I challenge you, Willow. The winner gets what he or she wants.

I'll make it easy.

You have five chances to surprise me before the semester ends. If you succeed, I'll teach you Ab Psych this summer, and you can be in next fall's Crimes class.

If you don't succeed, you leave me alone. Forever.

135

I don't have to ask if you accept the challenge. I
know you, so I know you do.

We begin now, Ms. Bolden. Do your best.

"Do my best? I'll beat you right now." *You arrogant
bastard.* I yanked out a second note I'd written for a *just
in case* scenario and extended it—with bravado—toward
NN. She glanced up with an all-too-cheery smile and
shook her head.

"What do you mean, no?"

She pointed to the corner of her desk. I hadn't
noticed. While I read, she'd placed another note there,
also with my name flourished across the envelope. A
postscript? I tore it open.

Don't bother to leave a backup note.
One down, four to go, Willow.

I growled and staggered from the office.

Chapter 18

I thundered across campus and clomped up the stairs to the cafeteria rooftop. Neither the warmth of the sun on a bright spring day nor the warmth of my best friend's embrace quelled the anger clouding the real issue deep-seated in my psyche: I didn't want to admit my predictability to anyone, including myself.

Logic dictated the best way out of this predicament—don't be predictable. A stranger offered a challenge. Was I up for it?

I grabbed handfuls of my hair and pulled straight out to either side. My eyes glided back and forth. In flaunting the one thing he'd missed, I'd made myself look exactly like the person I didn't want to be: a *predictable* oddity. I needed to break that streak, and I had to do it now.

Lela chomped a cucumber sandwich and cast a motherly frown from her corner of our lunch bench. Okay, I might've appeared odd.

"You're scheming, Willow, and sulking. Bad combination. I know you. You're upset. Let's see… We haven't heard from your mom in almost forty-eight hours. That's close to a record. That leaves Elliot, DD, and Professor Kirin. Elliot's history, DD is the future, so my money's on the professor."

I eyed my astute friend. "Do you *know* me, or am I that easy to read?"

"I know you, but I couldn't predict you if I didn't. To an outsider, you're out to lunch." She raised her sandwich. "You *are* out to lunch. I mean, you're off the wall. You know, Dog would say you're barking mad."

The devil crept into her narrowing eyes. Her grin said she teased, but her expression said I'd better listen.

"Professor Kirin finds you predictable, like a zombie eating you, brains first." She didn't wait for a response. "You realize allowing him to irk you makes you fall into his trap? Break out of the pattern." A smile tweaked the corners of her mouth. "This has to do with Crimes?"

"Uh-huh." I explained his challenge.

Lela nodded, and her grin broadened.

"What? What is it?"

"I might have an answer. If I tell you, it doesn't help. You need to come up with this yourself. It's simple. Close your eyes, click your heels together three times, and clear your mind."

On the second click, the answer struck me like a bus crunching a crone in the crosswalk. My eyelids flew open, and I hugged my best friend.

The last thing Professor Kirin expected me to do?

Withdraw my request to be in Crimes!

I grabbed my backpack, ready to dash to the psych building.

Wait, I had to be subtle about this. Professor Kirin expected me to charge into his office as soon as I thought I'd outwitted him. Somehow he knew what I'd do, and he nailed my timing too.

Okay, I'd wait.

I paced around our bench, skipped across the roof, then hopped back on one foot.

"Go home," Lela said.

I raced from campus, anxious to dive into a bubble bath as reward.

Steel beams leaned toward me, cracked pavement stretched ahead, gas fumes intermingled with the scent of giant pretzels. Grinding bus gears, the roar of underground trains, and a million conversations at once. An entire package of sights and smells and sounds filled my head with music and my psyche with vibrations.

I needed to rejoice before going home. I could catch the subway at Columbus Circle under the protective gaze of the Cement Man.

First I needed to walk in the heart of the city, Central Park. I refused to admit I hoped to see Mark and Fish.

The path wove in and out of shade by the lake. Reeds and pond scum flourished in clumps. Clouds scudded across the sky, mimicking ducks paddling in a pool. Strolling pigeons outnumbered strolling people. Flying Frisbees outnumbered flying pigeons. The dogs I passed were on leashes—many of them barked, but none of them spoke to me. I found my rock unoccupied, climbed up, dropped my backpack, and stretched out on my stomach, head up. I tested, tapping first my head, then the rock. Yep, just as hard as always.

I flipped over to gaze into the sky, lost in thought, empowered by ideas. I sat up, knees drawn to my chest. My eyes closed of their own volition, revealing a reddish-purple landscape on my inner eyelids. A few deep breaths relaxed me, and had it not been for a familiar bark, I might've fallen asleep. The bark drew happily close, and drool dribbled from the largest mouth I'd ever been this near to.

"Fish!"

"I'm pleased to see you."

Yep, someone beat me to those words.

A guy with a quirky smile ambled behind the mutt. Not Superman, not the man of my dreams with a steel body, extraordinary eyes, and a ruggedly handsome face. Not a six-foot-two-inch frame with rippling muscles encasing a charming personality resplendent with witty repartee. This boyish, unpredictable guy—I conceded six feet tall—pushed wire-rimmed glasses farther up the bridge of his nose and fumbled with his hands.

Would he ask me to dance again? That worked last time, but I was prepared now.

"Hi," I called, "out walking your dog? Happen to be going through the park, did you?" It came out more Jedi-master-sounding than I intended. *Hmm, young Jedi, happen to be going through the park, did you?*

"I was hoping to find someone who could help us," Mark said.

"With what?"

"Know anything about dreams, do you?"

He mocked the Jedi master. "I have them all the time," I said, refusing the bait.

"I mean, how to interpret them."

I'd read Freud's *Interpretation of Dreams*. Twice. Once for a psychology class and once for a philosophy class. I shrugged. "Try me."

"Okay. Fish gave birth to a vision last night that we don't understand."

"If Fish birthed anything last night, you should probably talk to a vet; otherwise, the park is full of dog-dream interpreters. Did Fish write it down when he woke up this morning?"

Mark squinted at me like I'd asked the most ridiculous question. "Fish can't write. He told me, and I wrote it down." He retrieved a folder from his backpack.

Silly me, of course Fish can't write. Mark had gone to a lot of trouble hoping for a chance meeting with me, though. For all I knew, he could've been coming here every day for the past week with those papers.

"Mind if I come up?" he asked.

I waved with a flourish, and he climbed my rock. Fish pushed off the side, followed him around to the gentle slope, and clambered past him into my lap. Mark settled cross-legged, and Fish licked my face and hands.

"Aghh. Did Fish dream about brushing his teeth? I don't suppose you've thought of pouring mouthwash into his water bowl?"

"Fish resists brushing and every attempt to inject mouthwash into his daily hygiene routine. I'm open to suggestions."

"Why don't you sneak a drop in his water? Every time you add water to his bowl, add a few more drops of mouthwash, and level off when you notice his breath improving. If you do it slowly, he'll never know."

"He will now. You've just told him."

Fish lay down between us, head resting on paws. His saucer eyes glanced at me as if to say, *What're you, nuts, girl?* The question didn't have a straightforward answer.

"Well, don't tell him what brand you're using or when you're going to start."

Fish renewed his *What're you, nuts, girl?* look and sighed. I dove to safer ground. "Tell me the dream."

One of them, Mark or Fish, cleared his throat. Only Mark read.

"Fish said he galloped through the city. The late-afternoon sun warmed his face and reflected off the mirrored surfaces of office buildings and windshields. The wind whistled around street corners and up alleys, and carried with it a dozen different scents, but Fish smelled spring: pine needles, blooming flowers, jasmine."

My nose twitched. I wore jasmine.

"City sounds assailed him: honking horns, the roar of jets overhead, the shouts of street vendors. Billboards flashed, neon lights blinked, concrete sidewalks blended into dirty streets, and cracked pavement traced myriad lines in a thousand directions. Which to follow? The press of the crowd, hundreds, thousands, millions of people swept him along."

Mark paused a moment. I didn't know if he meant to breathe or to create a dramatic effect.

"This is the most peculiar part. Fish said he could taste the city. It combined the sights and sounds and smells and feelings, and it lingered like a dog bone he couldn't bury." Mark shook the pages. "Fish thought of the title too." He flashed the papers in front of me. I couldn't read line by line, but I did catch the title, *The New York Symphony*, and today's date.

My head swirled, a dozen thoughts collided and dropped into my open mouth, and like Fish's dog bone, I couldn't bury them. The city symphony?

Not word for word, but all these things Mark described were the thoughts and feelings and senses that propelled me into the park today… so I could do what, taste the town?

Did Mark think he expressed his thoughts or mine? My gaze darted to the mutt, and his gaze mirrored me.

What're you, nuts, girl?

"What do you think?" Mark asked enough questions to be a reporter.

I blinked as though that would clear my mind as well as my sight. "I'm sorry, what?"

142

Mark smiled, placating me. "I wondered what you think and if you have any idea what it means?"

"A personification of your thoughts onto Fish?"

He nodded and massaged his chin. His eyebrows flicked once, up and down. "I've certainly experienced the same manifestations. However, this is Fish's dream the way he described it to me."

"I see." I didn't. Instead of describing his thoughts, or Fish's, I now believed he tried to describe mine. How could he possibly know? Mark watched me. No, he studied me.

"... other ideas?"

"Hmm? What?"

"I wondered if you have any other ideas."

"Okay. Sure. Yes. Yes, I do." I had to admit I wanted to impress him with insightfulness, but like the biggest dork in the world, I muddled along.

"Most people don't claim they can taste the city, but it's there for anyone to bite... apologies to the Big Apple."

He grinned, and warmth simmered upwards from my neck. "I-I didn't mean to make a pun. I'm serious. That just happened to come out."

"I'm sure."

My face burned, and I experienced trouble breathing. A single solution presented a way out. I arose, hands spread. "Would you like to dance?" I asked.

"Okay. Sure. Yes. Yes, I would." He arched an eyebrow, but I detected no sarcasm in his echoing voice. Fish rose too.

Mark's arms mirrored mine.

I asked *him* to dance? Am I a dork or what?

"Okay. Sure. Yes. Yes, I am." Did I say that out loud? Pins and needles tingled from my toes to my...

I slid into Mark's arms like a psychiatric patient

voluntarily sliding into a straightjacket. Electricity bopped through my body as if I held a finger centimeters from an outlet, about to plug myself in.

I don't know how long we danced. Swallowing was difficult, and fear of the emotional unknown tugged at consciousness. I needed to disengage.

Branches tweaked on a puff of air; pigeon toes clicked on the blacktop pathway. Fish's gaze roved from Mark to me. The scent of pine needles and jasmine fluttered around my rock, and the rock tilted beneath my feet. The taste of the city changed, and the symphony played a movement I didn't recognize.

"I have to go," I said.

His eyes registered my every movement. My backpack seemed three times heavier than normal.

"Thanks for sharing your dream. Fish's dream."

His glasses must've slid while we danced. He pushed them up the bridge of his nose again.

"I have to go now." I pointed into the park. My hand dove into a pocket, and I wrapped my fingers around Lela's gift, the green kryptonite.

Fish eyed me. *What're you, nuts, girl?*

"Don't forget the mouthwash, a drop or two at a time." That nailed it, in case I'd missed any earlier opportunity.

Self-consciousness dripped during my escape. I lacked the agility to back away without falling. Were my jeans this tight when I left the apartment this morning? I didn't want Mark to watch my derrière wiggle as I waddled away. The more I thought about stopping it, the more it shook. Don't shake. Walk straight. Don't shake, don't shake, don't shake!

What're you, nuts, girl?

I nodded. Another triumphant encounter.

144

Chapter 19

I blew into the bathroom like a parakeet on the wrong side of a giant fan. Oops.

Patchouli laced the air. Lela arched an eyebrow but waited in silence, knowing this mood didn't need prompting. I paced my perch, and Dog mimicked, dancing between my feet.

"Sometimes even I can't believe me."

I shook my head, then hiked up my jeans. Yeah, *now* they're loose.

Lela applied eye shadow and considered for a moment before she spoke. "I know you didn't go back to Professor Kirin's office, and DD would either have classes or practice in the afternoon. Elliot couldn't leave his job to find you—so who does that leave?"

"Whom."

"Who, whom, whatever. Mark and the dog, right?" She didn't wait for an answer. "What'd you do, meet them in the park again?"

"Am I that predictable?"

"Let me guess. Mark asked you to dance?" Lela's eyes flashed.

I cringed and shrunk beneath her glare.

"You asked *him* to dance?"

Innocence bathed my face.

"Clever, Willow."

Satan's tone clouded interpretation.

"Clever?"

"Totally unpredictable. I'm sure you took him by surprise."

"I don't know about him, but I took me by surprise."

"Did you sign up for a series?"

My brow furrowed.

"You know, a series of dancing lessons in the park. You, Mark, the dog…"

"Lela, I wiggled away."

"You did?"

"I couldn't help it. The more I thought about it, the worse it got."

"Your wiggling?"

"Yes."

"Why didn't you back away?"

"We were on my rock. What if I fell? Do you know how embarrassed I'd be?"

"As opposed to how embarrassed you are?"

"I can't believe I thought about wiggling. Or having thought about it, that wiggling in front of Mark would bother me." My mouth clamped shut, a dead giveaway.

Lela leaned into my reflection. "What else?"

I hung my head. "Witty repartee, 'Okay, sure, yes.' I don't think I repeated myself more than five times in our ten-minute conversation. Aghh." I tugged my hair out to the sides.

"He might be one of the biggest dorks in the city, but I acted like a top-ten candidate. I can't imagine what he thinks of me. We've met three times. I'm sure he's suffered enough. He hasn't even seen how wacky I really am. Believe me, Lela, he is one strange person."

"Are you talking about him, or are you describing yourself, girl?"

"Huh? Me. I'm talking about me."

"Would it matter if you never met him again?"

"No. No. No, of course not."

"When do you think it'll happen?"

"Soon, if I keep walking through the park."

"There must be something that draws the two of you together."

"Our joy of dancing?"

She tapped her cheek, ignoring my comment. "You must be connecting on some level."

"Not a chance. There's no way the two of us are on the same page or even reading the same novel. I'm not sure we're from the same universe. I'm telling you, he's strange."

"You haven't shared names or numbers?"

I shook my head hard.

"You've got nothing to worry about. If you're not connected, then the meetings you've had are coincidental. In a city this size, coincidences are going to run out quickly. You'll never see him again."

"Yeah, you're probably right." The music, smells, tastes, dream interpreters in the park. "I'll never speak with him again."

I signed on to Lela's computer to check her mail. "You've got another letter from Matterhorn Press."

"Read it. You might as well write the response too, if you don't mind."

"Giving up the relationship?"

"I'm searching for a real relationship. Go ahead. Knock yourself out."

I shrugged. "I can use a distraction from Professor Kirin, Mark, and Fish." I opened the e-mail.

147

Subj: Matterhorn Press Writer's Edition:
Psyche Confesses To
Power Plant
Pollutant Pumping

In an exclusive interview with this reporter, Psyche confessed today to being a major contributory cause of the worst power-plant pollutant pumping in the United States.

Her role in global warming is etched in history. A noted psychologist who wishes to remain anonymous stated that Psyche is emotionally scarred.

"She must live with the consequences of her actions. Guilt has undoubtedly made her quirky, self-conscious about her behavior and her appearance. She probably sleeps with a night-light."

The psychologist went on to say, "She'll hear music where other people hear noise. She'll surround herself with high walls, and won't reveal herself easily.

"If she ever becomes emotionally available, take the opportunity to know her. I guarantee it'll be a unique experience."

In related news, Verizon announced Psyche has received their coveted award for the most irreparably damaged psyche online.

Congratulations.

Yikes, not what I expected. Ron might know Lela, but how would he know me? He gleaned all that from the monster story? And because I capitalized Psyche at the end, he assumes that's my name?

I pointed at the computer screen. "This guy's either insightful or a good guesser." I rocked back and forth in my seat.

Lela anchored in the doorway, studying me. "Stumped, girl?"

"You'd better do something with your hair before it frizzes."

"I warned you, he's clever." She faded into the bathroom.

"Yeah, well, so am I, so am I." I clicked *Reply*.

Subj: Analysis

Certain people are straightforward, others are complicated. The more complicated, the more interesting, wouldn't you agree? A split personality, a necessity for a goddess to separate private life from public, lends itself to complications conducting a two-persona existence.

On the other hand, envious writers lacking a second persona create a different set of complications. Such a writer would likely project his thoughts and emotions onto others, onto a fictitious personality, or onto a pet.

Writers are loners. I'll bet you talk to yourself. Dress in a nonconformist manner. You probably live alone, or in a marriage and a reality resembling Walter Mitty's.

You hold the truth in high regard, but have no problem inventing stories and portraying them as true, if that suits your purpose. An Internet existence may well be the highlight of your social day.

I apologize for any damage I may've inflicted upon your psyche.

Do you realize what happened to the marine life caught in the Deepwater Horizon oil spill?

P

I ran spell-checker and clicked *Send*, confident in my analysis, then collapsed on the couch. The sofa sucked in my problems. How would I handle Professor Kirin if I ever met him in the psych office, or Mark the next time I saw him in the park? My eyes closed, and the cushions wrapped their arms around my arms, embracing me like a long-lost pillow. Plans formulated, and unconsciousness claimed me.

Chapter 20

All too soon, Wednesday morning spread across his brain like a bad commercial.

Fish and Ron arrived on campus late for their first class. Ron struggled through the morning and bagged his lunch break in favor of a rooftop bench. Fish agreed to join him. Ron's backpack substituted for a pillow, and he stretched out. Fish wandered nearby, circling like a plane in a landing pattern. He sat next to the bench for a moment, then paced. He waited until Ron drifted into semiconsciousness before nuzzling his hand, commanding behind-the-ear scratches. Ron growled but performed as commanded.

They chatted. Derek Forrester strode by with the unusual gait of a giant. By the time Fish and Ron headed back to class, Ron relaxed and remembered what he should've done had they awakened earlier this morning—check e-mail.

~ ~ ~

They scuttled off campus late in the afternoon, eager for the comforts of home. An odd twitch behind Ron's left ear convinced him to walk through the park instead of taking the train. Any excuse for not taking the subway would've worked today. Anticipation arced through his psyche as he crossed the park threshold.

Fish pranced, and Ron chased him, past the pigeons and the Frisbees and the strollers and the park pond. He tried to say that three times fast. "Park pond, park pond, park pond." Didn't work. He kept his eyes peeled for a parked chariot.

They approached Boulder Lane. Fish barked and pranced ahead to their rock. Elation spread over Ron like poison ivy climbing a traffic pole in midtown Manhattan. Fish hopped on hind legs, tail thrashing back and forth. This rock, foundation of their park experiences, the theater in which they watched the play unfold, the stage upon which they performed, provided unparalleled pleasure. Parked practically on the rock, the unseen conveyance they hounded.

Ensconced atop their kingdom, like a princess upon a throne, perched the object of Ron's desire, the girl of his haunted dreams, dancer extraordinaire, feeder of stray dogs, the enigmatic Lela, wearing a green sweatshirt, blue jeans, red socks, and purple canvas high-tops. At least when it was raining she valued dressing decisions. She faruffled, and Ron struggled not to laugh. His voice engaged of its own volition.

"I'm pleased to see you."

He couldn't wait to discover what other bodily functions would choose this moment to test self-determination. Like yesterday's meeting, the fleeting image of Master Yoda sprang to life with her first words. *Hmm, young Jedi.*

"Happen to be going through the park again, did you?" *Searching for something? Find something, you will.*

Well, umm, no, not yet, not exactly, Master. I—

You what?

Ron coughed.

Need help to speak, do you?

"Happen to be going through the park?" she repeated louder, as if he hadn't heard.

"Fish and I hoped to find someone to help us."

"You two need a lot of help, don't you?"

Ron leaned forward, eyebrows raised.

"I thought after yesterday's dream interpretation you'd be looking elsewhere."

"Your insightful analysis is what brought us back."

Lela squinted, sat cross-legged, elbow crooked, chin resting in her palm. "How can I help?"

Ron had no idea what he'd say. "Fish hasn't been eating well."

She glanced at the mutt. "How're you feeling?"

Fish barked.

"Use your words," Lela scolded.

Fish sighed.

She touched his nose. "It's warm. It should be cold."

Ron touched his nose. "Mine's cold."

"You're not a dog."

"Some people think I'm a seal."

"Navy SEAL?"

"Marine carnivore, midlist on the food chain."

"Being chased by polar bears?" She kept a straight face.

"I'm out of breath."

"Stay away from the water."

"No easier than staying away from the park."

"You may need to take Fish to a vet."

"Does it matter from which war?"

"An animal doctor. What do you feed him?"

"I've never fed an animal doctor."

153

"What do you feed Fish?"

Ron tugged his ear. "Worms?"

"Talking with you isn't going to be easy today, is it? What do you feed Fish, your dog?"

"Frosted Flakes. I've tried all the name-brand dog foods, extra nutrition, extra gravy, extra flavor. He's not interested in anything besides Frosted Flakes."

"Have you asked him what he wants to eat?"

Ron bowed his head. "I'm embarrassed to say that solution escaped me."

"Take him grocery shopping."

"They won't allow him into the food store."

"Put on sunglasses and pretend you're blind, like you did on the subway. Fish can pretend to be your Seeing Eye dog."

Fish glanced at Ron, as if to say, *What is she, nuts?* He blinked. Or it might've been a wink.

"Do you think that would work?" Ron asked.

"I'm sure Fish could pretend to be a dog." She laughed.

Ron's eyes reflected in hers, and they drifted on a chocolate sea of momentary silence. Little fish swam circles in his stomach. He wanted to caress her cheek, wrap her in his arms, and hold on forever.

Instead, he pushed off the rock and spread his arms in ready position. His turn to ask.

"Would you like to dance?"

Her eyes answered long before she arose.

She melted into his embrace, closer than in their previous encounters. Her hand squeezed his, and they swayed to music inside their heads. Her eyes kept his engaged. Her face flushed, and her palm perspired. Her eyelids drifted shut, and she leaned toward him.

He couldn't kiss her.

Not yet.

They had another bridge to cross first. He stepped back.

The scent of jasmine traced a delicate line around the soft curves hidden beneath Psyche's sweatshirt. It floated the short distance between them, like a sailboat dancing across a mountain lake. Her tawny hair drifted on the spring breeze.

Her lips parted, moist. Her eyes didn't express shock, but the anticipation of shock.

Blood warmed his face. She reengaged their dance, igniting that same electric anticipation that had nailed him as he'd entered the park. Hours ago, or minutes? Time disintegrated. When it reintegrated, she pointed into park nothingness.

"I have to go. I have to go now," she said.

Time halted again, clarified in a flawless moment at the caress of her hand disconnecting from his. Their personas played perfectly together, though her eyes grappled with what she didn't understand—no kiss? The sway of her hips, rendered irresistible by her charming innocence and the scent of her perfume, captured his id, ego, and superego, and delivered them bound and gagged.

Fish punched the air with his paw.

"Yes."

~ ~ ~

Needles prickled Ron's skin. He hunched down on the sidewalk, waiting, half a block from home, as Fish trotted ahead. Ron growled at a few passersby who neglected to mind their own business.

"Ready, set, go!"

He raced for their steps. Fish started a hop, skip, and a jump away, and clobbered him. Ron conceded the preferred couch seat and the remote and headed for the computer to compose a new e-mail to Lela. He had forgotten the e-mail from two nights ago, the one he avowed—with good sense—not to send.

Uh-oh.

He recalled having had the bad sense to send an un-reread e-mail yesterday morning. Fish's singing awakened memory dendrites, synapses snapped, and he hurried to his mailroom hoping to un-send the offending mail.

Too late.

Unsure of his memory, he reread the misbegotten note now. He described Psyche as *emotionally scarred and self-conscious.*

Uh-oh.

Lela's response stared back. He hoped she'd talk about their meeting in the park and dancing, maybe ask why he didn't kiss her, but she seemed intent on analysis reduction. *Did I grow up to be a loner?*

Ron glanced at Fish in repose on the couch, engaged with a vampire. After the *Mister Ed* marathon on Mondays, Fish had discovered back-to-back vampire shows on classic TV: *Dark Shadows* and *Forever Knight*. Ron's fault—he'd been reading aloud to Fish, vampire romance, *Love Without Blood*. Now Fish insisted Ron DVR the vampire shows on days they attended school together.

Ron refocused on being a loner. He wasn't alone. He lived with Fish. And now vampires. And occasionally he visited Diana. Hilary chased him. Howard adored him.

"Hey, buddy, do I talk to myself?"

156

Fish pulled his attention from the TV.

"Not out loud, right?"

Fish made a noise like clearing his throat.

"Okay, not often out loud. Besides, the operative word is *a lot*. No, that's two words. It doesn't matter. I don't talk to myself a lot.

"A lot would be, like, all the time. Someone who talks all the time would talk while he showers, dresses, and eats breakfast. I never talk while I'm eating. And what's wrong with the way I dress?" He surveyed his attire. Blue T-shirt, black jeans, forest-and-yellow-plaid flannel shirt, brown belt, gray socks, neon orange sneaks. "Yeah? So?"

He waved and continued to read. *Internet existence is not the highlight of my social day, it's my escape.* It was where he bolted to avoid the polar bear club. "The highlight of today, the highlight of the past week, happened when we danced, Lela."

He didn't feel particularly highlighted at this moment. A sour taste sloshed around his mouth, like yesterday's milk left on the counter overnight. He winced more than once, pressed his lips together, and twisted his mouth from side to side. An argument ensued between Ron and himself. *One of me has to win.*

He'd instigated the problem by describing Lela's emotional issues. She'd angered him with her scathing analysis. "So what if I talk to myself? And I *like* to make up stories." He slammed his manuscript on the floor and glared at the computer, unsure how to respond.

He didn't recall when he started to cook dinner, and that explained his not recalling that he cooked dinner at all, which explained the smoke, which explained the blaring smoke alarm. He knew the stove fan wouldn't work since Handyman Dave hadn't fixed it, but he tried the fan anyway.

It didn't work.

He snatched *Romantic Times* and fanned. Furiously. That also didn't work. He had to stand on a chair—he hated heights, anything above the second rung of a ladder—and remove the nine-volt battery from the smoke detector, which meant he'd have to stand on a chair again to replace the battery.

Smoked waffles have a peculiar aftertaste.

He tried to fill a cup, but the water filter pissed all over him. Wednesday wouldn't let go.

Chapter 21

I shook the shower curtain and crooned while Dog danced around the toilet. Lela had deposited a coffee cup with floaters on the vanity. I wiped steam from the mirror and checked under my arms to see if I should've shaved.

Lela banged pots and slurped coffee in the kitchen. "Going to surprise Professor Kirin today, girl?" she shouted.

"Yep."

"Going to the psych office before they open?"

"Nope."

"Guess he'd expect that, huh?"

"Yep."

"Waiting until later in the day to go?"

"Nope."

Kitchen sounds ceased. "He probably figures you'll arrive early. But he'd know you know that. So the less likely thing is for you to wander in sometime during the day. But you figure he'll figure that, so you *are* going to arrive the moment the office opens. Okay, okay, I approve."

I emerged from the bathroom not quite ready to tackle the day.

Lela cocked her head and eyed me. "What's plan B?"

~ ~ ~

The sun settled for second place Thursday morning. I beamed so bright the Cement Man needed to shield his eyes as I skipped past him. Despite Lela's misgivings, plan A swept in motion. I dashed through Central Park as ominous clouds stormed over the city, and I arrived at the psych office five minutes before normal opening time to see if Professor Kirin expected me and had ordered NN into work early.

I frowned at the locked door and took up residence in an alcove, out of sight. A couple of minutes later, NN marched down the hall. Not an altogether unattractive woman, if she kept silent. NN unlocked the office door, flipped on the lights, and settled behind her desk. I inhaled a deep breath and scuttled in.

NN cut me off before I could speak. "Ah, Ms. Bolden. Never one to give up, eh? I have something for you."

"From Professor Kirin?"

"No, this is from me." She laid her hand over her breast. "From my heart."

She presented me with a large manila envelope. I squinted, undid the metal clasp, and removed a single sheet of gray parchment with an embossed university logo.

Psychology Department Official Degree
This is to announce without further ado:

Willow Bolden has bypassed her remaining undergraduate classes and all of her graduate classes, and has been granted the title of Doctor of Psychology, effective yesterday, and ongoing in perpetuity, or until she discovers there might possibly be more she needs to learn.

Granted by this office, scribed by the Dean of
Spurious Degrees and Official Message Reader,
e-mail and otherwise, Clarisse Naughton

NN peered at me, one eyebrow up. If her ears were
more pointed, she'd pass for a Vulcan.

Before I spouted a clever retort, she cut me off again.

"I have two sets of instructions from Professor Kirin,
depending on what you say next."

"I only have two possibilities?"

Her eyebrows shrugged. "So it would seem."

"Where's Professor Kirin?"

"He didn't deem it necessary to be here today."

"He didn't think he needed to meet me face-to-face?"
An idea struck me. I straightened my spine and crossed my
fingers behind my back. "I've been waiting *for an hour* for
you to open the office this morning and—"

NN stopped me like a traffic cop and eyed an envelope
on the edge of her desk, my name swaggered across the
front, Professor Kirin's name stamped in the corner.

I opened my mouth.

She shushed me and pointed to the envelope.

I hesitated, put down my newly granted diploma,
seized Professor Kirin's envelope, and ripped it open.

Liar.

Heat rose in my face.

Two down, three to go.

The smugness of her posture meant NN knew the
contents of Professor Kirin's note. Undeterred, I proceeded

with plan A, official notification that I dropped my request to be in Crimes. I plunged into my backpack for the note with Professor Kirin's name flourished across the front. I thought it a nice touch, and passed it across the desk to NN.

She refused to accept the envelope and pointed to a rock paperweight on the left corner of her desk. Underneath, another envelope, partially obscured but plastered with my name. Throwing the rock crossed my mind, but I jerked the envelope instead and tore it open.

> Gosh, Willow, dropping your request to enroll in my class?
>
> Is that the best you can do?

A less outraged person would overturn the desk, pull down the bookcase, and rip the damn backward clock off the wall.

Plan B didn't yet exist, so I retreated, anger intact, before committing a rash act. NN's voice stopped me at the door.

"Excuse me. Excuse me, Dr. Bolden." She raised the pitch. "You forgot something." She waggled the gray parchment.

What's next in the embarrassment rainbow after scarlet?

Chapter 22

I waited at our lunch bench, eyes closed, feet tapping. The rain had ended, and haze parted. Passersby ignored me, thinking my color sun-induced, my behavior drug-induced. Calmer now, I gulped deep breaths and assessed the damage. Plan A had cost two of my remaining four chances. Plan B, when I thought of it, would likely take both the others. I needed to be certain this time.

I'd been certain last time. What had happened?

My eyes popped open, and I squinted against the sun. The music in my head played louder than normal. I hopped up and lurched around the roof. Professor Kirin had nailed me. He'd pegged me yesterday when we began this game. He'd expected me when the office opened this morning, anticipating my withdrawal.

Grudging respect for the celebrated doctor of psychology wrapped around my thoughts like cellophane around a CD. Understanding human nature, the religion of a psychologist.

The music stopped. "He will not make me a believer."

Heads twisted. I spun around. Gawkers. "Mind your own business." I snarled at a couple of other passersby who forgot to ignore me.

Two chances remained to beat this frustrating

psychology professor, Dr. High and Mighty who thought he knew me so well. I thought about regression analysis. He knew. I knew he knew. He knew I knew he knew… I considered returning to the psych office and submitting my withdrawal request, but quickly discarded that alternative. Analysis always ended on *he knows*.

I sprawled on our bench, ankles crossed, arms folded tight, lips jammed together. A pigeon landed on the far end of the bench. Its head jerked in robotic pigeon-head movements.

"What're you lookin' at?" Either my charming personality or my exaggerated, mood-induced Tennessean accent scared the crap out of the bird, and it flew away.

I popped off the bench and paced. I needed a plan I couldn't think of. If I could think of it, Professor Kirin could think of it. This led to a problem in logic. I lay on the bench, using the backpack as a pillow.

I dared to dream of the unexpected. I sat up, gripping the bench so tightly my knuckles whitened. He always knew when I'd show up in the psych office. He always knew what I'd say. An incredibly obvious solution had to be here. I lay back, rolled onto my side, and snuggled against the pillow.

My eyes refused to close. "How can you refuse to close? You're *my* eyes." Obstinate, they continued open in a sideways world, and I continued to wait patiently for Lela.

~ ~ ~

"Excuse me?"

Somewhere along the line, my eyes must've closed of their own volition, without informing me, because now they opened of their own volition, staring straight into shins.

"Did I wake you, Dr. Bolden?"

Who the hell is Dr. Bolden?

"I didn't mean to startle you."

Whose ankles talked to me? Whose ankles were that tall? I twisted my head toward the blotted-out sun. DD towered over my bench.

I was about to say, "Mr. Forrester, this is a *gigantic* surprise," when I realized DD probably put up with that nonsense all the time.

"Oh, Mr. Forrester, this is a surprise."

"So is this." He pointed above my head.

I sat up and maneuvered to see his target. My diploma dangled from my backpack, the newly anointed Dr. Bolden. *That* Dr. Bolden.

"I didn't realize you'd graduated already. I thought you were taking Dr. Coleman's Psychology in the Workplace with the rest of us. You just observing, then? Offering Dr. Coleman ideas on how to teach the class?" DD paused. "Now that I look closer, you're definitely more mature than the typical undergrad."

More mature?

Yep, he'd nailed me.

Wait a minute. Did he mean I *looked* older? I was younger than most juniors. How much older did he think I looked?

I contorted to glance straight up, about to say, "You're definitely taller than the typical undergrad," then realized the same thing I'd realized a minute before: DD didn't need this drivel.

DD tired of waiting for me to say something. "Your best friend is more mature too, and just as smexy as you are."

"Smexy?"

"Smart *and* sexy."

165

Good thing all the color hadn't left my face from this morning, as I had fewer shades to traverse now.

"Have you known each other long?" DD asked.

My voice reemerged. "We met here after I transferred. Lela advertised for a roommate, and we hit it off. We've been best friends ever since."

"Is she a psych major too?"

"What makes you think I am?"

"You mean, your diploma and doctorate notwithstanding?"

I forgot. *Dr.* Bolden.

"Yes, Lela is studying psych too. After grad school, we're openin' a clinic together." My twang always twanged more when I was flustered.

DD grinned and mimicked me. "Where're y'all from? Mississippi?"

"Tennessee."

"Mississippi, Tennessee... it's all the same, isn't it? One enormous state? Everyone's related. Your sister is probably your cousin." His grin widened.

Okay, he did a good job teasing me, and I continued to bite my tall tongue.

"I don't know anything about Mississippians. In Tennessee, we've outlawed conjugal relations between siblings. Hah. There's not enough money in a bubble-gum machine to make me do that."

DD eyed me. "Your best friend, Lela, she's not also your cousin, is she? You two aren't..." He twirled an extremely long index finger.

I masked a smile. "No, Lela's not my cousin, and we aren't..." I twirled my considerably shorter index finger.

"Is she also from Tennessee?"

"New Hampshire."

"New Hampshire, Tennessee... it's all the same, isn't it?"

"Yeah, pretty much."

"This is where I found you and Lela yesterday. Is this your personal bench?"

"Didn't you see the sign? Trespassers will be analyzed and discarded."

"Am I a trespasser?"

I eyed him with another theatrical gesture and nodded. "You'll still be analyzed and discarded, but it'll be with prejudice."

"With prejudice?"

"Subject to reanalysis at an undisclosed future date."

"Does Lela participate in the analysis?"

"I'm sure she does. Hello, Derek." Lela closed in. She unsaddled her backpack, and we exchanged wide-eyed looks.

What's he doing here?

I don't know. I didn't invite him.

DD's voice softened. "Hello, best friend."

"What brings you to our lunchroom?" Lela asked.

"Oh, that's what you use this bench for. Your home away from home. On my way between classes, I couldn't help but notice your roommate stretched out, apparently asleep on the bench. Concerned citizen that I am, I wanted to make certain Dr. Bolden was only dead to the world and not just dead. We were discussing culture in the Southern states when you arrived."

Lela cast a wary glance. "*Dr.* Bolden? You have explaining to do, ma'am."

DD extended a huge paw, unfurled my diploma, and presented it to Lela. Thanks for being so helpful, pal.

"At least NN confirmed your suspicions—she reads

Professor Kirin's e-mails." Lela tore her gaze from DD and scanned me with a quick up-and-down. "You certainly aren't pleased with yourself, which means you haven't been accepted into the class, have you?"

I shook my head once, meaning I didn't want to discuss that subject in front of DD. That wasn't what he latched onto anyhow.

"NN?" DD glanced at me.

"Ms. Naughton, the psych department administrative assistant."

"I thought her first name was Clarisse? That would make her CN."

"NN. Nausicaan Nasal. The Nausicaans are an alien—"

"Yeah, I know who the Nausicaans are. You call her NN to her face?"

"Not that I recall. I don't refer to anyone by their alliterated names."

DD laughed, a peculiar high-pitched sound emanating from a gargantuan body. "What does that make me? DD or FF?"

I flashed a look at Lela before confessing. "DD."

"I'm not sure I want to know. DD?"

Lela's eyes laughed. I'd trapped myself in this. "Derek."

"Derek…" He encouraged me with a ginormous gesture, spreading his arms wide.

I sought refuge in the harbor of my best friend. "So, Lela, how were classes this morning?"

Derek's smirk was not altogether unpatronizing, but he backed away gracefully. "I gotta go," he said. "I have one more class today. Nice to see you again, best friend." He dipped his head, and his gaze shifted to me. "Dr. Bolden." Long strides swept Derek from the roof.

Lela searched her backpack and produced lunch. She spread a paper towel like a placemat, unwrapped a sandwich, and nibbled and chewed with exaggerated motion. A smug smile suggested she knew I'd burst at any moment. It was remotely possible Lela had more patience than me.

"I didn't surprise Professor Kirin. I can't imagine how he knew what I'd do."

"Didn't you ask him?"

"He didn't show up. NN handled the whole thing for him and presented me with that." I pointed.

"Yeah, nice diploma." Lela spoke through a mouthful of sandwich. "What're you going to do?"

"I'm not sure. The solution is right here, I know it, but so far, everything I think of, Professor Kirin does too. I have to think of something I can't think of, know what I mean?"

Lela masked her expression, perhaps hoping we could both pretend I was on the right path. "I'm afraid I do."

"Well, until *I* figure out what I mean, I'm going to stay away from the psych office, and I'm not going to say anything to Professor Kirin."

Chapter 23

Thursday's *Dark Shadows* sponsor advertised Y-I-R—
yeast infection relief—5 or 7. *Hmm, do I want to keep this
yeast infection for five days or a whole week?* Ron
juggled his hands. "Five days, or seven?"

Fish munched Frosted Flakes before they wilted in
milk. Ron's lightning reflexes caught up to the speed of
thunder, and the water filter nailed only the edge of his
shirt. He gulped Swiss mocha decaf, gathered books and
papers into his backpack, and signed off the computer.
They trudged down three flights of stairs and the front
stoop before Ron realized dreary clouds draped over the
city like a tunic over a toddler.

Fish glanced at him. "It's the train all the way this
morning, pal." *Damn it, Dad.*

It was possible all those spinning things in Ron's
head spun slower on the subway platform. Tiled walls
were dingier, lights flickered more often, and the park
beckoned deep within the bowels of the city. *Columbus
Circle* was stamped on the walls like sanctioned graffiti.
The subway doors whooshed open, and on impulse, Ron
grabbed his backpack and slung it over his shoulder.

"Come on, let's go."

Fish cocked his head. *Yeah, right. It's beyond
overcast.*

"Come on. We can discuss meteorological issues along the way."

Fish followed him to the street.

The statue at the park entrance saluted his usual early-morning gesture and pointed at the ominous sky. *You're sure this is a good idea?*

They passed hundreds of pedestrians, none of whom entered the park. Suits carried briefcases, Ron's generation with suits shouldered messenger bags. Scruffy men pushed carts; they were the late-to-set-up street vendors who missed half the morning commuters. A woman pushed a stroller, unable to calm her wailing newborn; a few stray mutts allowed Fish a wide berth on what had become his turf; and a policeman reined his horse, the *clomp-clomp* of the animal's gait another instrument in the city orchestra.

Ron couldn't tell who spit at him—the horse, the cop, or the baby. It wasn't weather related, so they entered the park. Nope, not gonna rain.

The downpour didn't begin for a few minutes. Fish and Ron had a nine o'clock class. Ron scrutinized his watchless wrist. Fish didn't laugh. "Almost eight-thirty," he said. "No time to wait out the rain. Come on. Wetness is relative."

By the time they arrived at Goddard Hall, Ron felt like Fish's Frosted Flakes after an hour in milk. Like most long-haired, shaggy dogs, Fish didn't smell good wet, and he took exception when Ron suggested he not sit near anyone till he dried out. Fish flopped on the floor near the radiator and sighed throughout their first lecture.

Crowded hallways added to unpleasant conditions. Ron classified as drippy and didn't wish to consider how *he* might smell. Apparently not bad enough to ward off members of the polar bear club.

171

"Ron. Oh, Ron!" Howard Coleman rolled up, probably worried Ron might scurry away without talking. "I'm glad I caught you. First things first. Here," he huffed, and offered an envelope. Ron recognized Hilary Nixon's handwriting. The envelope held the feeling of command. *Come to my office this afternoon.* She probably knew the time his last class ended.

Howard blew his nose and stuffed the hankie into his jacket pocket.

"Miserable weather. Don't forget we're meeting tomorrow afternoon. Your paper is absolutely fascinating, by the way. Can't wait to discuss a few ideas with you. Well, I've got a meeting and another lecture before lunch. Try and stay dry. Ta-ta."

Fish and Ron stared at each other, then at the departing professor's back. *Ta-ta?*

A damp-induced shiver wheedled its way across Ron's shoulders. He always kept a clean T-shirt stuffed in his backpack.

Ron ducked into a lavatory, stripped from the waist up, and washed off the best he could. He twisted his upper torso around one of those hand-dryer thingies, the cheap kind without a swiveling head. He wasn't sure if he won the battle with the hand dryer, or if he dried by attrition. Either way, a clean T-shirt roused a smile. Fish tried the hand dryer too, and it fluffed up his coat.

By the time they arrived at the administrative building, the rain had stopped, and Fish and Ron were in good spirits. However, another obstacle blocked the path to Her Majesty the chancellor: the dean of Public Relations.

"Ron, what a coincidence."

More likely Diana had assigned an intern to scan the halls in case Ron approached.

Diana's sheer blouse exposed lace and curves. "I haven't heard from you since Sunday," she said.

"I know. I haven't called since then."

Diana arched her eyebrows, encouraging more of an explanation.

"I haven't been feeling quite myself since Sunday." Fish took the opportunity to sneeze. Ron ruffled his head. "Fish hasn't been feeling well, either."

Diana's forehead furrowed. "Who's Fish?"

Fish sat and raised one paw.

"You call your dog Fish?"

"It would be silly to call him Lassie."

"Why? At least that's a dog's name."

"But it's not *his* name." Like, *duh*.

Diana sighed. "I hope you're feeling better now."

Fish stepped forward and barked. Diana twisted toward him. "You too." She pivoted, face-to-face with Ron. He imagined the *Jeopardy!* song playing in her head while she decided if she wanted to continue this conversation. She glanced below his waist, and her lips puckered. Decision made.

"I'd like to get together again this weekend. We have freshman University Day on Saturday, and of course we invite the students who haven't enrolled yet. I may have to work until early evening Friday preparing, but the rest of the night can be yours."

Ron didn't want to give Diana too much rope.

A. His guts still hurt from two years ago.

B. He now knew her ultimate goal: to find Mr. Diana, fifteen years her junior.

C. Most important, Psyche pervaded his thoughts. Eyes closed, he inhaled the sweet scent of jasmine sailing around her, and imagined the caress of her hand as she drifted in and out of their dance.

His keenly honed intuition proclaimed him busy Friday night. Diana continued before he answered. "I read a book by Anne Rice—"

"About vampires?"

Fish's ears pricked up.

"Before her vampires gained popularity, under a different name, A. N. Roquelaure. She published a series of erotic stories about bondage and domination and how small pain can intensify the human orgasmic experience. Anyway, several interesting ideas came to mind, and I thought it might be fun… you know, to talk about… with you."

His humanity, at least the male part, raged to the forefront of his libido and stomped on his keenly honed intuition. "Okay. Friday night. Just talk."

Diana's raven hair glistened in the light of the chancellor's office. The gleam in her eyes accepted Ron's concession of victory. "Good. Let's say nine o'clock, my place. Bring a bottle of wine. I'll have everything else we'll need."

"What else are we going to need?"

Diana bestowed an evil smirk upon Ron. He cast Friday night from his thoughts and dredged up the task ahead of him, the command to appear before Her Majesty. Diana was but a helpful minion.

"Tell me about University Day. Does it include alumni? Bigwigs? Money people?"

"All of them. The dean of Arts and Sciences will give the welcome address. We anticipate thirteen hundred or more high school students and family members. General tours, show off highlights of individual schools. Lunch. An all-day affair."

"Catered?"

"Of course. These students haven't paid us yet. Many of them haven't matriculated. We want them to choose Huntington. Don't worry. We know better than to feed them university food."

She misunderstood. "Do you use the same caterers all the time?"

"The same caterers as what?"

"Will this be the same group of caterers who handled Hilary's party last weekend?"

She nodded. "Thinking about having a catered party? That's not the Ron I know."

"Me either. Just curious. Thanks." He jerked his thumb. "I'd better hustle inside before the royal guards come out to escort me."

Diana winked and faded into the university void. Fish chose to remain in the hall.

"Coward."

Ron swung open the massive doors. Elliot Collins glanced at him from behind a cherry desk.

"Don't worry. You're in the right place. Hilary has me working out of her office until mine is ready. A couple more weeks. She said you'd stop by this afternoon."

Ron's head bobbed. "I've entered at my own risk. How'd your first week go at the new job?"

"More hectic than I expected, and Hilary tells me this is the quiet season." Elliot shrugged. "I'm sure I'll adjust. Finished with midterms?"

"All wrapped up."

Elliot adopted the deep-pain-just-below-the-smile look. Experience told Ron not to dance around. "Have you heard from your ex-fiancée?"

Pain shoved its way through Elliot's mouth. "Nope. She won't talk with me."

"When someone you love breaks off a relationship, it can take a long time to heal. But the healing process doesn't start until you're ready to be healed." Ron rubbed his chin. At this point in an *ex*-relationship, many people don't know if they *are* still in love. "You want her back, right?"

Elliot's words choked.

"What you need is a plan." Ron almost added, *a plan so simple it couldn't fail.* His simple plans worked once in a while; he just couldn't think of any examples in the moment. If Elliot was still in love, he'd grasp any possibility. What qualified Ron to offer advice on love, though?

"Do you have something in mind?" Elliot asked.

"She hasn't contacted you, so you need to contact her without making yourself a nuisance." Wasn't that what Ron did by e-mailing Psyche? *Yeah, how's that working out for you?* Ron hesitated. Must be the other me asking that question.

"How do I avoid becoming a nuisance?"

"Be creative. Empathy often catches a woman's heart, or at least her attention."

"Empathy? I'm not sure I know what you mean."

The other Ron, the one who knew what he meant, seemed to be in charge of simple plans again today. "How's your singing voice?"

"I'm not Elvis, but I can carry a tune. You think I should serenade her?"

"I think you should write a song and sing it to her. Be personal, use her name in the lyrics, refer to things only the two of you understand. Women find a poet irresistible."

"I don't know anything about putting poetry to music."

"What matter are the words. Write the poetry, put it to her favorite music. She'll respond." If Elliot clung to true love, he'd do anything.

Before Ron could encourage Elliot further, a door whooshed open behind him. "Ron, I thought I heard you out here."

Elliot kept his back to Hilary and lowered his voice. "Thanks for the advice. I'm not a musician or a songwriter, and I don't know if I'm ready to start."

Ron grinned and half waved; Elliot's pessimism exposed another avenue. *Don't worry, Elliot. Since you've fallen out of love with your ex-fiancée, I have a simpler plan for you.*

Hilary opened the door wider, a silent command to enter from the leader of the polar bear club. She closed the door behind him, and his imagination heard the lock click.

"Would you like something to drink?" she asked.

I think I'll need it.

Hilary tilted her head. "What did you say?"

"Yes. Please. Caffeine-free diet soda, if you have it. No aspartame, lots of ice."

"Nothing stronger? I have wine, liqueurs, beer."

"Soda will be fine."

She located a can in the fridge behind the built-in bar, flipped the top, dropped ice cubes into a glass, then poured. Bubbles fizzed and overflowed the glass.

Pour the drink first, then add ice. You'd think polar bears, of all people, would have a better understanding of ice.

Hilary kept pouring. "You've been here a semester and a half. I don't know why we haven't found more time to spend together."

177

Ron remained baffled by Hilary's attention. Was she interested only because Diana was interested in him? Did Hilary think since he'd dated someone as old as Diana, one more decade wouldn't matter?

"My schedule never allows much free time. Between classes and writing, I'm busy."

The carnivore roved over him, mimicking the expression in Diana's eyes. Diana had caught him off guard in the hallway, but for Hilary, he'd developed a plan. One so simple it couldn't fail.

She handed him a glass, as much soda on the outside as on the inside. "Even scholars need to relax once in a while," she said. "I thought perhaps this Saturday night, after University Day—"

"Speaking of University Day, are you organized?"

"For what? All the major areas are covered. Diana's in charge of details."

"Details like the caterers? Hilary, are you prepared for the SDN and Rhiannon and whomever she's working with?"

"I knew you were teasing me at the party. I googled the SDN. Nothing."

"Our government has gone to great lengths to keep the SDN under the radar."

She studied his face. "You're serious?"

He shrugged. Eyebrows, shoulders, anything shruggable. "If I'm not, it'll certainly be easy for you to find out. Follow Rhiannon for a few minutes Saturday morning. She'll be conducting either SDN business or catering business."

"Can you—"

He used his best traffic-cop imitation. "I told you what Rhiannon said. It can't appear as if I'm interfering.

If they discover I talked with you about this, I don't know what they'd do. And I don't want to find out."

He averted his gaze, then slowly twisted his head and peered at Hilary. "Of course, if you're afraid of SDN repercussions, I understand. The SDN is using you as a political stepping-stone to gain financial support. It's not like you've endorsed their organization. They're just using your name."

"How're they using my name?"

"They point out to your guests that you've hired SDN-sympathizing caterers. Everyone knows how powerful Ms. Nixon is. She wouldn't allow the SDN to solicit donations without her approval. By doing nothing, you condone SDN actions. Like I said, it's understandable you're afraid. I am."

"Afraid? Ron, they've threatened you with bodily harm. I understand your reluctance to participate. But this is my university, and I don't approve of their tactics or the use of violence, and I'm not going to allow them or anyone else to use my good name to solicit money."

"These are dangerous people, Hilary. I urge caution. If you're going to collect data for the CIA, make sure you keep meticulous records: places, times, names, and whatever you can include of conversations you hear. The CIA will want it all. I mean, what else can you do?"

Hilary swigged a long gulp of white wine, slammed down the glass, and marched around the office, formulating plans. "Like you said, I can manipulate the SDN instead of letting them manipulate me. I suppose it's too late to create, what did you call them, plants? For University Day? But someone needs to shadow that girl."

"I think you'll have to do it. Remember, they work in pairs. You'll need help, but it can't be me." He scratched behind an ear. "Why don't you enlist Elliot? He

179

seems like someone you can trust. Next week, have him create fictitious people to enter into the database for future functions."

Ron cringed. "You and Elliot handle the surveillance this weekend. I'll keep an eye out from a distance in case I spot peripheral activity."

"Thanks, Ron. I don't know what would've happened if you hadn't alerted me to this situation."

He waved off her thanks. "How many different locations around the university will the caterers be on Saturday?"

"I'm not sure." She bowed over her desk and leafed through papers.

"You need an itinerary for Rhiannon, and you need to spot her cohort as early on as possible. Someone needs to stick to Rhiannon, and someone else will have to be a floater, prepared to go anywhere the caterers are. Hmm…"

"What?"

"I know I suggested him, but I don't know if Elliot is up to the floating job. I don't want to involve him over his head. Floating is dangerous."

She squeezed his biceps. "Don't worry, I'll take care of floating. I'll assign Elliot to watch Rhiannon." Hilary's eyes glazed.

Ron deposited his glass on the bar. "I'd better leave you to your planning."

"Yes, yes, of course. Thanks for coming by. And I do appreciate whatever help you can offer Saturday. The function starts at nine-thirty in the morning. Make sure you're there on time." She waved, immersed in the machinations of the nonexistent SDN.

Then her head popped up, and a frown creased her face. "You look serious. You sound serious. But you're pulling my leg about all this, aren't you?"

"If I am, we'll have a good laugh later. You'll know soon enough. If you don't want to spend your time investigating, at least assign Elliot to Rhiannon. *Someone* should watch her."

Hilary glowered as though discerning truth. "Send Elliot in."

Ron nodded. *Oh, Elliot… You're commanded into Her Majesty's throne room. Don't worry, though. Nothing but good fortune lies ahead of you. You just have to take an unusual path to claim it.*

Ron strolled through the outer office. The far set of doors whooshed open, and he peered over his shoulder at Elliot. "Hilary wants you."

Elliot winced, then smirked. "Thank you. Thank you very much."

~ ~ ~

No messages from Psyche.

Of course not. His turn to write.

He reread her last e-mail. Not exactly friendly. He didn't understand the dynamic. It was as if Psyche were two different people. She inspired intimacies in the park, then increasingly inimical e-mails afterward.

He dumped his first inclination to respond with sarcasm. He wanted to know this girl, and he wanted her to know him. His job was to change the tone of their correspondence. "This requires refinement," Ron said.

Fish laughed.

~ ~ ~

Ron woke in the middle of the night to Fish sneezing. He sneezed four or five times, dragged himself to Ron's bed, and flopped his head onto the blanket. His saucer eyes gazed at Ron with all the forlornness a dog could muster.

"What's wrong?"

Fish swiveled his head to sneeze twice more.

"Oh. You've got a cold. Let's find medicine."

Ears back, tail down, Fish followed him into the kitchen. His dinner bowl stared at them. Frosted Flakes beyond soggy, they'd solidified.

"Let me dump that. You don't want to look at it any more than I do. While I'm at it, I'll pour fresh water. When you're sick, you should drink more water."

Everyone knows lightning-quick reflexes are a daytime phenomenon. The water filter sprayed his shirt as he filled Fish's bowl. Fish didn't even laugh, and he ignored the water. Ron rummaged through the cabinet but remembered a friend once told him Tylenol and NSAIDs may be toxic for dogs, even in low dosages. He found leftover soup from the Chinese restaurant, heated it, and filled Fish's bowl. Fish sniffed, slurped, then smacked his lips several times and decided now would be a good time to lap water.

They headed to bed, but only one of them slept. Racing thoughts generated ideas for Ron's romantic comedy, how to deal with Howard's advances, Hilary at University Day, and Diana at their Friday-night talk-only orgy.

His mind finally focused on Lela. Imagination seized the reins. She melted into his arms, her body pressed tight against his. Her hand caressed his neck as they danced, and her perfume curled around them. The city symphony played their song.

His grin stretched wide. He wanted the next meeting in the park to blow her away.

How could he surprise Lela?

Chapter 24

He'd purchased a copy of Anne Rice's *The Claiming of Sleeping Beauty*, surprised that Barnes & Noble carried only one copy. The sales clerk informed him they stockpiled cases of the novel in storage but only shelved a single copy of one of the most shoplifted books in America.

What did Diana have planned?

~ ~ ~

Friday began with excitement and trepidation. Ron prepared to leave, and Fish retreated to the couch, remote in paw, ears drooping, tail down, as if he knew something Ron didn't. Ron convinced him to lap ice cream. Ice cream always made Ron feel better.

"I'll see you tonight. Remember, I'm gonna be late. I have a meeting with Dr. Coleman after class this afternoon. I coulda used your help on this one too, but don't worry, I have it under control." Fish slumped, head on paws, and sighed.

Ron rode the subway to Huntington. Queasiness dissolved quicker than normal. Classes he typically found stimulating bored him. A second consecutive day without Fish's witty repartee and the third time this week he lunched on the roof. *What's up with that?* He didn't understand the odd mixture of déjà vu and anticipation, but thoughts of Lela distracted him in every aspect of life. His libido refocused from a sure thing with Diana tonight to imprecise promises with his Central Park dance partner.

~ ~ ~

His last class finally ended. He gathered his backpack and all his notes and headed across campus. Howard agreed to meet at the student union center, where they could have a drink and discuss Ron's paper.

The professor rose and waved as Ron approached. Not surprising Dr. Coleman arrived early. His purple shirt and color-coordinated shoes projected a distinct image. Ron had to concede an appealing personality.

Dr. Coleman had located two high-backed chairs in the common room, near a corner window. He angled one to exclude the room, the other—where he sat—so he could keep surveillance on the main entrance. His broad smile reflected the reward for his efforts. Soda cans, one diet, sat on the low table between the chairs.

"Have a seat, have a seat." He repositioned his chair for optimum privacy. "Help yourself to a soda. They're both cold."

Neither was caffeine-free. "I prefer diet, if that's okay?"

"Anything you want. I drink either."

Caffeine would keep Ron up half the night. He was sure Diana planned to keep him up the other half. He popped the top and swigged. Dr. Coleman popped the other can and sipped.

Howard leaned forward. "How'd your day go?"

"Slowly."

"Which leads directly into a discussion of your paper, doesn't it? Relative time in everyday life. A dynamic concept. Allow me to applaud you. Your paper is well thought-out, organized, and provocative. I have a keener understanding of what you mean when you say your day seems to be going slowly."

Howard's chin wobbled when he spoke. Ron didn't recall ever noticing it before, a definite side-to-side oscillation. Transfixed by this revelation, he missed most of what Howard said.

"—don't you think so, Ron?"

Seemed best to agree. "Oh, yes." *Quite so, old chap, quite so.*

Not amusing. Maybe amusing.

They talked about the paper, mostly. Every so often, Howard sidetracked. He asked how Ron liked living in the city, how city life compared to life in Trenton—where exactly did Ron live, by the way? The more personal the questions, the less inclined Ron felt to answer. Howard never peered off into the distance, his gaze never darted to passing students. He remained fixed on Ron, flattering but not what Ron wanted. His favorite movie? Music? Where did Ron grow up?

Who said I ever grew up?

"What's your favorite place in the city?"

Not information Ron wanted to share with Howard, so he made up an answer. "The aquarium." A sign he'd once seen in an aquarium flashed in his memory. *Don't feed the fish.*

Ron's mind leaped ahead into the near future and pictured the professor asking him to dinner. He liked Howard. He seemed like an intelligent, friendly man, and

Ron was happy to discuss psychology or his paper, but Howard's objective was unclear. And Ron didn't wish to embarrass himself or Howard by asking his intentions. That would have been a simple plan, and when did his simple plans ever work?

Fish's illness fed an idea for retreat.

Ron glanced at his bare wrist and shook his head. "Look at the time. Excuse me. I have to find a bathroom and a phone." Ron treated his cell phone like a landline—it was always sitting on his bureau.

"The men's room is around the far corner." Howard curled his wrist and pointed. "Here, use my cell phone." He pulled it half out of his pocket.

Ron shrugged. "It's a personal call."

Howard smiled graciously and pulled it out the rest of the way. "Take it with you. Dial the number, push *Send*."

"Thanks."

Ron peed and explored calling options. Fish would've been perfect, but he'd never developed the hang of dialing, so he couldn't call back. Elliot would do, but Ron didn't know his extension. He knew Hilary's number, but why involve her? And he realized he didn't know Howard's number. He needed someone with caller ID. He settled on Diana.

"Do me a favor? Wait ten minutes, then call me at this number. You've got it there, right?... You're a doll."

He rounded the corner, and Howard literally shooed someone away. Two someones: Derek Forrester, unmistakably towering taller than anyone else, and a girl half his size whom Derek half dragged, half carried away.

~ ~ ~

186

I promised myself, but what do mild obsessive-compulsives do when compulsions conflict?

The only thing I wanted to do was talk with Professor Kirin and arrange to be in his class next fall. I realized immediately I was lying to myself. I also wanted to see Mark again. I wanted to dance with him. I wanted to wrap my arms around his neck and refuse to let him go, at least until he confessed his real name and cell number.

I refocused. I'd promised myself not to contact Professor Kirin until I was sure I could surprise him, and I'd promised to stay away from the psych office until then. I'd need Dr. Coleman's help again to surprise Professor Kirin, but Dr. Coleman maintained formality about certain aspects of student-professor relations and would never speak about personal matters in the classroom, so the only place I could speak with him was in his office, in the *psych* office. Conflicting compulsions.

Not to mention, I'd have to go through NN to make an appointment with Dr. Coleman.

No solution presented itself immediately. Friday afternoon, I headed to our bench to wait for Lela to finish her last class of the day. I stretched out, using my backpack as a headrest, and read *Love and Other Sides of Sex*. DD said it had been assigned, and I hoped the book would offer both a distraction and insight to Professor Kirin, the assigner.

I basked in the sun for half an hour, but the aromas drifting up through cafeteria roof vents overpowered my will. Two giant chocolate-chip cookies later, I returned to my bench, book in hand. I was surprised by approaching footsteps not belonging to Lela, then retracted my surprise when the largest sneakers I'd ever seen stopped just two feet away.

187

I smiled, the sun no longer in my eyes. "Hello, Derek."

"It's a pleasure to see you, Dr. Bolden."

Okay, that wasn't going away any time soon. I could deal, though. I sat up to allow him space to sit down and share our bench, confident I knew what he was doing here.

I glanced at my watch. "Lela will be here soon."

"I figured." Derek pointed. "Good book, huh?"

"I'm reading strictly on your recommendation."

He studied my face, like he was reading micro-expressions. "I doubt it," he said.

High marks for face-reading. My blush could've been confused with sun-induced color, though.

"Your doctorate notwithstanding, you've seemed out of sorts the past week or two," Derek said.

That was way too perspicacious. My eyebrows arched of their own volition.

"Surprise is the most common reaction when people get to know me," Derek said. "I'm sorry, I guess I was expecting something else from you."

Hadn't I lived through enough DD surprises not to be surprised again? Apparently not.

"I apologize," I said. "You deserve better from me. I promise you'll have to work fiercer in the future to surprise me ever again." Hadn't I made enough promises recently?

DD nodded. "It's okay. It's just that I pay attention to details. Paying attention makes me a fierce competitor on the basketball court and helps me understand off-court relationships. For instance, the other day when Lela mentioned registration closed for a class you wanted next semester, I'm guessing the look that flashed across your face has something to do with your out-of-sortedness."

My lips mooshed in a strange array of poses. "Keeping in mind the promise I just made to you, I'm betting you know which class."

He shrugged his shoulders. "Probably the same class that has the longest wait list in university history: Crimes in Psychology."

"If you fail to make it as a professional basketball player, you can always find a job as a mind reader in a circus."

"The tallest mind reader in the circus." He boasted what would've been the widest smile in the circus. "There's not much chance you'll get in," he added.

"To the circus?"

"To the class."

"Thanks for reminding me." I sighed.

"You can have my spot."

"What!"

He pretended to study his watch, then winced. "So that promise lasted about thirty seconds?"

Promises be damned. "You're in Professor Kirin's Crimes in Psychology class for next fall?"

"Where are those vaunted powers of deduction I've grown to know and love? Difficult for me to offer my spot if I weren't registered for his class."

"You're serious?"

"Which part is confusing you? Let's find your advisor and see about switching my class for one of yours."

"Why would you do this for me?" Charm the roommate by ingratiating himself with the best friend?

"I don't want to be in that class. Professor Kirin has preassigned three novels. I'm enjoying this book"—he pointed—"but I don't need any more of next semester's work added to the current semester."

Conflicting compulsions resolved. I hopped up and shouldered my backpack. "Let's go to the psych office," I said.

"He's not there," Derek said.

"Who's not there?"

"Dr. Coleman. He's my advisor too, and he's not in the psych office."

"How do you know? He might be there on a Friday afternoon."

"Nope."

"You can't be a soothsayer and a mind reader. That wouldn't be fair to the rest of us."

"I'm neither. I passed him on the way up. He's three floors down, in the student union center."

Derek escorted me, one step to every three of mine. We found Dr. Coleman sitting in a corner, walled in by two cans of soda—both open—but the professor was alone. He fidgeted like he was waiting for someone.

"Excuse me, Dr. Coleman. Could we have a couple of minutes?" I asked.

"One."

I swallowed, ready to speak fast. "Derek wants out of Crimes next fall. I want in. Can I just take his spot?" DD backed me up, like a looming shadow.

"No." He shooed us away with the back of his hand.

"That wasn't a minute," I said.

"Close enough," Dr. Coleman said.

"It's a perfect exchange." I whined. "Derek—"

"If Mr. Forrester wants out of that class or any other, he can fill out the proper add-drop paperwork and put it through channels. But you're not even on the first page of the wait list, Ms. Bolden. I checked with Professor Kirin for the favor, as I promised you, but he was adamant. If anyone drops the class, number one on the wait list will be invited in. He said, 'If two hundred and seven other students drop the class, Ms. Bolden will receive her invitation.' Assuming you've taken Ab Psych. Now, shoo." He flicked his wrist again.

I opened my mouth, but before I could speak, Dr. Coleman cut me off. "Go away, or I'll assign you each another paper to write this weekend. Go. Now."

Derek guided my elbow. Another paper would only bother me if I didn't win the argument, but Derek clearly didn't want extra work regardless. No chance to win, unprepared to concede defeat, I frowned. Derek dragged. It turned out his strength was in proportion to his height, and we glided away through an influx of after-class students at a rapider pace than I imagined possible, since I wasn't using my feet for anything other than stomping.

~ ~ ~

Ron didn't see her face, but her body language and floor-rattling stomp clarified her feelings.

Something about the departing view rang familiar before she was engulfed in a sea of undergrads rushing into their weekend. "Who was that?" Ron asked Dr. Coleman.

"An annoying student."

Ron spun for a second glance of swaying hips. Derek's head, shoulders, and half his back were visible, but the crowd swallowed the girl's body. Ron returned the phone to Howard. "Thanks."

"Did you reach whoever it was?"

"Nope. Stuck on hold."

"Sorry. Try again." He attempted to pass Ron the phone.

"If it's important, they'll find a way to reach me." Howard's tone, his expressions, his body language were suggestive.

Ron's preferences leaned one way, and he considered Howard's preferences to be Howard's business, not his. Ron hadn't meant to mislead Howard in any way at Hilary's party, yet somehow he had.

He realized then his behavior with Howard mimicked his behavior with Diana. By agreeing to meet Diana tonight, Anne Rice's book in hand, he was misleading her too. Also not what he intended.

He needed to control the flow of conversation until Diana called. "We were talking about the problem of roommates experiencing the same afternoon in the same environment. For one." He paused to slow the pace. "Time passes quickly; for the other, the same time passes slowly." He sipped his drink and sighed. "What happens when the two of them interact? Does one speed up, the other slow down so time passes at the same pace? Is relative time dependent on interpersonal experience?" *Could I cram any more questions into this instant?*

The phone rang. *Whew.*

"Excuse me." Howard kept his gaze on Ron and answered without looking at the screen.

"Hello... Oh. Hold on, please." He seemed perplexed. "It's for you."

Ron offered an apologetic look and accepted the cell. "Hello..." He tried to bring a measure of incredulity into his voice. "Really?... Oh, no... I'll be there soon as I can." He tapped *End* and handed the phone back. He couldn't cancel with Diana in front of Howard—that wasn't part of the plan—and he hadn't thought about it while he peed.

"Sorry. My sick friend. Have to go."

192

He grabbed his backpack. Dr. Coleman burped at Ron's sudden decision to leave. He slid to the edge of the seat and opened his mouth. Ron cut him off.

"It's been a pleasure chatting with you, Dr. Coleman—Howard. Thank you for taking the time to read my paper and for offering your invaluable insight." Ron slung the backpack over a shoulder while he spoke, unwilling to give the man a chance to express another thought. "Several of your ideas are intriguing, and I may have to address them in an addendum."

"Yes, but—"

"Here's one final concept. If time is personal, does that mean we can control relative time? If so, how far does that control extend in theory and in reality? Make a few notes if you have the chance? Gotta go. See ya."

He scurried away, sucking in his cheeks, relieved that he and Howard were still friends.

Chapter 25

A snoring dog never bothered him as much as a snoring Diana. Fish twitched and sighed.

Ron boiled water while thawing a small container of homemade spaghetti sauce. By accident he'd discovered Fish liked ditalini. They couldn't eat it too often because Ron always drank wine with pasta, and Fish needed to restrict the amount of alcohol he consumed.

Ron's mind raced as he prepared dinner. Guilt about meeting Diana tonight lodged a small headache in his temples. It had never been his intention to mislead her.

He still owed Psyche an e-mail. Every time he thought about Lela, his stomach twisted in knots and his appetite all but disappeared. Confusion reigned. He pounded the kitchen counter with his fist. He wanted to rant at her dime-store analysis. She barely knew him. Who'd she think she was?

She asserted he lived alone, talked to himself, and invented stories.

Notwithstanding the depressing accuracy, her analysis amounted to nothing more than cheap theatrics. If she wanted more in-depth analysis, Psyche's psyche could easily be discussed as Lela's psychosis.

He shook his head. That wasn't what he wanted. E-mail lacked the inflection and nuance that made their park meetings soar. He needed to transform the tenor of their online communication.

But how? Seeing Diana tonight wouldn't help.

"What do you think?"

Fish sprawled across the floor, ignoring TV vampires. He sneezed twice. Ron retrieved a sponge from beneath the sink to wipe the mess. Fish didn't have the hang of using tissues.

"No ideas, huh?"

Fish moaned and managed to roll his eyes, but not much else.

"I know how you feel. I'm sure there's a simple solution that continues to elude me."

Fish scrunched his face.

"Well, until I figure it out, I'm going to stay away from the park, and I'm not going to write to Lela." He stirred the pot. Fish struggled to sit. Ron scratched behind Fish's ear. "I'll go to the park once more, just to make sure it's not my imagination. Our time together is captivating. It's just our e-mails growing hostile, and I don't understand why."

Ron told Fish about his meeting with Howard. Fish continued to sneeze, although he seemed livelier and laughed at Ron's predicament, real or otherwise. Ron showered and put on a clean T-shirt.

"Listen, I'm stopping by Diana's. I'm not going to stay, but I owe Diana an explanation, face-to-face. You're welcome to tag along if you'd like."

Fish whined. *What're you, nuts?*

"Sure you're going to be okay alone?" Fish nodded, and Ron scratched behind his ears.

~ ~ ~

Ron's heart thudded long before he arrived at Diana's apartment. He'd done his best not to think about Diana's innuendos for tonight—it only stimulated his already overstimulated libido. He wanted a monogamous relationship with someone—not Diana. They didn't mesh emotionally, and as long as she realized he wouldn't become Mr. Diana, they might enjoy each other's company occasionally. Nothing more.

Living monkish while he waited for a girl he found emotionally and romantically challenging might not be a bad idea. This painted a complex picture, but his thoughts coalesced. He wanted the stars and the moon and the sun and rain and rainbows, not an older woman hoping to manipulate him with sex.

Diana answered the door wearing a bodysuit that clung like salt on a potato chip, every delicious bump and crevice outlined in glorious detail. She ushered him to living room center. On the way, he glanced into the bedroom. She'd knotted flowered scarves to the corners of her four-poster bed with a gift-wrapped carton at the foot.

"What's in the box?" Ron pointed.

"Don't worry, you're going to find out. Give me your glasses."

Diana shimmied into his personal space, removed his glasses, and produced a large bandanna. She glided behind him, caressed his ears, and slipped the bandanna over his eyes.

"What's this for?"

"I didn't say you could speak."

"But—"

She grazed his lips. "Don't move. You can talk soon enough. You'll be forgiven a first transgression, but from now on, you'll be punished for disobeying."

Footsteps retreated, the clink of crystal, a popping cork, a long-stemmed glass pressed into his palm.

"Drink this."

"What is it?"

"Wine. You're going to need it."

"Why? We're just going to talk."

"If you don't hush up, you'll be chastised."

"For what?"

"Too many questions. Wine will make it easier to deal with your punishment."

Punishment? He swigged alcohol. Diana transferred the glass to a table and caressed his cheek.

"Put your hands behind your back."

"What!" He yanked off the bandanna.

Chapter 26

Ron knew he didn't touch her.

Saturday morning rushed in like a leak in the Holland Tunnel. A ceiling other than his own yawned at him, and he imagined the suntanned face of a Southern California surfer, head bobbing.

"Duuude, way to go!"

His head throbbed and memories danced like a surfboard carving a wave. He kicked off the covers. Fully clothed except for shoes. Whew. He remembered no one had been tied up, though a second bottle of wine had been opened. Diana had finally promised to behave and just talk.

Her queen-size featherbed cradled him. He sat up and rubbed his forehead, encouraging eyes and ears into this plane of existence. Diana had to be somewhere—making coffee in the kitchen, shaving her legs in the shower, squeezing into Saturday-morning Lycra of choice in the closet.

No Diana sounds intruded. That lump under the covers… Nope, he didn't want to know.

He glanced at his wrist. His internal clock failed to register, the disorientation of what must be a hangover. He never got drunk, so he wasn't sure what a hangover felt like, but it couldn't be worse than this. A note at the foot of the bed captured his attention. Diana's eloquent handwriting filled the page.

> *University Day begins early, didn't want to disturb you. Can't believe you drank yourself into oblivion last night and you refused to touch me. No fun after you stopped being you. Relax.*
> *Stay sober.*
> *We have more to talk about.*

Memory reengaged, and a search for Saturday-night promises came up empty.

> *Help yourself to coffee or breakfast. Stay here.*

Stay here? "Sorry, Diana. I'm not good following orders." A memory search for University Day said Hilary commanded him on campus early. *What if I'm late? Hilary couldn't possibly know the exact moment I arrive.*

He performed one more memory search, on general principles. *Uh-oh. Fish won't be happy with me.* He had promised to be home last night. Sunlight stormed through Diana's bedroom window. Ron would suffer less guilt if Fish read his paper on relative time. He slipped on shoes and hurried home.

Ron winced when he opened their door and was forced to breathe through his mouth. Various messes scattered about the apartment testified to a difficult night. He mopped up quickly.

"I'm sorry, buddy." He rubbed Fish's head. "Grab your coat. I'm taking you to the doctor."

Fish barked.

"Yeah, I know, University Day. I remembered after I woke up. Hilary will have to wait. Let's go."

~ ~ ~

They returned from the vet's with good news, bad news, and horse pills. The good news: Fish didn't have diarrhea. The bad news: Fish suffered from pneumonia. The horse pills elicited Ron's best *Mister Ed* imitation.

"Whoa, Willl... bur, you're gonna need two glasses of water to swallow one of those."

Fish barely managed a grin. He flopped on the sofa, one of the few places not targeted in last night's multiple regurgitations. Ron opened windows for cross ventilation and re-mopped with pine cleaner.

~ ~ ~

Shaved and showered, Ron wore black jeans, black sneaks, and a black T-shirt, a perfect spy outfit.

"I won't be gone so long this time. Anything you need before I leave?" He set the remote on the sofa near Fish's head. "Dr. Grant said the best thing is rest. You'll be okay, I promise. Those pills will make you better." Fish's warm nose nuzzled Ron's hand. Ron unfolded the afghan. Fish rolled his eyes.

"You're right, don't cover up when you have a fever." He balled the afghan like a pillow and wedged it under Fish's head. "That's better, huh?"

Fish had no comment.

Ron waved from the doorway. "See ya soon."

His imagination often played tricks, but his head didn't pound when he descended the subway steps. Not so crowded Saturdays, or was he growing accustomed to the underground?

When the A train screeched at Columbus Circle, he

almost relented, forgetting his resolve to stay out of the park—or was it his resolve to face fears head-on? Instead, he hurried along Fifty-Ninth Street to the 6 train.

He arrived on campus in the early afternoon, with lots of unanswered questions. His stomach growled. University Day activities focused in the student union building, which seemed as likely a place as any to find Hilary and food.

Purple-shirted student guides dotted the landscape. Tours crisscrossed campus, dodging the usual Saturday activity of Frisbee fliers, book readers, sunbathers, rollerbladers, and a small crowd gathered around a singing guitar player. The sun radiated on a beautiful spring day. What high school senior in his right mind wouldn't choose to attend Huntington?

A smiling purple-shirted guide handed Ron a self-adhesive "Hello, my name is:" tag.

He grappled with images of a man sauntering into the student union, a label slapped across the lapel of a white tuxedo jacket, *Hello, my name is: Bond, James Bond.* The dorky name tag folded neatly into the pocket of Ron's black spy suit.

Various sandwich components, potato salad, and pastries rewarded his search for food. Long tables dressed with white linen were laden with a sumptuous spread. He sniffed freshly baked chocolate-chip cookies. Uniformed waitstaff milled about with pitchers of Saturday-afternoon-prospective-student-appropriate drinks. Rhiannon, her SDN coconspirators, and the newly anointed SDN hunters, Elliot and Hilary, were obligated to be nearby.

"Pssst. Ron."

He ignored the summons, encouraging Hilary to try again, louder.

"Ron. Ron."

He glanced in the wrong direction and yawned.

"Ron!"

He spun around. "Oh, Hilary. What a pleasure to see you." She leaned out from behind a post. "What're you doing there?" he asked.

"Shh." She signaled, as if he'd exposed a terribly clever hiding place. She waved him over.

He mouthed a big *Oh*, snatched a couple chocolate-chip cookies and a bottled water, then maneuvered around the table and various University Day guests. His gaze shifted from side to side, but Hilary didn't notice, her attention focused on the crowd.

He mopped his forehead with the cold bottle and dissembled. "University Day seems to be a success."

"I know who it is," she whispered.

"You do?"

"I found him just like that." She flicked her head in the direction of a hundred people. "When the caterers arrived first thing this morning, I still doubted you, but they split up."

"They did?"

"Uh-huh."

"That's great, Hilary, great. Umm, who's 'they'?"

She regarded him with disbelief. "Rhiannon. And her partner. I assigned Elliot to stick with Rhiannon, no matter where she goes, and I've tailed the other one." She palmed an iPad.

"That's him. Right there. With the pastry tray. Facing us now. Who's he talking to? Can you tell?"

Ron squinted and strained. "Nope. Can't make out the name tag through his back." Ron massaged his chin and studied the waiter as he angled toward them to serve another guest. "Are you sure that's him? The waiter with the handlebar mustache?"

"Your whole SDN thing on campus made me leery, but as soon as they got out of the van, he and Rhiannon fell deep into conversation. Rhiannon pointed, gave *him* instructions, probably making sure he knew where to go. He's acted suspicious the entire day, and you can't imagine the number of people he's stopped."

Ron tugged on his ear, then his chin, and nodded.

"What? What is it, Ron?"

"I've seen him before."

"You mean here on campus? At one of the other catered affairs?" She paused, hand pressed to her chest. "At my party?"

Ron shook his head. "No. Not on campus. Never. You may've hit on something big. Do you have any idea who he is? No, of course not, or you wouldn't be taking all this so casually. You're way too calm." He slapped the side of his head, chomped a chocolate-chip cookie, and chirped. "I *knew* I saw him someplace."

Hilary hopped from one foot to the other like a kindergarten kid who can't wait for show-and-tell.

Ron chewed diligently, swallowed, swigged water, and wiped his mouth. "When the CIA questioned me, they presented photos of known SDN operatives and party leaders. That's him. Magnus Ferguson. That's the Big MF himself. I'm sure of it."

"Who?"

"The Big MF is head of SDN Atlantic Coast operations. The CIA have never been able to find him, and here you are, first time out, you've nailed the top operative. I'm impressed. Say, do you think we could take a stroll across campus?"

Hilary's eyes bugged. "You've got to be joking. I can't leave here now. You know that's the Big MF. Who knows what he'll do or who he'll talk to? I have to maintain surveillance."

Ron forced the corners of his mouth down to keep from laughing. "I've been looking forward to spending time with you today."

"Don't you understand? This isn't a group of disgruntled students. It's serious. Besides, I need your help. Right now."

Hilary peered at Ron. "I have no idea where Elliot is or how he's managing with Rhiannon. For all I know, he's blown his cover. He's young, and he's inexperienced. Find him and Rhiannon, keep him calm, and make sure he doesn't let the girl know we're on to her. Got it?"

Ron saluted, left-handed. "Yes, sir."

Chapter 27

Each department prepared a presentation for University Day, and each one included food. Rhiannon could be anywhere. Almost two-thirds of the departments occupied offices in Goddard Hall, so Ron headed there first. Tours moved in both directions, up and down Goddard Hall steps, and hordes of people gathered in the immense lobby. He smothered a grimace. This couldn't be any worse than the crowded subway, could it?

Tables circled the periphery. Printed signs announced each department. He didn't recognize many of the presenters, but he assumed they were all professors. The few who recognized Ron smiled and waved, including Howard Coleman. Howard motioned for Ron to come over, but Ron waved a second time and headed in the other direction. Howard popped out of his chair, about to give chase. His forehead wrinkled when prospective students approached him, and his attention rounded on them.

Rhiannon's magnificent hair made her easy to spot as she worked the crowd. *Hmm, if I were Elliot and assigned to keep an eye on Rhiannon, where would I be? Behind a post? Under a table? Elliot, come out, come out, wherever you are.*

Ron strolled the lobby in an ever-increasing arc around Rhiannon, but Elliot remained invisible. Packs of people rendered searching problematic. Seemed like the basketball team, including JV, greeted visitors here. Lacking the height to see over everyone's head didn't help. Ron needed to be higher.

The back stairs led to a crossover connecting the halves of the building. A perfect spy perch to escape the masses.

Ron didn't give his mark enough credit. Elliot lounged on the crossover, leaning over the balustrade. Ron sighed and stopped far from the railing.

"You're hanging in space. What makes you think it's safe?" Ron asked.

"Life is all about trust," Elliot said. "I trust the architect."

Ron flashed a smile and munched another cookie. "This is good, by the way."

Elliot rubbed his belly. "Yeah, I'll try one if I ever get the chance." His attention refocused on the crowd, and he folded his arms across his chest. "I hope all the university affairs won't be so boring. Does Hilary always do this to her new employees? I could be wandering around, talking with prospective students and their parents, enjoying the beautiful weather, but noooo. I'm standing on the balcony all day."

Elliot crossed his arms. "Hilary mentioned you were somehow involved in this, whatever the hell this is. She told me to keep an eye on that redhead. The one in the uniform. There." He pointed.

"She's been doing her job since eight this morning. Hilary said to pay particular attention to who she contacts. Well, she's talked to almost everyone at University Day. She's efficient passing around those trays. What is it I'm supposed to do?"

Hmm. Ron studied Elliot a moment, edged closer—but not too close—to the railing. He spotted Rhiannon and followed the gentle curve of her hip as she sashayed across the lobby.

"Hilary didn't tell you anything else?"

"Nope."

"'Kay. Let me tell you what happened. Last week at Hilary's party, one of the guests accosted that young woman."

Elliot swung around to face Ron.

"Someone put his hand on her backside. He may've added some inappropriate comment. The whole thing upset Rhiannon. That's her name." Ron pointed at the girl, then spoke faster. "Rhiannon didn't want to make a big deal out of it—the guy being a guest of Hilary's—but she didn't want it to happen again either. So I told Hilary a story to enlist her aid. She assigned you to watch Rhiannon, but actually you're protecting her."

Elliot's attention fixed on the girl.

"Have you been up here the whole time?"

"Yep."

"Did you tell Rhiannon you're here?"

"Huh? Tell her?"

Ron nodded. "Relieve her anxiety about working a room full of strangers, a handful of whom may be the same people from last week's party."

"You think that's what I should do, tell her?"

"Elliot, you're this lady's special protector. Her personal knight. I think she'd be thrilled to know. Come on, let's go. Polish your armor."

"Go where?"

"I'm going to introduce you. Right now. How you handle it after that is up to you. You can keep her

207

company, escort her to dinner, make sure she gets home safely, or when University Day is over, you can run off and report to Hilary."

Elliot stole another glance to make sure no one close to Rhiannon appeared threatening. In the time it took them to arrive in the lobby, half a dozen more tours entered the building. People jostled, bumper-to-bumper. Masses swarmed around Ron. His breath grew ragged. Perspiration dribbled down his back.

"Where is she?" Desperation edged into Elliot's voice. His nervousness seemed to exceed Ron's.

Ron needed to calm Elliot. *Hell, I need to calm* me. Too many people too close. His pulse exploded rapid-fire. "She's over here." Ron lied to skirt the throng, if only for a moment.

When they arrived *here*, Elliot scrunched up his face. "Where is she?"

"She's not holding still. Silly girl. Come on, let's catch up to her."

Despite her shock of fiery hair, Rhiannon remained elusive in the unruly swarm. Ron and Elliot squeezed through the mob. Ron made a point of circumventing Howard's table. Rhiannon continued to elude them. Elliot scuffed the floor and twisted his head.

"Excuse me, would you care for a cookie?" Rhiannon found them. Her sea-foam-green eyes captured the spring sunshine and transported it indoors, her Scottish brogue as charming as Elliot's Southern drawl.

"Hello, Ron. I thought I recognized you."

"It's a pleasure to see you again, Rhiannon. I hope you're having a better party than last week."

She arched an eyebrow. "No one's propositioned me, if that's what you mean. I may've been groped once,

208

though. Someone bumped into me at the same moment, so I couldn't be certain." She maintained her smile. "I'm happy to see you again."

Ron grinned. "Rhiannon, this is a friend of mine, Elliot Collins. Elliot, Rhiannon Raeburn."

"Nice to meet you." She raised the tray. "Would you care for a cookie?"

Elliot shook his head. "That's unacceptable, Ms. Raeburn."

She frowned. "The cookies are good. I baked them."

Ron slipped a chocolate-chip cookie from the tray. "Yes, Elliot, the cookies are excellent."

Elliot shook his head harder. "I don't mean the cookies. I mean, I'm sure the cookies are wonderful. I'm talking about the other thing, Ms. Raeburn. That's just unacceptable."

Rhiannon balanced the tray, fingers splayed on her chest. "Something I did?"

"I don't mean you. I mean, whoever did that."

"Did what?"

Elliot flushed. Palms up, he shifted his weight from one leg to the other. "That." He pointed in the direction of Rhiannon's derrière. "You know." Elliot's hands fluttered. "That." He half pointed again. His face changed shades twice, approaching the color of Rhiannon's hair. "Th-That's just not acceptable."

"Really?" Her Scottish brogue accentuated, and she swayed ever so slowly to the side. "What is it you would find acceptable, Mr. Collins?"

"I-I-I don't mean to suggest you're not acceptable, Ms. Raeburn." He shrugged. "It's the behavior."

Rhiannon's eyes widened, her tone half-playful, half-belligerent, and she rotated her hips in a barely perceptible motion. "You mean my conduct is unacceptable?" Even Ron couldn't tell if she yanked Elliot's chain.

Elliot's mouth dropped. "That's not what I mean."

"Mr. Collins, whatever do you mean?" Rhiannon licked her lips, and her mouth curled up.

Ron forced a straight face. "Yes, Mr. Collins, fess up. Whatever do you mean?"

Elliot's hands flapped. The more he struggled for words, the more pronounced his accent became. "I guess I'm havin' a hard time explainin' myself. Y'all sure make it difficult." He glanced at Ron, as if Ron might make it less difficult.

"Dad insisted *Difficult* was my middle name." The crowd closed in, but no way was Ron gonna miss this. He took a deep breath. "Speak up, Mr. Collins, speak up," he said.

Elliot studied the ceiling, the floor, and finally captured Rhiannon's steady gaze, sheepish and courageous. Ron and Rhiannon struggled to hear him over the hum of a hundred conversations. "I mean, no one should touch you anywhere without your permission, ma'am."

Rhiannon blushed to match Elliot. Maybe she didn't know what he'd been talking about, but she maintained a firm grasp on the feminine mystique: the flutter of eyelashes, a shimmy way more subtle than Diana's, and the charming accent.

"Why, Mr. Collins—"

"Elliot, please, Ms. Raeburn."

"Elliot. You have to call me Rhiannon."

Didn't I perform introductions?

Elliot swallowed. "I'm going back to my spy perch." He pointed to the crossover.

Rhiannon's expression changed. "You're watching me?"

"To make sure no one touches you again when they shouldn't. I've followed you from the moment you stepped out of the van this morning. I came down with Ron to let you know as long as you're on campus, you're safe." They strained to hear him. "I won't let anything happen to you. I promise."

Tears blurred Rhiannon's eyes. Her focus shifted. Ron hid behind his hands.

"Don't look at me. I just performed the introductions, which you two did again anyhow. Watching you from there"—Ron aimed his finger in the general direction—"that's all Elliot."

Rhiannon's gaze flitted, and tears traced her delicate cheeks. "I don't know what to say."

"Oh, please, Ms. Rae—Rhiannon, you don't have to say anything." Elliot flashed a red-cheeked smile. "I'll be up there." He twirled and pointed, eliciting fresh tears.

The crowd engulfed him. Before Elliot could reach his perch, Rhiannon squeezed Ron's fingers. He bowed, raised her hand to his lips, and kissed it. He gestured with a flourish in Elliot's direction.

"Your knight, my lady."

He headed off to find Hilary. There remained one hook to set. This was way too much fun to stop now.

Chapter 28

Ron traversed the lobby from pillar to post, but Hilary couldn't be found. Perhaps someone had flushed her into the open?

The student union seemed more crowded than it had been an hour ago. Ron frowned. Purple-shirted guides grinned. Representatives from housing, financial aid, admissions, health services, and student activities circulated, along with deans, department heads, athletic coaches, and star students posing as typical students. Huntington boasted a fair number of 3.9 and 4.0 undergrads, all shined and polished for this event.

The high ceiling helped Ron locate the room's center. He planted himself, feet spread, eyes narrowed, and scanned the huge hall. What was Hilary wearing today? All black, her best spy outfit.

One of the uniformed caterers approached. Good thing he wore his handlebar mustache, or Ron wouldn't've recognized him: the Big MF himself, Magnus Ferguson. A bronze-plated name tag pinned above his breast pocket proclaimed his real name: Larry.

Hilary had to be close. The milling crowd was disconcerting.

"Can I get you anything, sir?"

Ron's eyes widened, his mouth curled up, and then

his gaze narrowed. Larry spoke with a Scottish accent to rival Rhiannon's. Ron needed to extend their exchange to sort this out: was it a wonderful coincidence, or had Hilary figured out the game and convinced Larry to play him? He glanced over his shoulder and spied Hilary behind a table. Ron motioned her to keep away.

"Can I get you anything?" Larry repeated.

Eight tour groups arrived simultaneously. The crowd swelled. Ron's head spun.

"A chair."

"Sir?"

"Any chair will do." Ron faked a grin and swayed.

Probably not the most bizarre request in Larry's waiting career, but probably not what he expected. Unoccupied chairs weren't at a premium; almost everyone stood. Larry returned shortly with a molded chair, probably easier to carry than one of the cushioned chairs near the lobby entrance. Blue plastic would do.

"Thank you, Larry." Ron leaned forward with both hands on the chair back, as if it were an elderly person's walker. People pressed too close, and Ron struggled against dizziness.

"Anything else, sir? A stool to put up your feet?"

Ron cleared his throat. "Tell me, Larry, what's the name of the catering company you work for?"

The waiter eyed Ron suspiciously. "Manhattan Caterers. If you're thinking about reporting me for the footrest comment, don't bother. You're talking to the owner."

Ron eyed him with equal suspicion. "The owner, huh? How come you're working the floor?"

"Big party night. Seven people called out this morning, and the temp agency only found three replacements, so I put on my old uniform. Still fits."

Ron nodded. "Yeah, it fits nicely. How long have you been in the catering business?"

Larry thumped his chest. "Over fifteen years."

"That's a long time to do one thing. It must be tough to own a business in today's economic climate."

"The government makes sure it is. Regulations. Who I can hire, who I can't hire, how much I have to pay them, benefits, overtime, insurances I have to carry. City taxes, county taxes, state taxes—the federal government wants the biggest chunk. And the work ethic of the younger generation... well, let's just say everyone over forty showed up for work this morning. The seven who didn't are all youngsters."

Ron empathized. "It's scary to think someday in the near future, this generation will run the country. As it happens, I'm an acquaintance of one of your staff under forty who did show up for work this morning: Rhiannon Raeburn."

A smile spread behind the mustache. "Rhiannon's a good kid. An exception to the generation rule. Shows up and does whatever is asked of her. A wonderful employee. She's actually a student here."

"I didn't know that. What's she studying?"

"Political science, I think. One of those undergrad degrees that sounds good but won't land you a job. You know, like psychology. Rhiannon wants to save the world. Good luck. I'm not going to tell her it can't be done."

"No, I wouldn't want to explain that to her, either. Quite an accent she has. Scottish?"

"Yes."

"Is that an accent I detect in your voice too?"

"Aye, a wee bit."

"Ever been there?"

"Where?"

"Scotland."

"Just returned from visiting my sister. Rhiannon's her daughter. My niece." He thumped his chest again. "Honor student."

"You and your wife must be proud."

"Proud, but unmarried. Never met a woman with a will strong enough to stand up to me. Ha. Listen to me tellin' a total stranger my whole life."

"It's fascinating, actually. If you don't mind my asking, what's your last name, Larry?"

"Scott. I don't put that on my name tag, though. Used to, but everyone called me Scotty. When I'd ask, 'Can I get you anything?' the standard answer was, 'More warp power.' Fifteen years and I still don't understand Americans."

"Yeah, well, I've been one for twenty-plus years, and I don't understand us, either. Don't worry, Larry, I won't report the footrest comment to Starfleet."

That elicited a grin. "Anything else I can do for you, sir?"

"Nope." Ron held up his hands, palms out. To someone watching from a distance, it might look as though Ron was being threatened.

"It's a pleasure, Larry. You know, I bet the school chancellor would like to meet you. Hilary Nixon. Ever talk with her?"

"When the university calls, it's Diana something-or-other." He massaged his chin. "Did a party at the chancellor's house last weekend. Sent the crew. I was still in Scotland."

"Hilary's a woman with a strong will. Never found a man who could stand up to her. She's here someplace. Look her up, introduce yourself. You do a lot of business with the university. Don't mention talking with me, though. I'd be embarrassed. She's too much woman for me."

The Big MF raised a finger to his nose. "You got it. Mum's the word."

Larry Scott melted into the crowd, and Ron sat, sighed heavily, and wiped his brow, as if in great relief. Hell, it was a relief. Too many people too close. His foot drummed an irregular beat.

Hilary charged to his rescue. "Ron. Are you okay?"

"Thank goodness you're here."

"What did he say?"

"Give me a minute to catch my breath." Ron pressed his hand to his chest, breathing yoga-style.

"Do you need water?"

He nodded as though he couldn't speak. Hilary Nixon, chancellor of all creation, scurried to fetch him a drink.

She returned a moment later, unscrewed the cap, and held the bottle to his mouth. He didn't want her to pour it down his throat, so he eased the bottle out of her hands and swigged. He sighed again and shook his head.

"I can't believe that happened."

"What?"

"Took me by surprise."

"The Big MF threatened you?"

Ron glanced at her, bug-eyed.

"I watched. I couldn't hear what he said, but I saw your reaction. He threatened you!"

Ron fought laughter. "Umm, no, you've got it all wrong. I thought wrong. He's not the Big MF. Honest. He… He asked if he could help with anything."

"And you reacted like that? I don't think so." She gripped Ron's shoulder. "I know you're afraid of the

SDN and the repercussions of discussing their activities. I'm sure he ordered you not to admit anything. Well, I know who he is and what he's doing."

"I don't think he's with the SDN."

"You don't?"

Ron waggled his head.

"What's the chair for?"

"Huh?"

"The chair. Why did he bring you a chair?"

Ron's face scrunched. "Because I asked for one?"

Hilary chuckled. "Yeah, right. Middle of a crowded room, you're ten steps from a slew of seats, and you expect me to believe you asked a waiter for a chair? I don't think so."

"He's not a waiter."

"I knew it."

"He owns the catering company."

"Come on, Ron, is that what he told you? We pay the caterers tens of thousands of dollars. If he owned the company, would he put on a waiter's uniform and work the floor? I think he brought the chair for intimidation." Hilary squatted to eye level. "What did he say?"

Ron pressed his lips together.

Hilary wouldn't relent. "What did he say?"

Ron struggled, as if the words were forced from his throat. "He said he'd just come from Scotland. Visiting his sister."

"What else?"

"He said Rhiannon was one of the best people he ever employed."

"He admitted working with Rhiannon and being from Scotland." Hilary tapped notes into her iPad. "What else?" she demanded.

"Nothing else."

"Nothing else? You leaned on that chair as if you could barely stand up. You talked forever. What else did he say?"

"Nothing related to the SDN. He said the government makes his life difficult. That's all, really." Ron gulped another swig of water and glanced away.

"Come on, Ron, it's obvious you're obfuscating. What is it?"

He pivoted and squinted at Hilary. "You're quite an interrogator. Were you a detective in a previous life? All right, all right, I'll tell you. He's looking for you." Ron let a deep groan escape.

"Looking for me? Whatever for?" Hilary clutched the iPad. "He thinks he's going to solicit a donation from me?"

"I don't think that's his intention, Hilary." Lips pursed, Ron shook his head in a jerky movement.

"What do you think he wants, then?"

"His company does a lot of business with the university. It's natural he'd want to meet you." Ron tapped his lips with his index finger.

"What?"

"You wouldn't want to."

"What?"

"Never mind. Drop the whole thing. Larry Scott isn't raising money for anything except his business."

"Is that the name he's using?"

"Aye." Ron fashioned a Scottish brogue. "The plan is a wee bit dangerous."

"What?"

Ron peeked away, scratched his shoulder, and slowly rounded back on Hilary. "It's not worth the emotional risk. Don't do it."

"Do what?"

They locked gazes, and Ron narrowed his focus. "I'm telling you, he doesn't know anything about the SDN. Nobody does. You'd only be proving his innocence."

"I don't want to prove his innocence."

Ron arched an eyebrow then winked at her. "I swear, Hilary, the SDN doesn't exist."

She eyed him. "Oh. Right... Do you think I could pull it off?"

"If you're determined, then find him. Be aggressive, but subtle. With a man like this, you need to assert yourself, but not all the time. You need to concede once in a while—the trick is to know when. Go ahead. Find him now."

She inspected Ron like he were a wounded duck. "I'll be fine." He quacked. "I'll sit here and collect myself."

She took two steps, then spun back on him. "What about Elliot? Did you find him?" She cocked her head. "Did he blow his assignment?" Suspicion edged into her voice.

"Elliot is fine. He's been watching Rhiannon all day, and if I'm not mistaken, he's going to charm Rhiannon to learn her thoughts. He's a brave young man. You should be pleased to have him on your staff."

"I am, I am. I didn't realize he'd take such initiative. Good for him." She paused and peered at Ron as though struck by epiphany. "Are you making up all this, about Rhiannon and Magnus Ferguson? The Internet makes no mention in any news articles about the SDN in our country or Great Britain."

Ron held himself immobile and stared into Hilary's eyes. *The truth and nothing but the truth, so help me.* "I swear, Hilary, there is no SDN. No one is soliciting money. Magnus Ferguson is in fact Larry Scott, food merchant, and Rhiannon is his niece and employee, nothing more."

Hilary studied Ron, and a grin of disbelief spread across her features. She nodded. "Right. I'm going to get to the bottom of this, and if you're putting me on, I swear—"

"Look." He swigged water and pointed at Larry scurrying across the lobby.

Hilary spun around again, tossing the words over her shoulder. "I've got to go, Ron. Don't worry, you'll be safe here."

She evaporated into the crowd, stalking the diabolic leader of a catering company.

Ron escaped from University Day and headed toward Central Park. He wanted to meet Lela again, convinced the tone of their e-mails was an aberration. Another face-to-face meeting would prove it. He swore he wouldn't e-mail until they settled these issues in person. All they needed was to have a simple, straightforward conversation. He'd arrived at the park entrance before realizing he couldn't go in.

Ron bore a responsibility today more important than his emotional stability: Fish. If Fish felt better tomorrow, Ron could come back. He couldn't leave Fish alone for more than a couple of hours, and University Day had already gobbled that time. If Lela found Ron in that small window tomorrow, if he found her, a few minutes could satisfy one need. She'd have to understand that they'd have other meetings.

He rushed down the subway stairs without a second glance at the gloom gliding over the city.

Chapter 29

I forced myself to stay away from the park Saturday. Homework was an excellent excuse. But I was efficient and was already ahead in all my classes. Sunday morning I could think of no other pretext.

I refused to admit I searched for Mark.

I wandered around Columbus Circle, jaywalking, sprinting ahead of onrushing traffic. Horns screamed, tires screeched, and I learned curse words in three languages. After I counted cracks in the pavement, I counted pedestrians in the crosswalk, then pigeons on the concrete—anything I could to steer clear of the park entrance.

I made the mistake of glancing in that direction one too many times. The Cement Man winked, waved, and called my name. I couldn't ignore him. Head bowed, I surrendered and entered my home away from home, Central Park.

The giant magnet hidden beneath the path must've latched on and dragged me to my rock. Somehow, I knew Mark would be there, and yet I avoided this meeting. He would understand my problem and lend a hand. I needed the answer, but didn't want his help.

He sat on top of the rock, knees up, arms circling his legs. He smiled when I approached and patted the surface next to him. I climbed and sat as commanded. He re-angled to face me but remained silent, expecting me to begin our conversation.

Something intangible drew me to Mark. I wanted to discover the secret behind my feelings. My head spun, and hot flashes erupted.

I came to the park to see *him.*

Three feet away and I'm tongue-tied. I wanted to tell him that every time we met, butterflies danced around my stomach. But those weren't the words that fluttered forth.

"Where's Fish?" I'd never seen him here without the dog.

"Home watching a vampire show."

"Fish likes vampires?"

"Scare the hell out of him."

"Why does he watch?"

"Must be the adrenaline rush. Sundays, *Mister Ed* isn't on, so he watches reruns of *Dark Shadows* and *Forever Knight.*"

"Do you string garlic over your door?"

"Crash helmets. Fish chases rollerbladers. Pretends he's a vampire. He figures if he terrifies them, their helmets become trophies."

"Your dog has a mean streak."

Mark waved. "Appropriating their helmets is better than hijacking their blood. Besides, he hasn't caught one yet. Good exercise, though."

"What do you do for exercise?"

"Dance, avoid vampires, circumvent carnivores, not necessarily in that order."

My laugh sounded nervous to me. Why hadn't he asked my name or mentioned his? No phone numbers, no e-mail, no way for us to reconnect except to meet here.

He must sense the same fascination. Why risk losing each other?

I tugged on my fingers, uncertain where to take our conversation. "I have a problem."

"Just one?"

"One bigger than the others at the moment." I didn't want to go into detail about Professor Kirin; I intended to solve that myself. I also didn't want to ask the questions Mark wasn't asking. Must be a simple reason, I just couldn't think of it.

It was as if he was trying to learn something about me before elevating our relationship to the next level.

What relationship? We were strangers who'd met a few times in the park.

Mark waited. We'd been joking, but he seemed to sense the serious intent behind my words. Or was that the serious intent behind my silence?

I clunked the side of my head. Duh.

If he felt the same connection, he was trying to learn the same thing I was. Why were we drawn to each other? The scent of budding spring puffed across my rock—*our* rock.

"Did you ever have an issue that didn't seem difficult, yet you couldn't find a simple, straightforward solution?"

He nodded.

"That's what I'm faced with."

"Most of my plans that are so simple they can't fail, fail," Mark said.

"Any of them ever work?"

"One did just recently."

"How many overall?"

"Counting that one?"

"Yes."

"One."

"That's encouraging."

His goofy grin made me laugh.

"If a solution to a simple problem doesn't present itself, step back," Mark said. "Take time away from it. When my writing is stuck and I don't know where the plot's going, I set it aside and come back to it at a later date. When it's fresh in my mind, the answer is often right there, staring me in the face."

Mark confirmed what I'd done intuitively: set aside Professor Kirin. The professor needed to go farther aside. Mark studied my face, my reflection captured in his eyes. I recognized his intentions.

"We're going to dance again?" I asked.

"Thinking about it."

I stretched out, leaned back, and crossed my ankles. "How do you do it?"

"I watch a lot of Nureyev and Fonteyn YouTube videos."

"No." I giggled. "I mean, every time I see you, my mood changes. You make me feel better. How do you do it?"

We smiled at each other and ogled each other's mind, passion exploding like solar flares in our eyes, and eternity lapsed in the next moment. Minutes passed, or hours. How would I know?

"Are you going to tell me your problem?" he asked.

I figured my problem was his problem. "I don't think I need to."

Mark nodded like he understood. "Did you just happen to come to the park today?"

Heat rose in my cheeks. Now I was sure he wanted

confirmation of the same thing I wanted to know. I just didn't want to admit it first. "No. Did you?"

"I came to meet you."

No fanfare, no suggestive leer. Simply a straightforward expression of emotion. My stomach flipped. It was what I knew, but it was what I wanted to hear, what I needed to hear. Our meetings couldn't all be coincidences.

He glanced at his wrist. I realized he wasn't wearing a watch, but it was the motion someone made when they checked the time.

"I'm sorry," he said, "I can't stay much longer."

Why not? Why couldn't we stay here all day? Why couldn't we stay here forever? I wanted to arrange our next meeting, yet I couldn't force those words from my mouth. I didn't think he wanted a prearranged date.

He squinted and swayed and, like me, struggled to form the words. "What makes you happiest?" he said.

That wasn't a simple question, nor did it have a straightforward answer. Especially if he enforced time constraints. My temples pounded. I wanted to say, for the past few weeks I was happiest meeting him. The way he held me when we danced, the caress of his thumb across mine. We hardly knew each other, so in our brief encounters, how could those things possibly make me happiest?

Seconds ticked away, and a sense of urgency surged through my thoughts. He couldn't stay much longer. "The park, this park, is like a home to me. This is my rock, in the center of my city, the focal point of the symphony that's played for me. I love it here. I come here when I want to be alone, and I come here"—I wanted to say, "because I want to see you"—"when I want to share myself with a friend." I swallowed hard, suddenly unable to read the changed expression in his eyes. Cramps wedged their way into my stomach. I lacked the courage to say what I truly meant.

"Being in the park makes me happiest." I had no idea why the last words emerged as a whisper.

Mark bit his lip and pushed off the rock. I thought he'd ask me to dance. Instead, he glanced down and fumbled with his hands, unsure—as he had been at our first meeting—whether to put his hands in his pockets or behind his back.

"I have to go," he said.

I couldn't be sure if the faintest whisper curled around his lip or if his smile had evaporated, but his tone had changed, his body language had changed, and this was our first meeting we didn't dance. Or, our second meeting we didn't dance if you counted the first one.

"I have to go now," he said, and pointed into the void.

He drifted away, and I watched his butt wiggle, nothing like mine, but even the thought on another day would make me laugh. Today it didn't register.

Did I say something wrong?

Chapter 30

"Come on, Fish, wanna race?" Ron inched ahead, racing stance captured. Fish knew the routine. He sat without Ron prompting, but his melancholy demeanor meant he wasn't about to comply.

They'd gone for a walk on the pretext Ron needed exercise. The subtext was Ron needed time and a strategy to deliver the news. Ron sighed and chewed his lip. Somehow, they found themselves in front of their favorite ice cream shoppe, where Ron ordered two milk shakes and one soup bowl, so Fish could lap his shake, an indulgence that wouldn't have occurred under normal circumstances.

Fish lapped a few times—to appease him, Ron suspected—but Fish's tail dragged between his legs, and his nose was warm.

Ron sucked in his cheeks and bit his tongue.

They'd visited the vet three times since University Day. Fish had seemed better that first night, but his condition continued to deteriorate from the moment Ron returned home from the park the next day. Dr. Grant supplied more pills Monday morning, did extensive tests at Ron's insistence Wednesday, and further tests the next week. Ron was with Fish every minute he wasn't required to be in class. Dr. Grant had called today, and her glum tone left little to imagine.

"It's cancer of the pancreas. Untreatable, I'm afraid. Fish doesn't have much time."

How do you tell that to your best friend?

Every time Ron thought about it, the lump hardened in his throat, preventing speech. Fish deserved to know. Dogs have a sense—Fish must—but they'd shared their lives so totally in the past several weeks, Ron committed to tell him.

They talked about everything else. Ron's classes, which Fish had skipped recently, most days unable to endure the journey to school; the research paper on relative time; their favorite *Mister Ed* episodes.

Fish chided Ron about Diana's failed attempts at seduction and Ron's ultimate solution of passing out. Ron had invented excuses ever since that Friday night to avoid meeting her. The more he resisted, the more she pressed.

Ron's thoughts refocused. Fish deserved to be told, but not tonight. He couldn't summon the courage tonight.

~ ~ ~

Fish and Ron shared another milk shake on Cinco de Mayo, the start of finals study week. The treat would prompt him to tell Fish. They talked about the rise in vampire television shows in the one-block journey to their second-favorite ice cream store. Ron was worried Fish might not manage the extra few blocks to their favorite shoppe. The sojourn lasted twenty-two minutes. Might as well have been twenty-two hours. Ron was unable to force words of finality.

He'd met Fish at their rock. He knew all along that was where he'd have the strength to discuss Fish's fate.

Fish didn't bother to ask why Ron had stayed out of

the park all of April. Other than classes, Fish was the sole focus of Ron's attention. Lela would still be there after—

They wandered home, both of their tails dragging. Fish refused to race. Ron granted him control of the remote anyway.

Ron fell into bed. Tears dripped onto his pillow, the room swirled, and darkness snared him.

~ ~ ~

Ron awoke on the second Saturday in May with a terrible headache. Morning crashed into consciousness like a wrecking ball into a condemned building. He checked that Fish still slept, then popped a couple of ibuprofen, drank Swiss mocha decaf, and glanced through last Sunday's *Times*. He froze under a hot shower for twenty minutes, attempting to wash away the pain. It didn't work. While he dressed, Fish moped around the apartment.

"It's beautiful out. Why don't we take a walk?"

The rain hadn't stopped, but the wind had calmed to mere hurricane gusts, tossing trash cans like scrap paper. The view from their window appeared damp and strewn. Fish gave him the familiar *What're you, nuts?* look, and they paced the small space for another ten minutes.

"Come on, we're going to drive each other crazy like this."

Ron grabbed a hoodie, and they headed out the door. They didn't talk about where they'd go, but they angled toward the Seventh Avenue subway. Campus could provide the perfect path for a Saturday stroll. Fish couldn't walk all the way to school anymore. Ron grimaced as their heads dipped below the sidewalk.

A crowded subway car isn't the most pleasant

situation, but wet people in a crowded subway car are like regurgitations in a crowded locker room. Ron and Fish made the mistake of taking the first train through instead of waiting for an express, thereby prolonging the agony. Breath labored. Ron's head spun, convincing him if they ever remade *The Exorcist*, he'd be cast in the lead role.

The time consuming trip to school seemed too much for Fish. They exited the train and climbed the steps at Columbus Circle, headed down Fifty-Ninth Street, and continued pacing on a grander scale. The drizzle tapered off. Ron hadn't visited the park since his last meeting with Lela weeks ago. He was sure she'd understand. She'd still be waiting for him. For them. Her image pervaded his thoughts as they skirted the park. He sniffed a breath of jasmine on the air.

If Ron and Fish were sitting on their rock, watching the pigeons, perhaps Ron could summon the courage. No, he didn't want to tell Fish. He wanted someone to talk with first, someone to share these feelings. Lela. Psyche. He wished her here. The more he thought about it, the sadder he became. He also knew he couldn't tell Lela before he told Fish. Emotions tugged in opposite directions.

What if he and Fish went to their rock now and Lela was there? Could he tell them at the same time?

They paused in front of the park statues. The skin tightened across Ron's chest, his cheeks sucked in, and the lump in his throat rose higher. The sun forced its way through the leaden sky; wind and warm rays dried the earth. The city hiccuped; street vendors hawked, buses ground gears, pigeons flapped, horns honked. Ron couldn't suppress a smile, but he could stop his feet. If they didn't go into the park, he wouldn't see Lela—but he also wouldn't have to tell Fish. They could walk back up Fifty-Ninth Street. Decision made. He headed along the sidewalk. Fish headed the other way.

"Hey, where're you going?"

Fish barked.

"Well, I'm not. I'm heading that way." Ron pointed.

Fish trotted a couple more steps toward the reclining statue, wheeled, and woofed again.

Ron shook his head. "Nah, we don't want to go in there. Come on, let's go this way."

The idea coalesced. At their rock he *would* have the courage to tell Fish, especially if Lela was there. If they didn't go to their rock, he didn't have to tell Fish, and if he didn't tell him, maybe it wouldn't happen. Ron knew the truth, but these thoughts clung to hope.

His clinginess lacked strength this morning. Fish's gait animated as he approached the park entrance.

"I guess we're going in."

Fish smiled for the first time in weeks. He wagged his tail and jogged. He growled at pigeons and chased an un-helmeted rollerblader for a few steps, just to give the guy a scare. Strollers strolled, squirrels squirreled, and Ron continued to avoid the inevitable. They passed the carousel and the large field, but every time he tried to aim them in another direction, Fish angled toward their rock.

Ron didn't want to think about it.

They hadn't been together long—not really—but they'd known each other their entire lives.

Fish flashed a mischievous look, then did something Ron hadn't done since adolescence. He chased his tail. Round and round, faster and faster. Ron laughed till tears filled his eyes.

Fish finally stopped, too dizzy to continue. He splayed on their rock, front legs stretched out, head down, tail up. Ron clambered up, still laughing, still crying.

Fish's tail thrashed Ron's legs, difficult to distinguish which of them was happier and which of them was sadder.

Fish licked Ron's hands and face, as if his giant tongue might stop his head from spinning.

"Are you all right?"

Ron admonished his recklessness. Fish pranced around. Ron wiped the tears from his eyes. Fish hadn't been this alive in weeks.

Can we come back tomorrow too? Please, please, Fish begged.

Ron closed his eyes and imagined Lela here with them. He'd ask her to dance. He'd grasp her hands. She'd drift into him like sand slipping through an hourglass, and like the sand, she'd accept her fate. Her surrender would be total, so complete, surrender would become existence.

He opened his eyes and blinked to clear them. Time slipped forward. Lela didn't show today, and without Lela, he still couldn't tell his friend. Cosmic winds guided Fish and Ron home.

He needed one more day.

Chapter 31

Mom's purple afghan covered my shoulders. A ceiling other than my bedroom watched me, forcing me to relive childhood memories of monsters. I rolled over and opened the blinds to force fiends to flee into closets.

Nighttime memories infiltrated my mind like mold on week-old bread. The strange ceiling belonged to our living room, where I'd drifted into an uncomfortable dreamworld last night. The apartment smelled stuffy. Perspiration soaked my neck and beaded between my breasts. So, Mark starred in at least one of my dreams.

I'd revisited the park every day since our last meeting, but Mark hadn't been there for more than a week. Hope of ever seeing him again faded. I realized going into the park was now making me sadder instead of happier. I skipped a day, then two, then I didn't go in for three weeks. I replayed our last conversation a million times. What had I said wrong?

Somewhere in the background, Lela answered the door, voice muffled. I shivered in nudity, arched my toes, and stretched my fingers. Grogginess maintained a stranglehold.

Memory pressed, but no independent timeline emerged in which I had removed my clothes. Lela and I had shared a bottle of wine and a lot of chocolate Saturday night to celebrate the holiday today. That might explain the throbbing over my eyebrows. My nose twitched as the aroma of cinnamon drifted from the kitchen. I flashed in front of the window, soaking in the Sunday sun. I figured the neighbors couldn't see through the reflection. Chocolate still tickled my nostrils. One of us—probably me—had left an unwrapped Hershey's bar on the windowsill, and the window acted like a magnifying glass. Goop oozed from the edges, like glue but with nothing to attach. The living room door swung open.

"Rise and shine," Lela said. "You have a visitor, and it's not your mother."

Mark? How'd he find me? My stomach flipped.

Lela's eyes gleamed. Elliot traipsed in behind her. Lela flashed a scheming grin. "Girl, you look beat. Want coffee? Ibuprofen? How about you, Elliot? Coffee?"

"N-no. Sure, I mean. I thought Willow might go out for breakfast with me, so we could talk."

They both observed me. Lela winked. "What's it gonna be, girl?" She sidled close enough to whisper. "Mother's Day breakfast with the redoubtable oak? Or you gonna hold out for a park picnic with a redwood?" She kept her hand close and pointed to remind me of my underlying nakedness.

"Ah!" I plopped on the cushions and hugged the afghan to my throat. "Sure, Elliot. I'll have breakfast with you."

I cast a glance at my evil, smirking roommate. I knew what she thought too. I still bombed with Professor Kirin. The semester was all but over, and I was about to lose the challenge. What happened to my resolve of six weeks ago? *Don't drop in, Elliot. Don't think about calling.* Hmm, let's see, what could the assistant to the chancellor do for me? Take me to breakfast?

"I'll need a few minutes to dress."

"Okay." He continued to gawk.

What? I glanced down. I had pulled up the afghan, but forgot Mom wasn't the tightest of crocheters. Girlish charms poked through in more than one place.

"Would you mind?" I twirled my finger.

"Oh, yeah, sure. Okay." Elliot offered his back. "Sorry."

Lela flicked her eyebrows. "I've got to study. What did you decide about coffee?"

"I'll take mine in the bathroom," I said.

"Elliot? Coffee?"

"Sure. I recall what Willow means when she says she'll be ready in a few minutes."

Okay, so Elliot knew me a little. I stepped out of the shower ten minutes later and dressed sexually neutral. Lela deposited French vanilla decaf with floaters on the counter, and I applied a trace of eye shadow.

"Where're you guys going? Did he say?"

"Not yet. Probably the Corner Café."

Dog pranced on the vanity, admiring his reflection. Lela settled on the throne and studied my reflection. "What do you think he's up to this time?" Lela asked.

I shrugged.

"You think he's worked it out with your mom?" My friend strained not to laugh.

"Another Mom-and-Elliot theory why I haven't called him in six weeks? It wouldn't surprise me."

"He has that I-have-a-plan look. I'll bet he's figured a way you two can meet up once a week for a few weeks, then twice a week, and build from there. You know, the way a tree grows? Start with a foundation and spread out."

A choked laugh was uprooted from my throat. "You don't really think so, do you?"

"Yep."

"What am I going to tell him? Elliot's a nice guy. I don't want to hurt him again. It must've killed him the last time we had this talk. Come on, I need help here."

"I'm not coming to breakfast, if that's what you mean. You two ought to work this out."

She scooped up Dog. "Don't run away this time, Willow. You have a habit of doing that when you reach an edge. Stay there, stay calm, talk with him. Repeat what you said before. I mean, I think you did a good job of explaining to him why your relationship had to end. Be more sympathetic this time. Hold his hand."

"I'm not looking forward to this."

"There's the other side to consider too. He's assistant chancellor, and you still aren't enrolled in Crimes. The way you're going, it doesn't look like it's gonna happen. It wouldn't hurt to ask a favor. I'm sure Elliot would be more than happy to oblige."

"That's just it. I don't want him to be more than happy. If he's going to do me a favor, it'll have to be with no strings attached. How do I tell him?"

"Exactly like that. Couldn't be any more straightforward. Elliot is levelheaded, but he's in love, and you know how that is. Love blinds us to many things. Stand in front of him, keep insisting you're not in love, and eventually, it'll sink in."

"You don't think that's mean?"

"Nope. I don't think Elliot will, either. It may take him more distance to realize that, but I'm sure he'll come to the same conclusion. Drink your coffee before it gets cold."

I sipped a chunk of undissolved French vanilla. Yuck.

~ ~ ~

Our conversation began much as it had last time, Elliot catching me up on minor events in his life till we safely settled in our café booth. He bristled with a plan. His shoulders arched back, head up, eyes sparkling. He exhibited an eagerness I hadn't seen in him for a long time. What did he expect from me?

I sipped decaf, Elliot knocked back an iced tea, and we considered the menu for breakfast. By the time the waitress took our order, Elliot's cheeks puffed out, ready to burst. Good thing he didn't have seams.

When he covered my hand with his, I jumped, despite Lela's suggestion, but reeled myself back under control. A crazy grin smeared across Elliot's face.

"Willow, in all fairness, I have to tell you…"

Oh, no, he's talked with Mom again.

"… I've met someone else."

Chapter 32

By the time I got home, curiosity puffed Lela like a balloon. Good thing she didn't have seams, either. She followed me for a few seconds in silence, then shrugged from her eyebrows to her toes.

"Well?" Her eyes bugged out.

"I was right."

"You were?"

"Yep. We went to the Corner Café."

"And?"

"And nothing. We didn't go anyplace else."

"I didn't mean, 'Where else did you go?' I meant, 'What else did he say?'"

"Oh."

Silence drove Lela nuts, like unscratchable fleas on Dog.

"Well?"

"Well what?" This would teach her to walk men into the room when she knows I'm naked.

"Can you tell me what he said?"

"Yep."

Lela followed me into the kitchen, then back to my room. I kept my lips sealed.

"You said you'd tell me," Lela insisted.

"You asked, '*Can* you tell me?' The answer is, yes,

I have the ability to tell you. You never asked if I *will* tell—"

She conked me on the head with a pillow.

"Not nice." I waggled a finger, grabbed my pillowcase with both hands, and swung a body shot. She smacked me on the head again. I walloped her a couple of times, pushed her onto the bed, and tickled her. I hated reversed roles, so I stopped before she felt the urge for retribution. I rolled onto my back, clutched my pillow to my chest, and contemplated familiar ceiling swirls.

"He said he'd only met a handful of professors, but the chancellor, his boss, is friendly with Professor Kirin, so Professor Kirin is in that handful." I admired my Nile-blue nail polish. "Yes, he'd be happy, but not too happy, to talk with Professor Kirin about letting me into Crimes."

"Way to go, Willow. Wait a minute, what'd that cost you?"

"Nothing."

"Nothing?"

"Good thing I sat down before Elliot told me."

"Told you what?"

I smiled, goofily. "Elliot met someone else."

"No way. That's perfect. It lets you off the hook completely."

"Yep. She's also a student here, and she was accosted on campus. Elliot was assigned to protect her, only she didn't know that, and one thing led to another, and voilà."

"Anyone we know?"

"Nope. Rhiannon something-or-other. There's a Rhiannon in Dr. Coleman's class. Could be her."

"After he told you this, that's when he volunteered to help you enroll in Crimes?"

"Lela, he must've talked about Rhiannon for an hour. Breakfast came, we ate, I downed a fourth cup of coffee, and he kept talking. He told me he's sorry, he knows I depend on him, he came to New York to be with me, and he hopes I don't think he's abandoning me, but he believes I keep pushing him away. At the same time, here's a beautiful, intelligent girl eager to share herself with him. He wants me to realize he's still an oak, he's just been transplanted into another forest."

"That's why he volunteered to help you, to make up for the transplant?"

"Kind of. I mean, I didn't have to ask twice. He understands Crimes is in high demand. He said Professor Kirin seems like a reasonable guy, all evidence to the contrary, and he'll talk with the professor sometime this week and see if he can encourage him to accept one more student in his class *without the prerequisite*. He'll let me know."

"There you go, you're as good as in. I told you he'd understand tree stuff. I'll have to remember next time I'm breaking up with a mountain man."

I shoved her shoulder, and we laughed.

Lela pushed up on her elbow and studied me. "You're not feeling regrets now that he's involved with someone else, are you?"

"A wave of the blues, that's all. I haven't seen my friend in the park for weeks."

Devil eyes glistened. "You haven't been in the park for weeks. I thought you loved it there. No wonder you're depressed. You've given up your boyfriend, and the park, and Ron has dried up online, and you're dealing with a bastard professor who knows everything you're going to do before you do it, not to mention he won't let you into a class you're required to take. And this professor has never even met you. Oh, I almost forgot, you're also wiggling your butt in front of strangers." She sashayed as if I needed reminding.

"My, oh my, it may've been a melancholy six weeks, *Dr.* Bolden, but concede, it's been a busy six weeks."

"I concede."

"Take your life back. You're allowing your behavior to be dictated by people you barely know: Professor Kirin, Ron, and Mark-in-the-Park, or is that Timmy and Lassie?"

I laughed. "Mark-in-the-Park. I like 'Mark-in-the-Park.'"

"It's a beautiful day. Pack your books, go to your rock, and soak in the sun."

"You're right. I'm going to regain control of my life. I'm going to the park."

~ ~ ~

The Cement Man smiled as I approached, a lost friend returning home. The late-Sunday-morning sun caressed my shoulders; the occasional car horn, accelerating bus, rumbling subway faded into the background in the city symphony unplugged. Pigeons flapped on the warm breeze. Helmeted rollerbladers wove their way between horse-drawn carriages and hawking street vendors.

"Veeee... nilllla!"

I hastened beneath the arch, and the park sucked me into a fantasy world as much a part of the city as Broadway and Forty-Second Street. Popcorn, pizza, roasted nuts, mustard—I sniffed again. I hated when sauerkraut intruded. Weekend lovers of all ages paraded across my path, hand in hand, arm in arm, strolling with purpose, the dance of passion. Nothing else mattered in the park. Unleashed love, life intruding on life, the vaccine for unhappiness.

I climbed to the top and dusted off my rock. Arms stretched skyward, face uplifted, I soaked in the city. I lost track of time and posed like a triumphant warrior come to reconquer my realm. Few passersby took notice.

I tilted my head back farther and twirled. Perhaps not the best plan I'd ever pulled off, pirouetting on the pinnacle of my palace. Arms outstretched, I spun, and the earth spun with me. I finally collapsed in a dizzy circle of trees and forsythia and a cloudless, pale sky.

They must've been hiding: a large mutt with wagging tail and a guy not with a six-foot-two-inch steel body, but tall enough and sturdy enough. He pushed wire-rim glasses up the bridge of his nose and studied me with eyes so penetrating, he didn't need x-ray vision.

The dog bounded forward. Mark either flew or leaped onto my rock. The world remained sideways, still swirling. I saw dog and boy once every revolution.

A gyrating performance is not the time I would've chosen for Mark to arrive, yet I exalted at his entrance. Did I long for a couch to crawl under, or a tube of Krazy Glue to attach myself to this moment? Flushed, sweating, heart pounding—how much worse could things get?

The mutt arrived first. He licked my hands and face, and his butt wiggled. Mark, I'm sure, would recall a previous encounter. *Come on, Fish, let's get out of here. I can't believe her butt wiggles like yours.*

"Are you hurt?" he asked. "Lie still, close your eyes, and relax. The spinning will stop."

He balled his sweater or sweatshirt or something and laid it under my neck. Music crescendoed. He cradled my head, and his touch electrified the city symphony.

He brushed a strand of hair off my forehead, and my skin tingled as if Tinker Bell had sprinkled fairy dust. Come on, Willow, fly.

I tried to sit up, but he pushed me down. "Uh-uh. Lie still. You're not Peter Pan."

How did he know my thoughts?

The dark red haze inside my eyelids continued to spin, but in increasingly slower revolutions. Soon it would fall in sync with my normal spinning, and I'd no longer have an excuse for not looking into the face of a savior, a hero, a… humongous dog.

My eyes flew open. At least part of me could fly. "Ah, Fish, I can tell you haven't been using mouthwash."

I stretched to re-aim doggy breath and scratch behind his ear. Fish twisted his head and licked my palm. Mark stroked behind my ear, and I considered doing the same thing as Fish. I performed a frantic memory search. Whew. At least I'd brushed and gargled.

I curled into his embrace, but restrained my urge to lick. "Are you all right?" Mark asked. "I thought you might fall and I might not be fast enough to catch you."

"Mark-in-the-Park not fast enough?" I couldn't prevent a full-body wiggle.

I'd seen his quirky smile before. My senses settled to earth, and I reconsidered the nature of my position. I pushed up on both elbows and shook off the caress that prolonged my embarrassment. "You and Fish just happen along?"

"Not exactly. Today seemed so beautiful, and, well, I had a feeling. I hoped you might be here again."

The heat in my face ratcheted up a notch.

"We saw you climb the rock, spin in celebration. As a kid I liked to spin till the grass tilted up to grab me. It always made me laugh."

"Where'd you grow up?"

"Krypton."

Of course. "I didn't realize they used grass on Krypton."

"That's all right. When I was a kid, I didn't realize they used grass on Earth."

"I'm not a kid anymore."

"No, you're not. You're a"—I thought he might say bizarre—"unusual woman."

"You're not exactly the run-of-the-mill guy."

"Thank you."

"You're not going to ask me to dance today, are you?"

He gestured with a flourish. "This is a giant ballroom, and the orchestra is playing for us. But no, I won't ask you to dance. Not yet, anyhow. I hoped we might spend time talking."

"What would you like to talk about?"

"Life, romance, Fish. Not necessarily in that order."

I sat up, crossed my legs, elbow on knee, chin in sticky palm. I wiped my hand on my jeans and resettled for a conversation that couldn't come fast enough. I tried to maintain composure. "Only the truth, right?"

"Of course. Tell me about meeting Fish. Did you ever feed him?"

"Bite-size hot dogs. I saw Fish for the first time that night." I never realized it before. The *dog* was the common denominator that drew us together.

At the mention of his name, Fish glanced at Mark,

glanced at me, and flopped his massive head on my unoccupied knee. At least he wasn't breathing on me.

I took a deep breath. I'd danced hand in hand with Mark, and I still didn't know his real name. That was okay, he didn't know my name, either.

Names no longer seemed necessary. "Are we alternating questions?"

He gestured, open-palmed.

"Is Fish really his name?"

"So he claims."

"Didn't you get him as a puppy from some kennel or something? A dog shelter? And didn't you name him?"

"No, no, no, no, and no."

"I didn't ask that many questions."

Fish angled his head away and sneezed. He rounded back to rejoin the conversation.

"That's a neat trick," I said.

Fish shifted his head and sneezed again. I eyed him suspiciously. Mark's smile captured half my frown.

"Anyway, no, I didn't get him as a puppy, no to the kennel, no to the something, no to the dog shelter, and no, I didn't name him."

No way could I let go that easily. "You didn't teach him that polite little sneeze, either?"

"Nope."

"Did he come with dog tags?"

"Nope."

"How'd you know his name, then?"

"He told me. It sounds odd"—Mark scratched his head—"but when you and I met, you were having a conversation with him."

Fish followed with his eyes, and his gaze settled on me, challenging. *You think I don't know my name?*

245

I know when to stand and fight. Now wasn't the time. "Your turn."

Mark didn't hesitate. "Ever take dancing lessons?"

"I took ballet for a few months when I was five or six. Do you know any girls who didn't?"

"Is that your question?"

"No."

"Okay, then, your turn."

"The second time we met, were you trying to follow me to Huntington, or did you have business there?"

"Business."

I wiggled, trying to resettle as the rock grew harder. Mark offered his sweater, my former pillow. I wanted to sit on his lap, not his sweater, but I maintained composure and accepted the seat cushion.

"What're you looking for in a relationship?" Mark-in-the-Park asked. "What does romance mean to"—his mouth wrapped around the words with a caress no less meaningful than when he rubbed my head—"Psyche?"

Sunlight reflected in his eyes, more hazel than brown. I swallowed hard. The leap his question took from feeding Fish to relationships caught me by surprise.

"Romance lives in understanding and empathy and communication and that oh-so-important chemistry that can't be explained, only felt. Most men I've known confuse sex with romance, hormones with love." Mark didn't flinch. I'd built momentum, and I let it flow.

"Romance isn't a thing, it's a feeling that makes your stomach flip, your head spin, and…" I almost said, *your butt wiggle*. "It makes you want to go to bed earlier at night because you can't wait to get up in the morning, but it keeps you from falling asleep. It's a milk shake, French fries, pizza, and strawberries."

I adjusted the sweater-cushion and gulped air. "Romance is a smile that comes with a thought, and that thought lifts you to a higher plane of existence. It's a feeling that your inner being is touched, a feeling that you want to know someone and be known.

"Men confuse passion with romance. Passion is what you experience when your partner touches you, the caress of skin, desire exposed in actions. Romance is feeling all that even when your partner isn't with you."

I paused and studied Mark, unsure if I could finish the thought. Butterflies flitted across my stomach. My mouth was dry. "I'm being swept off my feet." I could barely hear what I said, nor could I believe I said it out loud. I might as well have added, *by you*. Mark didn't grab my feet, but it would've been impossible to break eye contact.

"You've thought about it," he said.

"I recently left a long-term relationship. Thinking about this is what made me realize the partnership I was in didn't match my idea of romance." Did I mean to tell him I wasn't currently involved? Yep, yep, yep.

"What does romance mean to you?" I asked.

He didn't waste time considering.

"Romance is holding hands and bumping thighs as you walk down the beach at sunrise. It's skinny-dipping in a mountain pool, and making love in the grass during a thunderstorm. It's sharing straws, and T-shirts, and spoons, but not toothbrushes. It's sleeping as close as possible, and showering together, and leaving secret notes in each other's pockets.

"It's sharing fears and dreams and having both met with acceptance and encouragement. It's not idle prattle, 'Hi, how was your day?' It's sharing the emotions behind

247

what made your day *your day*. Romance is sharing your physical self, and your emotional self and your intellectual self with someone who is physically respectful, emotionally available, and intellectually challenging.

"It's the mutual sharing that charges passion, the exposed psyche as much as exposed flesh that ignites desires." Mark's smile broadened. "And romance is holding hands."

"You already said that."

"I know. I really like holding hands."

I struggled with my hands. One hand wanted to jump out and capture his hand, and the other hand wanted to stop the first one. Did a real guy exist who'd put this much thought into his idea of romance? That couldn't've been off the top of his head. I needed that tube of Krazy Glue to attach him to this moment with me.

My hand shot out but landed on Fish's head, and I scratched frantically behind his ear. Mark appreciated something of my struggle. I'm not sure I did, except since holding hands meant that much to him, I wanted him to take my hand first.

He released my eyes, and his gaze settled on my guilty hand, acknowledging my true desire. No sooner had he focused on that when he reengaged my eyes and wouldn't let go again. Yikes.

The man in my dreams jumped in with his next question. "Ever hear of the IRA?"

"Individual retirement account, or Irish Republican Army?"

"The Irish. How about SDN?"

I cast about in my memory. "Shiites damning nationalism? Sycophants doing nasties? Scottish Democratic Navy?"

He grinned. "Scottish Navy."

"Something from your imagination?"

He nodded sheepishly.

"Why'd you make it up?"

"To avoid a polar bear."

His gaze remained intense. We still spoke the truth. I worked out polar bears were metaphorical. "Anyone I know?"

He offered a small shrug. "Hilary Nixon."

"The… What is she? Chancellor?"

He nodded.

"My turn," I said. "Ever been to the redwood forest?"

"Yep. What did you think of it?"

Go ahead, assume I've been there. "Of all things in nature, Redwood National Park is the most incredible. The trees are alive in a way that no other trees can compare. The air surrounding them is so thick you can taste it." I inhaled thick air surrounding Mark. "You're passionate about life, aren't you?"

He shook his head. "Uh-uh, you don't get two questions in a row. My turn."

"You asked what I thought about the forest."

"Didn't count."

"Sounded like a question."

"Sorry, my turn." He patted his chest.

I rolled my eyes, allowed my lips to curl up, and gestured with a flourish.

He pushed off the rock and extended a hand toward me. "Wanna dance?"

I cocked my head and squinted. "If that counts as your question."

His expression didn't change. "Of course."

I accepted his hand. "Excuse me, Fish." I held Fish's

chin as I scootched my leg from beneath his head. Fish acknowledged with an approving murmur, as if he comprehended what our dance meant.

Mark pulled me up, and on the uneven rock I slipped into his embrace, an embrace that swept me away, forced the air from my lungs, and compelled my toes to stretch skyward. His grip softened as he caressed my hand. My hands. Somehow, my other hand found its way into his other hand, and he held them both, pressed between us, as the length of my body folded into his.

My muscles, my will, nothing obeyed me anymore. Surrender no longer optional, it became existence. We swayed to the shared city symphony. The perspiration on our hands belonged to me; the exuberance pressed against my thigh belonged to him.

I understood what he meant: an exposed psyche igniting desires. We'd laid ourselves bare. I didn't wish to intrude with incongruous words. Biting my tongue only resulted in a sore tongue. I thought long before I said anything else. "Tell me about your passions."

He leaned back, opening a gap into which our eyes refocused, and he spoke to my psyche. "I'm passionate about writing. I'm passionate about my schoolwork, about my friends, and I'm passionate about Fish." Fish's gaze shifted from me to Mark. "Being swept away is a shared experience."

Mark drew me close, his hands pressed tighter to mine, as if he could capture this moment in relative time. I closed my eyes, and my head spun every bit as much now as when I'd fallen. Mark lent me the strength to continue standing, and Fish offered his approval, barking and prancing around the rock.

We danced the dance of madness, the dance of desire, the dance of love.

Mark's voice softened into a whisper. "I'm passionate about the city, and I'm passionate about sharing my feelings, and I'm desperately passionate about holding you."

As if someone flicked a switch, a feeling snaked its way across my shoulders and gripped the nape of my neck like a vise. It wasn't in his words, but in the tone of his voice, a chilling sadness, so powerful, so enduring, my eyes welled with tears.

Chapter 33

Ron pulled her up into dancing position, their hands trapped between their bodies.

Psyche glowed. Ron leaned back to create a gap between them, more like elastic than actual space, unwilling to let go of her.

"Every time you smile at me, it's an affirmation of how happy you are and that I'm playing a part in that happiness."

Fish danced around them and barked. Ron inhaled the park and plunged in. "It thrills me to make you happy. Did we meet just a few weeks ago? Part of the thrill, part of the joy is how fast these feelings have raced over us."

She beamed at him, and they swayed to the same imaginary music.

"You said you're being swept away. I assure you, that's a shared experience."

There was so much he needed to tell her.

He wanted to express the importance of dancing.

He wanted to say he came to the park to see her, and even when she wasn't here, to sit on their rock and think about her. And smile. They might be separated by distance but not by thought.

Around them, trees greened, flowers budded, and forsythia bloomed, the most vibrant colors of any spring in history.

He wanted to tell Psyche she'd become part of his life.

Emotions swept over them like an aphrodisiac, feelings of familiarity and trust and understanding. Before he told her any of that, he wanted to tell her about Fish, but his mouth clamped shut. A lump welled into his throat. He wanted to describe the importance of Fish's friendship, that Fish was the catalyst to bring them together. Tears blurred vision. Fish's tail thrashed them both. How could he describe Fish's dreadful condition now? How could he tell Fish in this moment when he seemed so happy? Was Fate or Freud about to murder Fish's soul, only to replace it with…?

Psyche seemed to sense his somber mood. She didn't speak, but clung to him the way he clung to her.

They communicated with their hands, and he didn't know sign language. Under different circumstances, he might've purred. If she caressed his neck one more time, he believed he'd surrender and tell them both.

"I'm passionate about the city, and I'm passionate about my friends, and I couldn't be any more passionate about holding you," he said.

He screamed inwardly. Thoughts conflicted. He and Fish had to leave.

After struggling for so long to find this woman, he'd walk away? Had their meetings been fated by the universe? He didn't believe in fate.

Still no names, no phone numbers, no addresses.

"There *will be* another time."

~ ~ ~

A glint in Fish's eyes said he wanted to race. Ron knew Fish no longer possessed the strength. He glanced

253

at Ron when they approached the starting mark, and Ron kept talking as if he didn't notice where they were.

"I'm pretty sure it's an episode we haven't seen before, Willll… bur."

Fish struggled up the steps. Ron thought about carrying him, but he knew that would wound Fish's pride. Fish plopped on the sofa, exhausted from their park excursion and their perhaps-not-chance meeting with Lela.

Ron headed for a hot shower, hoping to lose his thoughts and delay for a few more moments telling Fish. He had to tell him, and it needed to be tonight. Between now and then a cascade of new Psyche memories reflected and refracted in relative time. She never said it, but Ron knew she journeyed to the park to meet him, at least half the same reason he trekked to the park. Their previous meetings stirred the pot, even the first one when he made such a dork of himself.

Why didn't he tell her Fish was dying?

He never expected to have issues crying in front of a girl. He assumed emotional involvement would guarantee her understanding the reason he cried. He knew the real reason, emotional conflict finally resolved when he admitted it to himself: he owed it to Fish, to his friend, to tell him first.

Water pounded into his flesh, and he adjusted the temperature up to the bearable extreme. He wished he weren't showering alone. Perhaps he should've invited Lela home? No, that would've been a mistake. Too early in their relationship. He had enough trouble saying goodbye.

He lost his willpower while they danced, but now he wanted to talk.

Duh. He clunked the side of his head. He had her e-mail address, and he owed her an e-mail. He dashed from the bathroom dripping, a towel draped around his shoulders. Fish raised his head enough to laugh at his nakedness.

"Oh, shut up." Ron tossed a small pillow at him on his way to the computer.

Fish barked.

"Yeah, I know, I'm a lousy shot."

His mailbox opened. He clicked on the filter for her messages and reread Psyche's last correspondence. Acerbic, mirroring his previous e-mail to her. They were too anal, so neither of them could pass up the opportunity to answer a challenge.

Don't respond!

Ron needed to break out of the publisher format and write a letter from his heart.

Subj: Passion and desire

I wish to be known. Here's a glimpse of me I've never shared with anyone else...

Finished without proofreading, he clicked *Send*.

Ron had to prepare for finals, but his nerves tingled and energy arced across his shoulders, as though he could tackle several problems at once. Fortunately, he didn't need to. Fish slept, his breathing labored. Ron decided to work on his novel until Fish woke up; then he'd tell him, no more delays.

He worked through the afternoon and into the evening. Fish squirmed and sighed, but didn't wake up for hours. Once when Ron patrolled past, he covered Fish with an afghan and opened a window to allow cool spring air to breeze through the room.

Darkness enveloped the city when Fish came to, perhaps forgetting where he was or who he was for a moment. He raised his head. Ron smiled, pushed back from the computer chair, and angled to the sofa. Fish rolled onto his back. Ron sat. Fish handed him his paw.

"Thank you. Nice to see you too."

Fish wanted to be scratched behind his ear, and Ron obliged. His saucer eyes fixated on Ron's, and they stared at each other, waiting for someone to blink. Thirty-one clocks ticked off a slice of life before Ron finally forced the words out.

"We have to talk, buddy..."

Fish lent him the moral support Ron couldn't offer his friend. Tears blurred Ron's vision, no comfort that Fish accepted his fate. Roles reversed, Ron couldn't have been so gracious. They fell asleep on the sofa. Neither of them felt like eating dinner, so neither of them needed to go out.

The majority of the clocks said 3:00 a.m. or later when Ron jerked to consciousness. He hated waking suddenly, but tonight he was blanketed by foreboding.

"Fish!"

His friend gasped for breath, his sides heaved in convulsions. There was no twenty-four-hour animal hospital nearby, and he couldn't reach Dr. Grant. They had to muddle through on their own. Ron rubbed Fish's head and held his paw until Fish's breathing eased into a steadier rhythm. Ron dragged his laptop to their seat on the floor, shook the mouse awake, and surfed to WebMD. Maybe they'd be willing to help.

Excuse me, I'm sorry to bother you, but it's my friend. We're home, it's the late stages of pancreatic cancer. He woke up in convulsions...

They asked about his meds. Ron scuttled and collected bottles from the kitchen and typed in all the names.

Give him the muscle relaxant. Keep him warm. Call your doctor first thing in the morning.

Fish licked his hand a couple of times, and they both tried to sleep again. It seemed as if neither of them succeeded. At 6:10 Ron called Dr. Grant. He knew her office wouldn't be open, but lots of people go to work early.

A lot earlier than she probably wanted to talk, but he did reach her. She listened diplomatically, and said he could bring Fish in if he wanted to, but only one option remained to alleviate suffering.

"No!"

~ ~ ~

Ron had to rush, already late for his first class Monday morning. He promised Fish he'd come home at midday. Fish's tail flopped.

Showering took two minutes since he skipped shaving. Papers gathered into a messy pile were stuffed into his backpack. He stopped at the door, but didn't have the courage for words. The stairs squeaked.

Honking horns and grinding gears greeted him on the street. The rush of the subway, a jet overhead, smog and flashing signs and metal bars across doors and millions of people crowded onto one tiny island. The stench of garbage overflowing cans; cat-fighting; rodents munching breakfast; someone blaring rap; a homeless woman, bedraggled and dirty and stinky, pushing a shopping cart overloaded with her life.

The city symphony played a different movement this morning. Ron scuffed the sidewalk, and he kicked an empty soda can without stopping to recycle it.

Chapter 34

"Lela?"

"Back here, girl."

My voice strained. How'd I manage a sound, let alone call her name? I drifted into the mirror-fogged bathroom. Dog pranced behind me, his tail hooked, seeking attention.

Lela snuggled in a towel, a second towel wrapped like a turban around her head. "Oh, my, you must've had some morning in the park. What happened?"

Lela didn't give me a chance to answer. "Obviously, you met boy and beast again, or is it beast and dog? Seriously, Willow, you're not just flushed, this is an expression I haven't seen before. You're glowing and you're about to cry all at the same time. How is that possible?"

One look and Lela understood everything in my life.

I sat on the throne to talk, but hopped up and paced. My hands gestured, and I continued the silent conversation I'd started with myself when Mark left. What afflicted me, this feeling of sorrow? Why did he leave? I figured it still wasn't time for our first kiss. Tears clouded his eyes, and despair laced his tone as we parted.

Lela must've sensed I couldn't talk, wrapped up in unexplained events, in need of companionship and understanding to prevent sadness overwhelming me.

"You need a hot shower." She spoke over her shoulder. "I know you, Willow. You danced with the guy again for sure, but this isn't butt-wiggling issues. This is something much more. I'm making us coffees."

Lela exited the bathroom. I stepped out of my jeans.

"This is about romance, isn't it? Did he ask you out on a real date?" Kitchen sounds jumbled her words. "Nope, that's not it. I'm willing to bet you two haven't traded names yet, have you?"

Acquiescence in silence.

"I knew it. So, we're still calling him Mark. Funny if that's his real name, 'cause then we'd have to think of something else to call him." She laughed. I couldn't even smile.

"This is big-time, but not a date. Dancing means physical contact, but not enough for all this."

I stepped into the shower and pulled the curtain behind me.

Lela deposited mugs on the vanity and spoke over the sounds of banging pipes. "It must've been something he said. And you're still talking to yourself too. I can hear your thoughts, girl. You're asking the same questions. How'd this happen? What'd he say to elicit such a powerful response? Or is it all your intuition?" She stooped to stroke Dog.

"The kicker is the sorrow you dragged home. Such overpowering sadness. What? Is he gonna die or something?"

Tears streamed down my face.

~ ~ ~

I'm not sure if I showered for two minutes or two hours. Hot water soaked my flesh, and a sympathetic best friend altered my mood. I toweled off, dressed in comfort clothes, and discovered the reheated cup of French vanilla decaf on the vanity. My voice returned.

"Whoa. No floaters. Good thing the counter is here for me to lean on, otherwise I might fall over."

Enter Lela. She stuck out her tongue. She'd dressed in short shorts and a cutoff top, one tighter than the other. This time she sat on the throne, petting Dog, waiting for me to speak. What insight did I have to offer? Dog leaped off Lela's lap and scurried out of the bathroom. I explained what Mark didn't say while Lela brushed her hair.

"We don't know exactly what has you so whatever it is you are, Willow, but you're convinced, we're convinced, it's something tangible."

"Yes."

"What—"

Dog pranced back in and gave us the doorbell look.

"I didn't hear anything, did you?"

"Nope."

The doorbell rang. Who said cats don't make good watchdogs? I hauled the brush through my hair, rushed to open the door, and gaped straight into a belt buckle.

"Derek. This is a surprise." I arched my eyebrows and tilted my head back. "Isn't it?" I opened the door wider and gestured him in. "Close the door behind you, please."

I scampered across the floor and poked my head back into the bathroom. "You look beautiful. I'm sure he'll approve."

Lela preened in the mirror. "Who?"

"Your new double-decker boyfriend."

"DD? Here? He's not my boyfriend. Willow."

"He's waiting. Hurry up." I closed the door to prevent her from hearing the next bit of conversation.

"Well, Derek, what brings you our way? Need my psych notes again?"

He frowned as though I'd asked him to eat liver for lunch.

"No, thanks. You have odd ideas about note-taking, you know: what's important, what's left of mainstream note-takers."

I poked my upper lip with my tongue. "You know what they say about beggars."

"Don't offer wine when cold beet soup will suffice?"

I waggled a finger at him. "Would you like some soup?"

DD cracked a smile. He remained one step inside the door, absorbing his surroundings as though he were a building inspector. That put me off till I realized he was obliged to check for headroom. Doorways, chandeliers, things the rest of us didn't think twice about posed hazards for him.

"Nice digs," he said.

"Yeah, we couldn't afford the Village if Lela's aunt didn't own this apartment. Would you like something to drink? We have diet soda, with or without caffeine, water"—anyone who lives in New York realizes if they're offered water by another New Yorker, it's likely to be city water because it tastes as good as bottled—"and if you want wine, I'm sure I can scrounge some."

"Diet soda. With caffeine."

"No problem. Grab a seat."

I ducked my head into the bathroom on the way past. Lela remained glued to the mirror. "Hurry up, pokey. By the way, you didn't give DD our address, did you?"

"Not a chance."

262

"That's an awful lot of prep for 'Not a chance.'"

She stuck out her tongue farther this time and continued to apply eye shadow.

I grabbed a couple of soda cans from the refrigerator, flipped one to Derek, and sat across from him. He caught it two-handed and wisely waited a moment before popping the top. I couldn't resist a grin.

"Always pushing, aren't you, Willow?"

My eyebrows waggled. "How'd you find us? Our address isn't posted in the student guide."

His waggle dwarfed mine. "One of the perks of being a professional, er, not professional college athlete. On the team we call it 'Ask and ye shall receive.' Works for almost anything. In fact, there's a university employee whose sole function is to keep school athletes happy. We call him 'The Felicitator.' You know, kind of like The Terminator, but different."

"Yeah, that's different. You call this guy and…"

"Give him a name, and tell him I need an address. He goes right to a keyboard. I obtained my address, umm, your address in twenty seconds."

"That's convenient all right. You have someone who discovers girls' addresses for you. Does he arrange your dates too?" I called over my shoulder. "Lela. Come out. I've been replaced as your social director."

Derek laughed. I squinted at him. "You're not dangerous, are you?"

I hadn't noticed before, but Derek possessed the hugest mouth. I forced my eyes to continue examining his face and not drift downward. Derek laughed again. I wasn't sure what he laughed at.

"You must be a blast at parties. No, I'm not dangerous, except on the basketball court."

He hopped up, gazing past me. Lela. Had to be. Different reaction from when I'd sauntered into the room with sodas.

"Hello, best friend."

"Hi, Derek."

I rolled my eyes. "If you two will excuse me, I've got studying to do." They zoned me out. Didn't matter. I sniffed romance in the air. "Play nice, children."

~ ~ ~

Ron hadn't e-mailed in weeks, our playful banter disintegrated. After my last e-mail, I never expected to hear from him again.

A new letter surprised me. Gone were all references to *Matterhorn Press* and Psyche. In their place I received a self-description from a guy I'd never met but used to dream about. A guy Lela must've dreamed about too. I sat with my mouth open and read it again. And again.

I didn't know what to write in return. I'd already met a super man. Um, Mark. In the park.

Chapter 35

The next morning spread out like low-fat peanut butter on fresh bread. Flossing hurt, and one of those thousand-leg thingies disappeared under the closet door. Eughh. I cringed at the thought that a critter might be in one of my shoes. Dog deposited a surprise on the bathroom floor instead of the litter box, and I enjoyed the god-awfullest cramps.

I had an early final this morning too. Lela yawned when she tossed me a warm towel and left French vanilla decaf with the usual floaters. My jeans didn't want to zip, and my shoes were definitely too tight, though thankfully bugless. At 6:50 a.m., that had to be the limit on the bad side of things today.

My cell rang, caller ID blocked. Lela ran shower water, so that meant either me or voice mail. Too early for anyone I knew to be calling. I deepened my voice. "City morgue. You stab 'em, we slab 'em."

"I'm sorry, I must have the wrong number."

"Elliot? Is that you?"

"Willow?"

"Who were you expecting? Oh. The morgue guy. Sorry, he can't come to the phone right now. He's dead to the world."

Silence.

"Elliot? It's okay, really. Shall we start again? Hello, this is Willow. To whom am I speaking? Ohhh, Elliot Collins. What a pleasure to hear from you so soon after the sun has risen. To what do I owe this joyous surprise?"

Silence.

"Elliot. Come on. Lighten up. What can I do for you?"

Elliot sighed. "I wanted to catch you before you left for class. I spoke with Professor Kirin."

Okay, I take back the morgue stuff. Elliot promised a colossal favor. "Oh, right, Professor Kirin. I appreciate your help, Elliot. You know, I got nowhere and—"

"Don't thank me, Willow. I'm afraid you're still getting nowhere. Professor Kirin was immovable. I asked if he would consider doing me a favor, and he said, 'Sure.' I asked if he could enroll one additional student into Crimes next fall. He said he could arrange that for me. I added, 'What if one prerequisite hasn't been met?'

"He got this funny look in his eyes and said, 'No, no, no, no, no.' Couldn't be any clearer, Willow. Five times. I didn't know what else to say. I never mentioned your name."

I kicked the floor and rolled my tongue under my lip.

"That's all right, Elliot. Thanks for trying." I hung up.

Hell. I so wanted to be in that class. Only two chances remained to surprise Professor Kirin, and I still had no idea how I might do that. Time was up. Classes had long since ended, and the last final would be over in a few days. The professor anticipated everything I planned. How could anyone know me that well? I stomped around the kitchen, retrieved Lela's towel from the dryer, and tossed it over the curtain rod without a word. My back ached.

Lela had already dressed by the time I finished packing. "See ya at lunch."

"Willow?"

I slung the backpack over my shoulder and reached for the doorknob.

"What's wrong, girl?" Lela's inflection stopped me.

Tears formed. "Elliot. Professor Kirin. No, no, no, no, no."

Lela darted over and hugged me. I loved Lela.

"I know how bad you want into the class. I wish I could help. You still have your two chances, don't you? Have you thought of a way to surprise him yet?"

She answered before I could. "No, of course not. If you had, you'd have done it already. All right, tonight, after we finish studying for finals, we'll brainstorm. We can ask my Ouija board."

I laughed through my tears, squeezed her back, then headed for school.

Pissy and sad. That's a lousy combination, especially walking into a final exam. The city usually lifts my spirits. The symphony plays to me, my gait changes, and burdens are less burdensome. This morning's symphony struck discord. Instead of sounding like music, shifting bus gears sounded like, well, shifting bus gears. Horns honked, loud irritants. Too many people surged along the sidewalk. Buildings that should've stretched to the clouds leaned in instead, making me claustrophobic in one of the largest cities in the world.

The rush of the subway overwhelmed me, and I covered my ears. Jostled by curves and harsh braking, I opted off the train, wobbly, head throbbing. It took me longer to recognize off-kilter this morning. Even the Cement Man forgot to wave to me. Dumb statue.

I drifted past the carousel and the chess pavilion. I didn't have much extra time, and I didn't expect Mark to be here, but I wandered within sight of my rock.

No Mark. I sniffed and caught more than a trace of dog poop. My backpack seemed heavier than normal. I dragged on to school.

~ ~ ~

I exited the exam shaking my head and muttering, an hour to kill before Lela finished hers and met me for lunch. First thing first: find a bathroom. My mood latched onto all bodily functions.

This bathroom visit broke records. By the time I arrived at the roof, an underclassman framed in sunlight was sitting on our bench.

Shy of noon, I shuddered to think what the rest of the day held in store, and parked myself on a nearby bench, waiting for the miscreant to realize he trespassed on private property. I popped up after a minute and paced. Book in hand, I pretended to study for tomorrow's final, but failed to take advantage of free time.

I growled at the bench intruder. He ignored me. I edged closer to try again and plopped down one bench away, clutching my bulging backpack in my lap. I squeezed the sides so tight, I thought something would burst. The psychology world has a term for my behavior that escaped me in the moment, some kind of substitution.

In a vain attempt to feel better, I closed my eyes, and inhaled deeply, trying to will the air into every tense muscle and fiber of my being in order to relax. Since I knew the air couldn't actually pass beyond my lungs, intrinsically the effort was doomed to failure, but I made the effort anyway. I don't know how I missed it, but I didn't see the heretic leave our bench. I opened my eyes. Someone had supplanted the squatter.

Lela. Smiling. Waving like a petite dork. I rolled my eyes and pushed off the temporary bench as pain expanded in my back. Lela's beam broadened as I slugged across the roof. Unlike me, she probably aced her final.

"Come on, girl, sit down." She patted the bench next to her. "Your mommy called."

Yeah, this was gonna cheer me up, all right. "Let me guess, she wants to know if I drank my orange juice this morning, did I finish my homework last night, and when am I getting married to Elliot?"

"You're too cynical. She didn't mention anything about orange juice. Come on, smile. I brought lunch and an e-mail surprise."

"I'm not hungry, and I don't like surprises."

"Since when? You're always hungry after class, and you love surprises. I happen to know you're especially going to like this one. Come on, sit down." She patted the seat again.

I fell onto the bench, backpack on the ground between my legs, chin lolling on my chest.

"Willow, Willow, Willow, you better read this." Lela waggled a single sheet of paper.

"I don't feel like reading."

"You'll feel like reading this."

"No I won't."

"I checked our mailboxes before I left for class, and when I saw this, I figured you wouldn't want to wait to read it. It's been so long since you heard from him."

I didn't bother to look up. "Yeah, yeah, I know, Lela,

269

there's mail from Ron. I read it last night. Nice, different from our other mail, but so what?"

"You're not interested in reading this, then?"

"I told you, I already read it."

"Really? So you know what Professor Kirin says?"

"It's not from Professor Kirin. It's from Ron."

She held the paper close to her face. "Hmm, no, it's pretty clear. This says, 'Pro-fes-sor Kirin.' But I guess if you aren't interested, I'll toss it." She crumpled the message and threw it on the roof in front of our bench. The wind snatched the paper, kicking it twenty feet away.

I spun sharply to study her. She arched an eyebrow like a Vulcan woman, and I knew she wasn't joking. I shot off the bench at warp speed, chased the paper halfway across the building, scooped it up, then unraveled and smoothed it as best I could. Professor Kirin's e-mail smirked at me.

Subj: It is with deep regret...

That I concede victory to Willow Bolden. I'm sure I'll hate myself in the morning. Mr. Collins' attempt to intercede on your behalf notwithstanding, it's been six weeks without word from you, Willow, and that is a surprise! Honestly, I expected to be approached by administration next. However, I expected that long ago, so technically you've won.

Professor Kirin

I couldn't stop jumping. I yanked Lela off the bench and made her jump with me, hands high overhead. I didn't even snarl at the passersby who weren't minding their own business. It didn't matter. Nothing mattered. Professor Kirin would teach me Ab Psych this summer, and I would be in Crimes next fall.

"Yee-ha!"

We attracted a small crowd. I ignored them. I couldn't stop. Derek and two almost-as-tall basketball buddies—I could tell by their jerseys—emerged from the throng, waving, soaring with us. Derek's empathy endeared him to me.

"What're we jumping for?" he asked.

Arms stretched over his head, his fingertips scratching the sky, a silly grin sandwiched by his ears. I couldn't help laughing any more than I could stop jumping. Lela answered for me.

"Willow got into a class she wanted."

"I hope I'm around if she ever wins the lottery."

Derek jumped. I have no idea why his buddies jumped, but they laughed with us and scored such a good time that other people joined in, everyone waving hands high overhead. The throng swelled, and more people jumped with us. It would've made a good paper: "Crowd-Jumping Psychosis."

~ ~ ~

By the time we arrived home, off-kilterness latched onto euphoria. "That miserable bastard knows I can't live without details. I want to know when we're going to start Ab Psych, and how it's going to work. Is he going to take me up on my offer to teach him, or is he going to lecture me? What books do I need? Where're we going to meet?"

"What're you so anxious about?" Lela poured tea.

Oolong for her and PMS for me, never too late. "We're not done with finals yet. Don't you want a week or two off before hitting the books again? A couple days at least?"

"Yeah. No, I want Ab Psych over with, and I want to know when and how we're going to get it over with. That bastard. He could've told me."

I booted up the computer. I owed Ron a response, and didn't feel like studying. Lela dripped concentrated lemon juice into our tea, stirred, and handed me a mug. The devil sparkled in her eyes.

"You're right, Willow, Professor Kirin is a bastard. Did you tell him yet?"

"Tell him what?"

"That he's a bastard."

"Think I should?"

"How's he gonna know if you don't tell him? You want him to go around thinking he's not a bastard when he actually is? That's liable to cause him confusion, and what would you gain? You're gonna be taught Abnormal Psychology by a *confused* bastard. I don't know, it's not high on my list."

Another e-mail from Professor Kirin goaded me from my mailbox. Lela dangled over my shoulder. "He knows everything else about you, he must know you're talking about him." I glanced at her with one eye shut.

"Let's find out."

Subj: Okay

Willow, I know you must have twenty questions. When are we going to meet, where are we going to meet, how're we going to structure this class?

272

Our first meeting will be this Friday afternoon at three-thirty in the psych office. Finals will be over by then, and we'll discuss the particulars.

Professor Kirin

Lela rested on my shoulder. "He forgot to answer one of your questions."

I frowned. "Wanna bet?"

"What do you mean?"

"There's one more e-mail from the almighty, all-knowing professor."

"You're kidding."

I closed this mail to prove my point. Glaring at us from my mailbox were three messages from Professor Kirin, the two we'd already read, and, undoubtedly, the answer to my other question.

Subj: P.S.

You know what this e-mail is about, Willow. Yes, you're going to read one of my books—no, you won't have to purchase a copy, you can read mine—and we're going to use a number of collateral readings. You'll receive the list Friday.

He didn't sign this one.
The bastard.

~ ~ ~

Sadness dragged inexplicably into the next few days, a bizarre offshoot of my mood. Normally, within a day or two, something breaks me out of this: food, exercise, partying. Finals week is not the most convenient time for concentration difficulties.

My thoughts were overrun by my success with Professor Kirin, the park meeting with Mark, and the last e-mail from Ron. Lela's best coaxing failed. Professor Kirin declared me winner of the challenge. I surprised him. I refused to acknowledge I'd done anything, though.

How could the absence of doing something be doing something surprising? Had I truly won?

After weeks of silence, why had Ron picked now to contact me again? I tried to place his e-mail in my semester timeline. Previous contact coincided with Professor Kirin's last contact.

How'd Mark-in-the-Park fit into this timeline? Other than a few days ago, our last park meeting also happened about the time of my last contact with Professor Kirin. Life seemed to revolve around Professor Kirin.

The bastard.

Chapter 36

Every once in a while, a burst of energy flashed through Fish. Ron asked Dr. Grant, who had no good answer. "Indulge him. I'm sorry, Ron, it won't last much longer."

He indulged Fish every way possible. Fish wanted company, someone to talk with, to hold his paw, scratch behind his ear, share a milk shake. Occasionally he wanted to go for a walk, or a run.

Ron wasn't sure if Fish knew what a pancreas was, but Ron knew from his eyes he understood death.

They shared the week as best they could. Ron had finals, but he managed to come home for a couple of hours each day, having nearly perfected subway riding. He usually found Fish lounging on the sofa. His tail thrashed the cushions when he saw Ron, and they talked about the morning exam or the blossoms spreading in the park or *Mister Ed*. They didn't talk about summer plans. Fish knew.

Fish kept him laughing. *Willll… bur. You dance like a horse.*

Of course, that evoked memories of Lela in the park. Who'd taught Fish psychology anyway? He wanted Ron focused on something happy, instead of floundering in melancholy.

Why hadn't Ron told Lela his name? E-mail didn't count; she didn't seem to make the connection. She hadn't mentioned her name, either. Didn't she realize he knew it was Lela?

"What tangled webs weave our lives?" That wasn't quite the quote, but Fish laughed when Ron told him about the group roof jump. Ron was waylaid in Howard's office with Howard's newest idea about relative time, and during one of his chair's 360 spins, Howard stopped at 180 and gaped out the window.

"What on earth is going on out there?"

Ron hopped up. Dozens of students on the roof waved their hands high over their heads and danced. Well, jumped mostly. Derek Forrester caught his attention. He towered above the group, a goofy grin plastered on his face. Ron was wondering what ignited mass jubilation when he noticed, dancing near Derek, the woman tangled in his thoughts—Lela.

A single ray of sunlight kissed her cheek. Feelings rushed to the outer edges of Ron's body. His toes curled. A rainbow arced across the sky. Emotions he'd never successfully calculated now formed a single elementary equation.

He needed her.

He snatched his backpack and headed for the door. "Excuse me, Howard. I just remembered something. Gotta run."

Howard frowned. "I had another thought. There's a problem in the example you used about two friends spending the afternoon together. One of them is having the most marvelous experience, and for him, time flies. The other is bored, unable to focus on anything, and for him, time drags."

Ron tried to leave gracefully, but Howard wouldn't stop talking.

"Doesn't this create a paradox? If spatial coordinates are different, we can claim time passes differently in different places. But here, the spatial coordinates are identical. Two people are sharing the same time, and we want to say time is passing at different paces. We also—"

Ron gripped the door handle. "Seems paradoxical, but it's not, and I'll explain why, only not now. I have to run."

"I understand, for you, time is passing too slowly." Howard refused to let go. "For me, sharing the same time-space with you, time is passing too quickly. We're presented with a real-life example, but I don't see why there's no paradox here. Perhaps—"

"Perhaps I could explain this to you later? How about Friday afternoon? After everyone is finished with finals and we have time to take a breath and concentrate?"

"Friday afternoon would work. You'll explain it over a drink?" Howard laughed. "It might make more sense diluted with alcohol."

Ron forced a grin. "Yeah, it might. I've gotta go. We'll talk Friday."

By the time he reached the roof, most of the people had stopped dancing, but the crowd hadn't dispersed. He fought his way through to where he remembered Lela jumping. He found Derek easily enough, but no Lela.

"Derek, did you see where she went?"

"Who?"

Ron flashed a quick smile, as if Derek should know whom he meant. "Lela."

"She went home to study for tomorrow's final." He pointed over the heads of his fellow students. "That way."

That way. Ron laughed to himself. Not enough of a clue.

Chapter 37

Friday dawn broke upon his consciousness like a day of sailing on the ocean. The water is wonderfully calm, but you know there's a storm beyond the horizon. Not just any storm. This is the one they make movies about. The old sea dog can smell it in the air.

Fish barged into Ron's room. He seemed to have undergone a miraculous recovery. He danced on his hind legs, and his huge forepaws splashed on Ron's stomach. *Wake up. I wanna go outside. I wanna run.*

Lethargy had chased Fish for weeks. How could Ron be angry? It wasn't that dark outside.

Come on, get up, get up.

Ron showered and dressed, and he and Fish greeted the scraggly old men opening their newsstands for the day and the street sweepers washing gutters before traffic started. The sky lightened. The sun would rise soon. He hugged Fish.

What're you, nuts?

They ambled home for breakfast. Fish kept him company while he dashed off the next chapter in his romance. Fish insisted he read it aloud, and to Ron's surprise, Fish insisted on coming to school with him. They rode the 6 train from Astor Place all the way to Huntington. Fish peered at him like, *How come we didn't get off at the park?* But they needed to arrive on time for their last final.

Ron barely noticed that they were underground, or that throngs crowded the subway for the morning rush. A calm day at sea morphed into high winds across campus and tousled his hair and Fish's coat long before they arrived in class. Hard to tell who was the bigger mess.

~ ~ ~

They zipped through the morning and early afternoon, and the semester finished with only a couple of odds and ends to wrap up, like Howard and the paradox in Ron's theory of relativity. He recalled offering Friday afternoon to talk but not to have a drink like Howard was probably expecting. No chance of misleading. Ron and Fish approached the psych office without an extrication plan.

Fish lay down on a patch of Oriental rug in the lobby. Sunlight streamed in through high windows. "Big day, huh?" Ron held Fish's head in both hands and scratched as his friend sighed, no interest in accompanying Ron into the psych office.

"Hey, buddy, when you see someone coming, you know, like Howard, how about a heads-up bark?"

Fish flashed a mischievous grin.

The administrative assistant flagged down Ron as he entered.

"Ms. Naughton, what can I do for you?"

"When you have a few minutes, I'm trapped between universes."

"Ha, ha." Ron leaned over her desk in a conspiratorial posture. "If I'm trapped with Dr. Coleman for more than ten minutes, make the phone ring or something and save me."

She smiled in sympathy. "Will do." She tilted her head and glanced past his shoulder.

"Hello, Ron. Glad I found you." Diana promenaded into his personal space. The slit in her skirt exposed leg way beyond normal exposing in a psychology office. Her blouse fit like wrapping paper on someone else's birthday present. She pulled him away from Clarisse's desk to have a private conversation, her sultry voice seeking his libido.

"There's a sequel to Anne Rice's *The Claiming of Sleeping Beauty* that describes exquisite punishments. It's Friday. I'm willing to bet you don't have plans, do you?" She squeezed his hand hard against her arm, near a place it didn't belong. "I need you tonight."

"Actually, I do have plans. With Dr. Coleman." He arched a suggestive eyebrow. Not his fault if Diana misinterpreted. Well, not *entirely* his fault.

"Really?" Diana sounded skeptical but maintained her grip. "Howard Coleman?"

Before Ron could answer, Clarisse's voice caught their attention, like a miniature warning flag. "Mr. Forrester. What can I do for you?"

Diana refused to let go. Ron shifted his stance and smiled. "Hiya, Derek."

"Hi." Derek waved like a giant kid. "I'm looking for Dr. Coleman."

Ron pointed to the backward clock. "He'll be here momentarily."

Derek plopped into a chair, his knees now higher than his hips. "That was a tough final he gave us today," Derek said.

"Yeah, Dr. Coleman is one tough character. You have to watch out for him."

"Watch out for me? Why?" Howard had sneaked up on them. "Ron, I'm glad you're here early. I—" He frowned at Diana holding Ron's hand pressed too close to parts he didn't possess.

"You have a student waiting for you, Howard," Ron said. "First things first, isn't that correct, Ms. Naughton?"

Clarisse gestured toward Derek. "Mr. Forrester is waiting to speak with you."

Derek popped out of his chair. "Dr. Coleman, it's about today's exam. You see, I have to maintain…"

Diana slipped into the opening and described a chapter in Anne Rice's book, the husky tone in her voice unmistakable, though he hoped her words were inaudible to the crowded room's other occupants.

Howard, in mid-discussion with Derek, eyed Diana suspiciously.

Two-thirds of the polar bear club present and accounted for. What more could Ron ask?

Chapter 38

"We going to celebrate, girl?"

I smiled at my best friend. "You bet. Listen, I want to stop by the chancellor's office to thank Elliot for trying to help, then I'll go meet the bastard professor. Heading home to change before we go out?"

"I am." Lela cocked her head. "Is it all right if Derek meets us later? I don't want him to intrude on our time."

"Of course, silly. Bring him along, or have him meet us there. Whatever you want is fine with me."

Lela radiated like the midafternoon sun. "Too bad you don't know how to reach Mark-in-the-Park. We could make a foursome and go dancing or something." She snorted like a horse, then encircled my arm. "I'll go see the chancellor with you. I'd like to meet this bastard professor myself, then we can ride home together."

The scent of blooming lilac blew across campus. Students scurried, anxious to leave the city. We strolled toward the administration building.

Double cedar doors led to Chancellor Nixon's office. No one answered our knock, so we wandered into the foyer. Plush burgundy carpet, dark wood-paneled walls, a massive cherry desk, and Louis Quinze high-backed chairs adorned the outer office. I sniffed copier ink, an anachronism in this place.

Elliot emerged from the inner sanctum. "This is a nice surprise," he said.

"I stopped by to thank you again, Elliot, for trying to help me into Professor Kirin's class. You'll be glad to know I made it. I'm in. He told me."

"After 'No, no, no, no, no,' he still let you in?"

"Yep, yep, yep."

"I don't know what to say, except, congratulations. I'm sure you'll enjoy his class."

"Thanks. I really—"

"Mr. Collins, I don't think we've finished our discussion." An attractive older woman in a tailored suit stomped out of the office from which Elliot had emerged. "I didn't realize we had visitors. Sorry. I'm Hilary Nixon, university chancellor." She extended her hand.

I grasped it and tried not to cringe at the frigid exchange.

Elliot jumped in. "Ma'am, these are my friends, Willow Bolden and Lela Thompson, juniors."

Chancellor Hilary shook Lela's hand too. "I'm pleased to meet you both." She rounded on Elliot. We were already paying students; dismissed. "Mr. Collins, you're sure Rhiannon Raeburn is not a member of the SDN?"

"Positive, ma'am."

"I can't believe it. I saw her solicit donations in my home."

"You actually heard her do that?"

"I know what she was doing. Ron said—"

"What?"

The chancellor pounded fist into palm. "I can't believe this. We need to talk with Ron, now. Do you know where he is?"

Elliot shrugged. "The psych office? Want me to call?"

"Let's surprise him. I don't want to give him time to think up more stories. Walk with me, Elliot. Ladies, excuse us. We have a meeting."

I glanced at the grandfather clock standing guard along the wall. "If you don't mind, we're headed in the same direction. I have an appointment in the psych office with Professor Kirin in fifteen minutes."

The chancellor eyed me. How could I possibly have an appointment with Professor Kirin? "Please excuse us if Mr. Collins and I continue our discussion while we walk."

Lela and I didn't mind. If Chancellor Hilary thought it appropriate to discuss university business in front of us, go ahead. Mark-in-the-Park once mentioned a fictitious SDN, and Rhiannon Raeburn must be Elliot's Rhiannon. Lela and I pretended to be deep in our conversation while we listened to Elliot and the Chancellor.

"Miss Raeburn told you this?"

"She says she's never heard of it. You'd think a Scotland native would be aware if the group existed."

"Ron said it was a secret organization, like the IRA."

"We've all heard of the IRA, ma'am. There's documented evidence of its existence. Television, news-papers, magazine stories. Rhiannon is a good person. I've gotten to know her in the past several weeks. She wouldn't belong to that organization if it did exist."

"What about the Big MF?"

"Who?"

"Her boss at the catering company. Larry Scott. I've met him several times and pumped him for information."

Lela and I soaked this up big-time. The big MF? We understood "met him several times" to mean they'd dated. Rumor implied that dating Hilary Nixon didn't mean holding hands and strolling through the park.

"Ms. Nixon, Larry Scott is Rhiannon's uncle, her mother's brother. When Rhiannon arrived from Scotland, Mr. Scott gave her a job, which allowed her to obtain a green card and establish residence. That's not a crime. She should be commended. She works twenty hours a week and maintains a three-point-seven average with a heavy academic load."

Ms. Nixon stopped abruptly, hands on hips, facing Elliot. Lela and I lurched up on our toes to keep from crashing into them. The chancellor's face burned scarlet.

"I've never for a moment believed they were related. Do you have your cell phone with you?"

"Yes, ma'am."

"Call Mr. Scott, and have him meet us at the psych office pronto."

"What if he's busy?"

"I'm sure he doesn't have many clients the size of our university. He can drop whatever else he's doing. While you're at it, why don't you contact Ms. Raeburn and have her meet us there too. We're going to have a chat with Ron."

Serious trouble lurked on Ron's horizon, whoever Ron was. I didn't know any Rons except Lela's online friend.

We glided down white marble steps heading away from the administration building. The feeling of sadness—never fully dissolved—resurfaced. Lela and I trailed Elliot and Chancellor Hilary into the huge two-story lobby of Goddard Hall.

Hilary Nixon screamed.

I peeked around Elliot. A monster of a dog sprawled across an Oriental rug in a patch of sunlight streaming from second-story windows. He barely raised his head to

285

acknowledge the official university reaction to his presence.

"Fish?"

His head popped up, and he spied me at once. He struggled to stand and waddled the way a big dog does when the entire back half of his body wags. I stooped, and he licked my hands and my face.

"I'm pleased to see you too."

Chancellor Hilary regained her composure. "Ms. Bolden, does this animal belong to you?"

"No, ma'am, our Dog is a cat."

"Excuse me?" She shook my words out of her head. "A friend, then?"

I smiled all the way to my ears and scratched Fish's head.

"Yes, ma'am, Fish is a friend of mine."

"Not the dog, Ms. Bolden, his owner."

"The owner doesn't belong to me, either, ma'am."

Hilary took a deep breath. "Ms. Bolden, I'm trying to discover who owns the dog." She squirreled her eyebrows. "Did I hear you correctly? You called the dog Fish?"

"I didn't name him."

Lela caught my attention. "The dog in the park?" she whispered.

I nodded.

Hilary cleared her throat. "The dog's owner?"

My weight shifted. "Fish doesn't belong to anybody, do ya, boy?"

Fish bellowed a big dog bark that reverberated in the high-ceilinged lobby.

"Who named him?" the chancellor asked.

"It's the name he came with."

"I don't see dog tags. I suppose they could be hidden beneath that mass of hair."

Fish shook his head.

"Fish told him his name."

"Told whom?"

Lela stepped around to make sure I could see the devilish gleam in her eyes. She whispered, "Yeah, told whom, Willow? Mark-in-the-Park?"

"Ms. Thompson, you have something to add to this?"

"Oh, no, ma'am, Willow is doing fine without my help." She gestured toward me. "Willow?"

"He told my friend, Fish's roommate."

"That's what we're trying to discover, Ms. Bolden, your friend's name, please."

I mumbled, "I don't know."

"I'm sorry, what did you say?"

Lela glowed. "I couldn't hear you, either, Willow."

"I said, I don't know."

"You don't know your friend's name?"

"Nope." My head shook with a staccato burst.

"Good friend, is he?"

"Yep."

"A good friend whose name you happen not to know?"

"Right."

"Are you always this helpful, Ms. Bolden?"

Lela darted forward. "I've only known Willow for two years, Ms. Nixon. Her mom calls every day, sometimes twice a day, and assures me that from the time Willow could crawl, she's been a helpful person."

I squinted at Lela. Laughter danced in her eyes. She wasn't done being helpful herself.

"Willow does have a name for Fish's roommate."

I tried to shush her.

"You do know his name?"

"Not exactly, Ms. Nixon. It's what I call him because I don't know his real name."

"At this point, I'll settle for that. What do you call him?"

"Mark."

"Mark? That's all?"

Lela chimed right in. "Oh, no, ma'am, that's not all. Is it, Willow?"

My wicked friend, wait until tonight. "In-the-Park," I added, fast and faint, hoping Hilary would hop over it.

Elliot's helpful nature surfaced. "Mark… in-the-Park? And he has a dog named Fish? Is that anything like *The Cat in the Hat*? Does Fish eat *Green Eggs and Ham*?"

Fish woofed again, and I swear he nodded his head. Thank you, Elliot.

"Ms. Bolden, your good friend, Mark-in-the-Park, doesn't actually own this monster, they're just room-mates?"

"Yes."

"I see. Mr. Collins, we can't have dogs wandering loose in our halls. Bring him along, please, until we locate Mark-in-the-Park. And if you don't mind, make it clear to Mr. Park there are leash laws, and this dog—"

"Fish," Elliot interjected.

"This *dog* needs to be on a leash."

Fish pranced around and headed up a hallway as if he understood "leash" and didn't want one. Coincidentally, we headed into the same hallway. Hilary shook her head, her heels fired a determined beat on the marble floor, and she mumbled as we all followed the dog.

"Fish. Mark-in-the-Park. Wait till I rip up Ron."

Chapter 39

Howard retreated to converse with Derek, Diana reengaged Ron, and Rhiannon Raeburn waltzed into the office.

A deep bark echoed down the hall. "*Now* he signals me."

"What was *that*?" Diana asked.

"A friend's poor attempt at humor," Ron said.

Rhiannon aimed for Clarisse, but her mind must've been wandering. "Hi, Ms. Nausicaan, uh, I mean, Ms. Naughton." She repeated it, in case Clarisse missed it the first time. "Ms. Naughton, I need to see Dr. Coleman as soon as possible."

Clarisse, not a devout Trekkie, raised a Vulcan eyebrow and pointed across the office. "Take a seat and wait your turn, Ms. Raeburn."

Rhiannon's attention searched for Howard instead of a chair.

"Dr. Coleman, I'm so glad you're here. I have to talk with you about the final. I—" She noticed the tower beside Howard, her classmate. "Sorry. Didn't realize you were speaking with someone. Hi, Derek." She ogled south of Derek's waist—her eyes widened—then tilted her head back.

Clarisse hopped up to corral her.

"Tough test, huh?" Rhiannon continued, unfazed. "Is that what you're doing here too? Talking about the final? Go ahead." She shooed them with the back of her hand. "You two finish. I'll wait."

"Thank you, Ms. Raeburn," Howard said. Rhiannon seemed to miss the patronizing tone. Clarisse returned to her post.

After a second bark, and a third, a premonition crawled over Ron's skin. That's when Rhiannon spied him, backed into a corner.

"Ron. I'm so glad you're here too. I've been dying to thank you."

She charged over. "Excuse me," she said to Diana, who took a shaky step back. Rhiannon wrapped her arms around Ron and planted a kiss on his cheek.

Diana and Howard eyed Rhiannon with pungent distaste. Ron's face pressed in Rhiannon's rush of hair.

In tromped the chancellor.

Uh-oh. "Hello, Hilary," Ron managed to say. No reply.

Hilary probably recognized Rhiannon from behind, which explained the smoke emerging from Hilary's ears. Hilary's entrance explained Fish's first bark.

Enter Elliot, who probably also recognized Rhiannon's lips pressed to Ron's cheek, which explained the smoke emerging from *his* ears. His entrance explained Fish's second bark.

Diana, Howard, Hilary: polar bear club present and accounted for. Ron couldn't wait to see what Fish's third bark meant. He didn't have long to wait.

His stomach dropped, somersaulted, and disappeared from this plane of existence. A noose tightened around his neck. His head pounded like a herd of hippopotamuses splashing across a stream. Rain and rainbows, the sun, the moon, and every star in the galaxy collected in a tiny crucible called the psych office.

Fish had delivered fair warning. Posed in the doorway, in all her splendor, soared the woman of tortured months, dancing dreams, and inexplicable e-mails: Lela.

Rhiannon maintained a powerful grip around his neck, the full length of her body pressed tightly against him, not to mention her lips still attached to his cheek. This situation wouldn't be easy to explain. He offered a wan smile to all.

Too late.

Hilary fumed. "Ron, what is the meaning of this?"

"Monthly meeting of the polar bear club, plus friends?"

Hilary didn't laugh. "We need to straighten out this SDN thing right now."

"Does it have to be *right* now?" Ron scratched his head. "Hi, Elliot."

Rhiannon disengaged enough to glance and point her chin. "Elliot, I'm coming to your office as soon as I finish talking with Dr. Coleman."

Elliot's mouth teetered into a frown. "That's Professor Kirin."

Rhiannon leaned back to gawk at Ron. "You're Professor Kirin? *The* Professor Kirin? I want to talk with you too. I want to register for Crimes in Psychology next fall."

Lela, mouth agape, pointed an accusing finger at her favorite dance partner. "*You're* Professor Kirin?"

"A rumor increasingly difficult to deny," Ron said.

Howard, exhibiting extraordinary single-mindedness, pointed at the backward clock behind Clarisse.

"Ron, if you'll excuse yourself from all this, I believe we have an appointment. Hello, Hilary."

Hilary afforded the professor a cursory glance. "Hello, Howard." She snapped right back to Ron. "I demand to know, right now, what you're doing in the embrace of an SDN operative."

Diana, silent since the club meeting began, decided now was a good time to be helpful.

"Yes, Ron, exactly what is she thanking you for?"

Lela ventured another two steps into the office, followed closely by a shorter, equally beautiful woman.

"You're Professor Kirin?" Lela repeated. The shorter woman peered past Lela's shoulder.

Thinking it his chance to be helpful, Elliot answered Diana's question. "Presumably, she's thanking him for introducing us and encouraging me to take her out."

Hilary spun on Elliot. "You're dating her?"

Enter the Big MF. "I got your message, Hilary, and rushed over. What's going on?" He paused to absorb the scene. "You should've told me it's a party. After all, I am a caterer." He laughed, and so did Clarisse, Derek, and the shorter woman.

"Uncle Larry!" Rhiannon said.

Hilary pointed, and her weight shifted. "She really is your niece?"

"Of course she is," Larry said. "I was hoping to catch you alone, Hilary." He edged closer and cupped his hand next to his mouth as though no one else would hear. "I don't know what time to pick you up tonight."

Elliot spun on Hilary. "You're dating him?"

Hilary Nixon, chancellor of the world, blushed. "Ron introduced us. He—"

"Ron seems to be making a lot of introductions." Diana's brow shot up.

Thanks, Diana, for the valuable summary.

Lela inched forward, barely uttering the words, "*You're* Professor Kirin?"

Clarisse arched an eyebrow, spread her thumb and pinky, and positioned her hand beside ear and mouth like she was rescuing Ron with a phone call. Ron could only add a silly grin.

"Hi, Lela." Derek waved, followed by a ludicrous laugh. Lela ignored him, focusing on Ron.

"Hi," the smaller woman answered Derek.

A boisterous bark in the doorway made everyone jump.

Hilary, encased in scarlet, focused on Lela, finger waggling. "The dog's owner, Ms. Bolden?"

Ron's mouth shaped the words, but no sound emerged. *Ms. Bolden?*

Ms. Bolden raised the accusing finger a second time. *He's the owner, Your Honor.*

Hilary resembled a cross between a Vulcan and a Nausicaan. "Professor Kirin?"

"Yes," Ms. Bolden said.

Fish barked twice.

Ron processed the conversation, replaying perspective in the undercurrent. "You're Ms. Bolden?" It didn't seem right; at the same time, it seemed perfect. "Willow?" Ron's turn to point. "You mean, *she's* Lela?"

Willow glared at Ron. "You're Mark-in-the-Park." Now the shorter woman's mouth gaped. She danced into Ron's space, held out her hand like a lady-in-waiting, and crooned, "Hello, Professor Kirin. We haven't been introduced. I'm Lela Thompson, Willow's roommate. You're Mark-in-the-Park? And Fish's roommate?"

"And advocate for Carl and Carl," Ron mumbled.

Willow gasped. She must've heard.

In a moment of insightful inspiration just behind Willow's, Lela added, "Ron? Ron Kirin? Oh my. I thought my roommate was schizophrenic. Fish. You poor thing."

After that, everyone talked at once. The real Lela discussed evening plans with Derek. Howard tried to discuss drinking plans with Ron. Diana wanted to discuss dating plans with Ron. Rhiannon cozied into Elliot's arms, but Ron couldn't distinguish what they were saying. Hilary squeezed close to Ron's face.

"Let's straighten this out now. The SDN—"

"What did I tell you at University Day about Mr. Scott?"

Hilary pressed her lips together. "You said Larry had nothing to do with the SDN."

"Have you seen evidence to the contrary?"

Hilary pushed on. "What about Ms. Raeburn?"

"I told you, she's not a member, either. At your party, a financial-giant alumnus harassed her. Rhiannon didn't want to create an incident. I invented the SDN story. I knew if you kept a close watch, harassment would stop, and the university would still have its benefactors."

More smoke billowed from Hilary's ears. "I don't care how big a money man, if it ever happens again you tell me immediately because we are making an issue of it." Her gaze narrowed. "And if you ever invent another ploy to—"

Clarisse waved a phone in the air to grab Ron's attention. *Yeah, ha, ha, Clarisse.*

Larry grabbed Ron's hand and pumped. "I want to thank you," he said. "You were right. Hilary is everything you said, and then some."

Hilary pivoted, face flushed. "What did you tell him?"

Clarisse maneuvered from behind her desk and handed Ron the phone. "It really is for you."

"Who's calling? Everyone's here." He covered his other ear to dull the office rumble. "Hello?"

"Dr. Kirin? This is Dr. Grant at the veterinary hospital. I'm going out of town. I want to give you the number of another doctor in case you need to talk with someone over the weekend."

"Wait a sec, let me grab something to write with." Clarisse handed him a pad and pen. "Go ahead," he said to Dr. Grant.

"Her name is Kerry Rand. She's not a vet, but she's a good psychologist, and she happens to be my cousin."

Ron laughed. A *good* psychologist, in case he needed grief counseling. "Okay, thanks, Doctor. Fish is having a great day. He's been running and jumping, and he came to work with me for the first time in weeks."

"I see." Dr. Grant failed to mask the emotion in her voice. "It's a beautiful day in the city. You and Fish enjoy it. Call me Monday."

She thinks this is Fish's last hurrah.

Fish yapped as though he required Ron's attention. By the time Ron wormed his way through the office, he guessed why Fish fussed. The artist formerly known as Lela-Psyche-Willow Bolden, his newest student, his most annoying, anal, pain-in-the-ass pupil of all time, ever, vamoosed. Fish nuzzled his hand to remind him Ms. Bolden wasn't enrolled in the class yet and, therefore, wasn't officially his.

Chapter 40

Lela found me on the library steps. "I didn't see you leave, Willow."

"I appreciate you coming after me, but I don't want to talk."

Lela nodded, hands on hips. "You don't have to talk, girl. Just listen while I recap." She took a deep breath. "You meet an enigmatic guy in the park. He's handsome, engaging, and every bit as quirky as you, and a strong emotional bond develops.

"Turns out your stranger is also this bastard professor, but he's still the same stranger. Do I have the story straight?"

She probed beyond my external façade. "Every time you face an intense emotional issue, you run away. You did it with Elliot when you couldn't break up, you did it with Professor Kirin when you couldn't surprise him, and you're doing it now."

"Look how much I hurt Elliot."

"Forget Elliot's feelings for a minute. When you finally confronted him, didn't *you* feel better? You can't keep this stuff bottled inside. You might've hurt Elliot, but in the long run, he'll thank you for it."

"Thank me? I kicked Elliot in the gut. Twice. It hurt me to do it as much as it hurt him."

"Confronting him allowed him to move on with his life. It may be coincidence, or maybe Professor Kirin interceded, but look how happy Elliot is." She sat and draped her arm around my shoulders. We didn't move for several minutes.

"Don't run away from Professor Kirin or from Mark-in-the-Park or from Ron. You've managed emotional issues before. Do it again. Put yourself in his path."

I sucked in my cheeks, like a fish avoiding a hook.

Lela grabbed my hand, and pulled me up. "Go to your rock, Willow."

I sighed, and my lips vibrated like a horse's.

Chapter 41

Fish and Ron left without being noticed, heading to the park. If they saw Willow again today, Ron knew it would be on their rock.

Fish pranced beside him as though he understood something Ron didn't. Ron's breath came fast. He itched with no good place to scratch. He knew where to go, but a tiny voice kept urging, *Don't go there.*

They entered the park. Ron headed for the usual path leading past the carousel. Fish aimed down East Drive.

"What's up? You're goin' the long way."

Fish stopped and glanced at him with a familiar look. *What're you, nuts?* Ron did a double take. *Willll… bur, our path leads this way today.*

The usual vibrations drifted through the park: bus engines and the squeal of speeding taxis, an occasional vendor, and the grinding labor of a construction site. And something out of place: an unrelenting high-pitched drone.

Ron sniffed, expecting a trace of hot dogs and pretzels and mustard and a bit of exhaust and a bit of spring. Instead, his nose wrinkled. Unfamiliar distaste.

A contingent of pigeons flew by, wings spread for landing. People strolled, but no one held hands. A black squirrel scurried across their path, and Fish ignored him.

Ron kicked a stone, and Fish ignored that too. Too many bicyclists and rollerbladers and joggers weaving, speeding, independent of all else New York, thumping their chests, proclaiming their space on East Drive—they didn't need the rest of the city.

A homeless person, tattered in clothing and spirit, unable to discern a pattern in the speeders and unable to cross, lingered by the curb, frustration wrapped around his unshaven cheeks.

Up ahead, a small boy on roller skates bounced a large ball around a young mother. Mom struggled to control boy and ball on the uneven path beside the road.

A discordant symphony played to Ron.

What happened to his city?

They crested a small hill, passing mom and boy.

A few more steps, and Ron glanced behind. East Drive took off into space. Like an arcade game, people on wheels shot over the ridge and flew down their side.

The ball bounced down the path, away from the boy. He yelped with delight and gave chase, followed by mom. Her call stopped him, but he must've thought it a wonderful game: follow the ball, Mom follows me.

Mom caught the ball and rolled it uphill to the child. Instead of rolling it back, he pushed the ball into the street and chased again. Mom shrieked. The boy squealed. Fish bounded after the ball.

Never had Fish galloped so fast in all their racing days. A car flew over the crest of the hill, bearing down on the child.

"Fish!"

Perhaps Fish pushed the child or bumped him as he flew past, but the car never veered, and barely missed the boy.

A thud echoed through the park nonetheless.

The car sped off, never stopping, never slowing. The boy cried out, the mother screamed, bicyclists and rollerbladers wheeled by as though accidents were none of their business. Pigeons flew away, a hawk narrowed its circle, and Ron squeezed his eyes shut as tight as he could.

Fish.

Chapter 42

My rock.

I'd been here twice in the past six weeks, and he'd been here as well. Mark-in-the-Park. Professor Kirin. Ron. They all knew me. Mark pretended not to know me. Professor Kirin had made me jump through hoops as though he knew me intimately, predicting every thought and every movement. What game did Ron play? He'd written to me pretending to be a stranger, when all along he knew me in the park, and he knew me in school.

Lela called it—he was schizophrenic.

I hated confrontation, but he needed to know how deception compromised my feelings. He could forget everything that happened between me and all three of him, except that Professor Kirin would still teach me Ab Psych this summer and I'd take his class in the fall. I'd earned it. The bastard.

I arrived at the uneven path and drifted so far off-kilter I barely recognized myself. Footsteps didn't coordinate with sounds, and my mouth developed an acrid taste that wouldn't dissolve. I'd carried the kryptonite pebble in my pocket for months. I squeezed it for reassurance.

I hunkered down and caressed the rock where we'd danced. The cold surface yielded nothing. No one waited there. I glanced around, half expecting Fish to hurtle forward. The barren landscape appeared parched in a spring inundated with rain. Children did not jump gleefully on the playground, old men did not toss bocce balls, and trees did not whisper my name. Instead, a high-pitched whine wailed in the back of my head and refused to go away.

I heard it then: a shriek, squealing tires, and someone yelling, "Fish."

A woman screamed, a plea for help. I shuffled in the general direction. An echo, like a homing beacon, pulled me toward East Drive. I heard it again.

"Fish!"

A young woman, hysterical, hugged a child as though she couldn't capture enough of him. A homeless person, unshaven, hair unkempt, parked by the curb, gesturing with exaggerated motions, talking to himself, but his eyes were misted and his cheeks wet.

A few passersby stopped to snoop.

Professor Kirin knelt in the road, shoulders sagged, head bowed like he'd lost a terrible battle. The sensation flooding my mind went beyond foreboding. Fish lay limp on the blacktop.

I covered my mouth as a sick feeling spread like wildfire through my stomach and knotted my insides. Professor Kirin's shoulders heaved.

I wanted to run to Mark-in-the-Park, throw my arms around him, hold him in a moment of shared grief, but I couldn't intrude. I didn't want to have anything to do with Professor Kirin or Ron. Empathy latched onto my neck and shoulders, and as Mark cried, so did I.

Gawkers yakked about what had happened.

"Did you see that? The dog saved the boy."

"Did not."

"Did too. Pushed the kid out of the way, and the car hit him instead."

"You're imagining things. The dog darted into the street. Probably chasing the kid's ball. Simple hit-and-run. That's all. The car never would've hit the kid."

"Think what you want. I know what I saw."

I know what I saw: Professor Kirin sobbing as though he'd lost his best friend. I leaned against a tree for support. I don't know how long I remained motionless; it might've been thirty seconds, or thirty minutes. Time is relative, and I suspect the latter time passed.

Eventually, a vehicle pulled up, *Something Animal Hospital* embossed on the side. A guy in a uniform slid Fish into a bag, loaded him through the back of the vehicle, and drove away.

I've never seen anguish such as that exuding from the man left standing alone in the road.

I wrapped my arms around the tree to keep from running to him.

~ ~ ~

Through renewed tears, I explained to Lela what had happened and why I hadn't confronted the bastard professor. We agreed the best thing would be to wait. Professor Kirin and I hadn't worked out our meetings for Ab Psych, so he needed to contact me.

I figured grief through the weekend, and he'd be back to business by Monday.

~ ~ ~

By Wednesday, I paced our apartment, staring at the phone, jumping on the computer every half hour to check e-mail. I checked Lela's e-mail on the off chance Ron had something to say.

Perhaps he knew me so well, he expected me to show up at the psych office for another note. I refused to visit the psych office without an invitation, but if he knew me that well, maybe I should.

Lela smiled when I left the house. I took the train all the way to school, opting to stay out of the park.

"Excuse me, Ms. Naughton, I was wondering if—"

"Nope."

"Excuse me?"

"Professor Kirin did not leave you a note."

I frowned, angled to leave, but spun back. "I'm sorry, how'd you know what—"

"He won't be in the office for the next couple of weeks." She waved a paper. "He left *me* a note."

"That says I'd be in to ask if he left *me* a note?" Her head bobbed.

Ms. Naughton's voice nailed me at the office door. "He didn't say this, but you know he's waiting for you to contact him."

I didn't want additional prompting, so I headed home to mope and pace.

~ ~ ~

Thursday morning dawned with a plan so simple it couldn't fail. He must be at our rock. He and Fish had wandered there so often, all I needed to do was go there now and wait for him.

~ ~ ~

On the third day of my simple plan, I realized another plan might be necessary.

I e-mailed Professor Kirin at his university address. After a couple of hours, I still hadn't received an answer, so I e-mailed Ron. None of his personas responded. I checked the status of the mail: he hadn't opened my messages.

Lela eyed me from afar. "You have that scheming look."

Dog jumped into my lap and nudged me to pet him.

"I'm going out." I jumped up, and the cat flew off, exchanging my lap for Lela's.

Lela pretended she talked to Dog, but I knew she intended her words for me. "I hope she doesn't trigger trouble."

How much trouble could I trigger in a pet shop?

I figured Mark-in-the-Park needed a Fish replacement. Puppies are puppies, and once you stagger beyond the store odor, how could you not find them the cutest things on earth?

One fuzz-ball sat at the edge of his cage, pawing me, his huge eyes imploring, *Take me home.* I decided to walk away and come back in a few minutes, and if the same puppy said the same thing, he'd be the one.

I examined dishes, water bowls, leashes, collars, the squeaky toys. Professor Kirin undoubtedly owned all these. Or not. After the death of a loved one, don't some people pack up the deceased's belongings and give them away?

I wandered back to cage row. Fuzz-ball sat where I left him, waiting for me.

A clerk peered down the aisle to see if I needed assistance. I shook my head. This wasn't right.

How could I present Mark-in-the-Park and Professor Kirin and Ron one puppy? My ear itched. I tugged handfuls of hair out to the sides.

What about three puppies?

I closed my eyes and twirled around and around until my head ached. My feelings were as jumbled as my thoughts.

The past refused logic. Three puppies made no more sense than one.

I spun and blended timelines and images in my mind. A dance of passion at my rock, butt wiggling as I wandered away from a surprising boy with rain dripping off his glasses, childhood memories, envelopes with my name flourished across them, notes anticipating not just my arrival but my actions.

My first meeting with Mark had coincided with the first time Professor Kirin said no. My most recent meeting had happened around the time Professor Kirin finally said yes. Ron had followed every meeting with an e-mail. Didn't I secure exactly what I wanted? Was it what I deserved?

Spinning gelled history.

Mark-in-the-Park, Professor Kirin, and Ron almost melded into one man.

Spinning stopped, but my heart thumped. Scattered ideas congealed in perfect understanding. I hadn't won the challenge. Yet. I clamored to do something to surprise them. *Him.*

Chapter 43

Professor Kirin wasn't in the white pages, the operator wasn't inclined to give me unlisted information, and the university directory referred me to the psych office for contact. Fair enough, NN it would be.

She didn't seem surprised to see me.

"Good morning, Ms. Bolden. The answer is, 'No, I can't.'"

"You can't what?"

"I can't give you Professor Kirin's phone number."

"Don't want it, although I do need something else."

She maintained a faint curl of her lips and waited for me to continue.

"His address."

"Can't do that, either."

"Why not?"

"He said so."

"He told you not to give me his address?"

She waved a piece of paper. Maybe the same paper as last week, maybe not. "A list of dos and don'ts for Ms. Bolden. Says right here: 'Do not give out my home address.' Sorry, Willow. I promised."

I believed her. Not that she couldn't give me his address, but that she felt genuinely sorry. I didn't want her to break her promise.

My frown lasted a few seconds. I banged the side of my head. Ask and ye shall receive.

I'd forgotten my phone. "May I use your phone?"

She gestured. I dialed. "Lela? It's me. I need DD's phone number... Okay, thanks." I hung up and dialed again. "Derek? Hi, it's Willow. Listen, I need a favor. I need Professor Kirin's home address."

"Hold on. I'll use my other line."

His other line? Less than a minute later, I scribbled an address.

NN's eyes widened.

I needed more. How much did NN know? "Did Professor Kirin tell you what happened?" I asked her.

"Yes."

"I mean a week ago Friday, after we were all here in the office and he went to the park?"

"He told me about Fish. Though I don't think he realizes how fortuitous that was for him and for the dog."

My face contorted. "Fortuitous?"

"Pancreatic cancer in its final stages is heartrending. Fish had little time left. I think the dog knew that."

Yikes. I didn't know that. Memories of Mark-in-the-Park and Fish swam around the office. Tears I thought were past renewed.

"Ms. Naughton, did he tell you we danced in the park?"

Her eyebrows arched. "That was you? He told me he met the most fantas—"

What?

She eyed me. "Are you aware he didn't know *you* were Willow until that Friday afternoon?"

Something else I didn't know, but certainly had dreamed about.

I leaned on her desk, perhaps for support, perhaps because I wanted to prevail upon her. "I need a favor, Ms. Naughton."

~ ~ ~

I didn't have long to wait. A tenant showed up within fifteen minutes, and I rushed up the steps in hot pursuit. I pretended to be an innocent kid—jeans, white T-shirt, my hair pulled back. A shy smile and a sweet "Hello" were enough to fluster the guy as I entered on his key. By the time I climbed to the third-floor landing, my heart raced, my mouth was dry, and I itched in so many places, scratching seemed futile.

No response to my first knock. I tried again, more forcefully.

"I'm busy."

Not what I expected.

I knocked again.

"Go away."

I deepened my voice in an effort to disguise it. "Building inspector. Sorry to bother you, sir. I can't go away."

"Come back some other time."

"Sorry, sir. Inspection reports are due today, and I can't skip anyone. I'm on the third floor, and so is your apartment." What? "It'll just take a moment, sir."

The chain clinked, the bolt slid, the door squeaked open. "Make it quick."

That's when he eyeballed me. I posed, half a smile and half a shrug.

"You."

He flipped the door closed with his fingertips. I

blocked it with my foot. He trudged away. I took that as an invitation, or as close to an invitation as I'd be offered.

I entered the apartment and locked the door behind me. My nose wrinkled. The air stunk, as if he hadn't left for a week. Or showered. The second thing I noticed was the incessant ticking. What did he have, like, a thousand clocks?

He plopped on the sofa, ignoring me, a notebook in one hand, a pen in the other.

I opened a window. A spring breeze rushed in. Dozens of papers rushed to the floor. Oops. I rationalized the apartment needed air more than his desk needed documents.

He didn't react, so I gathered everything without regard to organization, weighted down the pages with a tennis trophy, and took a deep breath.

He wore a T-shirt and sweats, much as I might do around home, only my clothes would be four or five days fresher. He wrote—expressionless—undisturbed by my intrusion, or the horse who seemed to be singing on the TV.

His cheeks were sunken. All of him appeared sunken. He probably hadn't eaten much the past few days. Okay, we could start there.

I found the kitchen, instant Swiss mocha decaf, a loaf of bread with no overt blue or green growth, and an old-fashioned, push-the-knob-down toaster.

I pushed, and bread disappeared as ordained. Then I marched around the kitchen, hands on hips. A crimson bowl on the counter contained solidified milk with what appeared to be Frosted Flakes frozen in place. Yuck. An azure blue bowl half-filled with water sat on the floor next to the table. I dumped Frosted Flakes in the garbage and rinsed the bowl, then searched the refrigerator for butter, but a burning odor distracted me.

Sure enough, smoke streamed from the toaster. No biggie. I forced the toaster button up and rescued partially blackened bread.

I jumped out of my skin when the smoke detector screeched. He still didn't react. I flipped the stove-fan switch. Nothing happened. I shut it off and tried again.

"Hey, your fan doesn't work."

Mister Ed answered over the unrelenting alarm. "Watch out, Willll… bur."

I scanned for something to stand on so I could switch off the mutant thing, spied a pile of *Romantic Times* magazines instead, and fanned. "You might want to call a handyman."

I toasted two more slices of bread, then located two mugs so he wouldn't drink coffee with floaters. I twisted the water filter downward and turned on the tap. The damn thing squirted me.

"Nothing's going to explode in here, is it?" I arched an eyebrow and tapped numbers on the microwave. "I'm standing kinda close to this nuke machine. Will I be glowing tonight?"

The microwave counted down the final seconds to hot water, and residual smoke must've drifted to the alarm. It screamed. I screamed. "That could grow annoying," I shouted.

I fanned until the alarm stopped again, then found a clean plate and brought him coffee and reasonably unburnt toast. He wasn't interested.

I tried feeding him. He took one bite and continued to scribble. I swallowed and frowned, swiveled my head away from his view, my chin resting in my palm, and rolled my head around and around. I deposited his food on a coffee table, then positioned myself between him and the TV. He didn't try to look around me, but he did look at me. His face remained unreadable.

No more asking. "You have to come with me. Now." I snatched the notebook and pen, grabbed his arm, and tugged. "You're going to shower and change first. It wouldn't hurt to brush your teeth, shave, gargle. You know, the usual bathroom stuff."

He slogged across the apartment, and I placed him in front of the bathroom sink. He failed to perform.

No bathroom booby traps were evident, so I squeezed toothpaste onto his brush and brushed for him. "Okay, spit." He neither helped nor resisted.

I spread shaving cream next, wiping it from the corners of his mouth. He tolerated me, tilted his chin when requested—well, when I kinda pushed it—and not once tried to give me directions. I knew enough to shave downward, and no blood dripped from his cheeks when I finished.

I started the shower, adjusting hot and cold knobs until the temperature balanced. I pirouetted to leave the bathroom so he could take off his clothes, but he just deadpanned into the mirror.

Must've been enamored of my wonderful shaving job.

"Come on, I'll help." I hoisted his T-shirt over his head to give him the idea to undress, and I tried to back out of the room. He remained immutable, bare-chested, frozen.

I nodded. No cup on the vanity. "I'm thirsty. Don't go away."

I found a glass in the kitchen, poured cold water,

returned to the bathroom. My charge mimicked a statue dressed in sweatpants, shower steam fogging the mirror.

"Don't you want to enjoy a nice warm shower?" I angled until situated between him and the mirror, then dumped the water over his waistband. His eyes bugged out, and I knew I'd finally impressed him.

I put the glass in the sink, pointed, and giggled. "Looks like you peed." I gestured toward the shower.

He inhaled steam and gritted his teeth, determined not to succumb to my antics.

I knew when I was defeated.

This wasn't it.

I maneuvered behind him and yanked down his sweatpants. He raised his feet one at a time, on command, to step out of his sweats, kind of like shoeing Mister Ed. I shoved him into the shower and resisted the urge to peek. He remained motionless under the stream.

I twisted off the hot water.

He sputtered, spun around, and adjusted the controls. "What do you want?" he shouted.

"I want you to come with me, and I need you clean and dressed first."

"Come with you where?"

"Uh-uh. Clean and dressed first."

"All right, all right." He slid the curtain shut.

I waited a moment to register the sounds of someone washing, then retreated to the sofa and a talking horse. Clocks shined and ticked in varying stages of disagreement, more than half reasonably close, others way off. Majority ruled: we still had time.

When I'd explained to Ms. Naughton what I wanted to do, she supplied names and phone numbers. I called Dr. Grant. Yes, her animal hospital retrieved the body in the park, and yes, they held remains for ten days. If no one claimed the body, it would be disposed of.

"Please, please hold Fish for another couple of days. I promise I'll be there to collect him."

She agreed, and I hustled home to begin my next task. Pet cemeteries, even the cheapest, were way out of my price range. I chose one nonetheless, went to visit and pick the spot, left a small deposit, and assured them they'd be paid the rest of the money.

I called his friends, explaining what I'd done, and asked for donations to help defray the cost. Elliot, Rhiannon, DD, Clarisse. I even called his textbook publisher. I decided against calling Dr. Coleman, Ms. Nixon, and Ms. Burnett. Lela overheard and plunked forty-seven dollars on the table.

"It's all I can afford, Willow." I hugged her.

We were dramatically short, and I worried half the afternoon until the phone rang. Larry Scott, Rhiannon's catering uncle, said he'd pay for the whole thing.

They were all coming to the funeral, including the people I hadn't called. I imagine Clarisse told them.

I didn't tell *him*. I held his hand and directed him from the apartment. "Trust me." I didn't speak other than that, and I didn't let go the entire trip.

His grip tightened when I pushed open an iron gate. An embossed bronze plate glinted in the sun: Rockaway Pet Cemetery.

His friends were gathered, and I think that blew him away.

Tears welled into his eyes, and I figured he couldn't speak. The cemetery guy conducted a brief ceremony, he lowered the casket, we bowed our heads and said goodbye, and everyone offered condolences.

He trembled when the casket disappeared. Friends departed, and we remained alone beside the grave.

I hugged his arm. "Fish was a wonderful companion. I know you'll never forget him." I tugged to take him away, but he resisted for the first time since I'd taken his hand. I glanced into his grieving face.

"Thank you, Ms. Bolden."

I offered a thin smile, and we left the cemetery.

His blank expression didn't change when we got off the subway at Columbus Circle. The Cement Man winked at me. Sunlight danced across his face. I know he knew where we were headed. Too soon, though.

I spied a luncheonette across the street.

"Come on, I'd like a cup of coffee."

We sat at the counter on round, swiveling stools. I twisted and did a thing I often do: I sighed and made my lips vibrate. I sounded like a horse. Why wasn't there a word for that?

He didn't have anything to say, and I didn't want to force him to talk, but silence seemed suddenly awkward, so I talked.

I told him about our plans, Lela's and mine, to continue with grad school, earn our degrees in psychology then open our therapy practice here in the city. We loved New York.

I rambled on until it was time to go, then tossed a few crumpled bills on the counter. I aimed him into the park, toward my rock. Our rock.

Couples strolled across the playing fields, hand in hand, arm in arm, lost in each other and found in each other. People—several with eyes closed—sat on benches, undoubtedly dreaming of the city. Vendors with carts hawked what every person in the park might want: watches, ice cream… nuts.

315

I sniffed mustard and sauerkraut. My stomach rumbled, but we didn't stop for food. Rollerbladers, skateboarders, and bicyclers rolled past, gathering momentum for life.

Pigeons paraded. Baseballs, footballs, bocce balls, Frisbees, moms pushing carriages, children skipping and laughing, the clippety-clop of horses' hooves, the rustling of trees, a squirrel chomping on an acorn, a child picking wads of cotton candy, the distant squeal of tires, grinding bus gears—the city symphony renewed.

He didn't object when I captured his hand again, but as before, *I* held on to him. Gusts kicked up, dark clouds rumbled into place, leaves twisted and displayed shiny undersides. We climbed our rock, the wind whipped our hair, and an occasional drop splattered our arms. We'd shared this rock with Fish, and a few moments of silent tribute seemed appropriate.

A compelling bark intruded on our silence.

We pivoted. The medium woof of a medium dog. A mutt tied to a nearby tree, nobody around. I scanned the paths leading away. DD jutted above the landscape. Once I found DD, I recognized Lela's graceful hips beside him.

I don't think *he* noticed their departure, and I led my charge off the rock, toward the mutt.

He peered as we approached, as if the dog's owner must be waiting to jump out from behind a tree. The scraggly animal wiggled his entire body. He licked our hands and hopped around. The mutt had no tags, no collar. I untied the rope at the tree.

"You can't do that," my charge said.

"Sure I can."

"No, you can't."

"Why not?"

"That's not your dog."

I nodded. "True. It's your dog."

"I don't own a dog."

"Well, not in the sense that the dog belongs to you, but I happened to be at the animal shelter yesterday, and this mutt and I got to talking, and he said he needed a place to stay while he was in town, and I mentioned I knew someone who might have an apartment.

"He said that sounded perfect. He asked if he could meet you, so…" I gestured with my hands and shrugged. "I didn't say a word about the ticking or all those papers on the floor."

He eyed me, I thought with anger, but the mutt kept nudging him.

"You brought this dog here to meet me?"

I bit my lower lip and nodded.

He scratched the dog behind the ears. The dog sat and waved a paw at him. "What's his name?"

The dog barked immediately. I leaned in and cupped my ear. The dog barked again. I offered my best Mister Ed imitation. "He says his name is Willll… bur."

Wilbur barked in agreement. Mark-in-the-Park-Professor-Kirin-Ron gathered me into his arms. I melted into him like the chocolate on my windowsill. Heat—or the chocolate—fused the three of him into one man, Ron Mark Kirin.

I buried my face in his chest. He buried one hand in my hair. Our exposed psyches danced in the park, swaying to strains of the city symphony, both new and familiar.

Our fingers laced, and jasmine wafted around us. Our lips brushed, then pressed together, and the warmth of his breath caressed my skin, elevating us onto a new plane of existence. Time crystallized into a perfect moment frozen in the late-spring embrace of an approaching thunderstorm. Wilbur pranced around us.

Ron pushed back, and our gazes locked. I surveyed his eyes and saw the sun, the clouds, rain, and rainbows. And a redwood.

"You surprised me today," he said.

"I know."

Rain pummeled us then. It soaked through my white T-shirt, searching for flesh, and it matted the hair to the back of Ron's neck. He shook like a dog.

"Want to wait this out under a tree?" he asked.

I waggled my head and pulled a faded green pebble from my pocket, dropped it, and stomped it into the softened earth.

"What's that?" he asked.

"Kryptonite," I replied.

We roamed through the park, hand in hand, arm in arm, lost in each other and found in each other. Wilbur pranced around us, stopping every once in a while to cock his head and convey that look.

What're you two, nuts?

About Raz Steel

Raz Steel was born in a chalet in Frisco, Colorado. His alter-ego was born farther east—or farther west if you go the long way. A storyteller his entire life—his father may not have appreciated that 100% of the time—Raz finally put stories to paper. He's a pilot, a teacher, a recycler, a dad, and now a granddad! He holds a degree in Philosophy from Lafayette College and currently resides in Bucks County, Pennsylvania. His stories are character driven, and many take place in Bucks County.

Raz's writing career began after he became a pilot.

Being terrified of heights—anything over the third rung of a ladder—the choice didn't seem difficult: fly or write.

His father always said, "Son, face your fears head-on." So, Raz tortured himself to earn his pilot's license to cure his fear. Didn't work, but Raz now feels qualified to offer advice to other acrophobiacs—"Let me assure you, if there's anything more terrifying than flying a single engine airplane at 2000 feet, just you and the flight instructor, it's flying a single engine airplane at 2000 feet—alone." You have to fly solo to earn your license. What could he have possibly been thinking?

Writing is Raz's passion, and that passion is expressed in his storytelling.

His first two novels, *Love Without Blood* and *Blood Between Lovers*, are vampire romance. Vampires scare the hell out of Raz, but the romance of life eternal was too compelling, so those stories are psychological thrillers.

PASS THE KRYPTONITE is a sweetheart young adult romantic comedy—no vampires!

Raz has conducted writing workshops, *Heroes With PMS (Phony Male Syndrome),* for the Bucks County Romance Writers, Valley Forge Romance Writers, and at the Romantic Times Booklovers Convention in Orlando, FL and hosted a blood drive for the city of Orlando. He's taught fiction writing for ten years, and he recently taught a unique class: *Producing A Novel Instead Of Writing A Manuscript.*

You can follow him at his website RazSteel.com and on Facebook @RAZSTEELAuthor.

Made in the USA
Middletown, DE
01 September 2025

13343942R00183